'A compelling tale of two young people whose destinies are inter-twined, a witch-hunter and a witch. But is she really a witch? This meticulously researched account of a bigoted man's inhuman-ity to women in the seventeenth century will make the modern reader grateful to have been born in an enlightened age.'

Mari Griffith, author of *The Witch of Eye*

'*Widdershins* gives a compelling and nuanced account of the clash of cultures that claimed so many lives. Steadman's carefully inter-woven narrative conjures a world of herbal lore, folk practice and belief and convincingly portrays the psychological and ideologi-cal forces that form a perpetrator, and the social structures that sustain him.'

Helen Lynch, author of *The Elephant and the Polish Question*

'Her writing reminds me of Hannah Kent's bestselling novel, *Burial Rites*, which follows the final days of a young woman accused of murder in Iceland in 1829. Helen's writing has a simi-lar persuasive and empathetic force, weaving together historical fact with modern concerns about the treatment of women.'

Helen Marshall, award-winning author

'*Widdershins* is a dark and wonderful novel, rich in historical details, herbal lore, traditions and superstitions. Steadman's clear-eyed storytelling and colourful period voice give life to a vibrant cast of characters drawn against the backdrop of tragic historical events. A compelling and memorable tale!'

Louisa Morgan, author of *A Secret History of Witches*

'Infused as it is with aromas of rosemary, fennel and lavender, even the healers' herbs do not mask the reek of the injustice that sits at the heart of *Widdershins*. Powerful and shocking.'

Wyl Menmuir, author of *The Many* (longlisted for The Man Booker Prize 2016)

SUNWISE

Helen Steadman

IMPRESS BOOKS

First Published 2019
by Impress Books Ltd
Innovation Centre, Rennes Drive, University of Exeter Campus,
Exeter EX4 4RN

The right of the author to be identified as the originator of this work has been
asserted in accordance with the Copyright, Designs and Patents Act 1988.
Typeset in Garamond by Swales & Willis Ltd, Exeter, Devon

Printed and bound in England by Short Run Press Ltd, Exeter, Devon, UK

British Library Cataloguing in Publication Data

A catalogue record for this book is available from the British Library

ISBN: 978–1–911293–25–5 (pbk)
ISBN: 978–1–911293–26–2 (ebk)

For Oliver and Leon

'Honour the Lord with your wealth, with the firstfruits of all your crops.'

Proverbs 3:9 *NIV*

Sunwise: 'Righthandwise, towards the right; motion with continuous turning to the right, as in going around an object with the right hand towards it, or in the same direction as the hands of a clock, or the apparent course of the sun (a practice held auspicious by the Celts).'

Oxford English Dictionary

CONTENTS

Acknowledgements

When *Widdershins* was released, a small army of book bloggers reviewed it and told the world about my first novel. I have been astonished at the amount of reading you all do and your dedication to literature. You are all amazing people, and I can never thank you enough. Thank you also to everyone who read *Widdershins* and took the time to review it, and to everyone who came along to readings and asked questions – it really is lovely to hear from readers. I am eternally grateful to my wonderful friend, the novelist, poet, painter, singer and plain-speaker, Marita Over, who did the heavy lifting when it came to critiquing *Sunwise*. I am grateful to my PhD supervisor, Dr Helen Lynch at the University of Aberdeen, for not so much as raising an eyebrow when I announced to her that I was writing a sequel to *Widdershins*, and that everything would be fine with my PhD work (and it will be, honestly). Once again, I am very grateful to everyone at Impress Books, but particular thanks must go to Laura Christopher and Julian Webb for their painstaking efforts and care in editing and publishing *Sunwise*, to Megan Symons for her careful proofreading, and also to Natalie Clark and Richard Willis for their sterling work and creative ideas for publicising *Widdershins* and *Sunwise*, respectively. Thanks to Move Design for the beautiful cover. I am grateful to Michael Murray for providing me with a sheaf of two-row barley so I could make kern babies, and one of these days, I promise to stop calling him

Martin. Finally, special thanks to Neil, Oliver and Leon Steadman for keeping me happy and healthy, and to Eddie and Elsie who force me to take them for long woodland walks to prevent me becoming entirely chair-shaped. Any errors and omissions are my own, and I apologise sincerely for them in advance.

1

John

On God's Errand

Instead of sweltering in the hellish heat of a Newcastle dungeon, I was now on the coastal path to Berwick. It was God's will and my heart eased with every mile put between me and the cursed town of Newcastle. Now that the great tract of Northumberland was largely behind me, the land began to look more akin to Scotland than England. To the right was the huge sea and to my left were gentle hills. Yet, even the plentiful forests with their silver brooks, and the vast expanse of the sea with its briny air, failed to buoy my spirits. Although I'd escaped with my hide intact, it still irked me that Jane Driver had escaped the hangman's noose.

Had Driver gone to her death as intended, I'd be in Newcastle now, hanging witches at twenty shillings a piece. Instead, that snatcher of unborn infants roamed free to practise her dark arts. She'd cost me my good name and much silver. At the thought of these losses, rage suffused my blood. That witch must not be allowed to live and pollute the good earth. This would mean going back to mete out justice.

But Driver would keep a whilst. Her powers were so great that I must strengthen myself for the final onslaught else she best me again and her powers be increased. For now, it would be wise to conserve my strength and replenish my coffers. Once strong enough, I would return to relieve the witch of her duties, the imp in her belly and the air in her lungs.

It amused me to consider her end. Might it be possible to put her to the flame in Scotland? That would despatch her immortal soul straight to the great fire, and a pyre was always good for deterring innocents on the cusp of darkening their souls. But it was futile to dream of home, for great English armies had marched ahead of me and my country was not presently a safe haven. It wouldn't do to return there and become embroiled in a war commissioned by men. Besides which, God still needed me to fight His war in England. I would bide in Berwick a whilst. After my recent travails, God would forgive me for indulging myself a little.

My path was gilded by fields of barley swaying in the sea breeze. But this shallow beauty didn't deceive me. Aye, the countryside might look innocent enough on the surface, but beneath, for those prepared to use their eyes, it brimmed with evil potential. Witches waited for the celestial bodies to align and then used the power of God's earth for their own ends. Even simple food crops were not safe when hags like Driver would pick plants and enchant them for use in their wicked deeds.

On closer inspection, the crops were somewhat sparse. Might this be due to hordes of hungry soldiers? Surely the English would never let their men march on empty bellies. Was it the result of a poor harvest? If so, this might be a good sign. When harvests were poor, townspeople tended to be more willing to point fingers at the women responsible.

The fields were scattered with serfs, who looked up from their toil as I rode past, but they didn't tug their forelocks or offer any greetings. Doubtless, my fine boots and cloak made them commit the sin of envy. Or, more likely, they saw the fervour in my eyes and were awed.

When I paused to enquire about any queer happenstance of late, the cross-eyed dolts just gazed at their feet, afraid to give up their womenfolk. These rural fools were not worth my breath. In any event, towns were always better for unearthing witches since people forced to live in close proximity were more inclined towards gossip and spite. Berwick was a town smaller by far than Newcastle, so my gain would be considerably lower, but its coffers would be deep enough to suffice for now.

When my mare clattered over the bridge crossing the Tweed, my heart began to hammer at the sight of the massive ramparts looming before me. There would be guards at the gate. What might they make of a Scot entering their town? Might they see me as a spy? Berwick's people were currently for England, but might they hold a secret sympathy with Scotland in their hearts? That might bode well for me. Added to which, the soldiers of the realm were so light of pocket of late that it lightened their consciences also. The prospect of being once again trapped within a fortified town troubled me, but the travelling papers resting against my chest soothed my racing heart.

A lanky guard addressed me. 'Halt! What brings you here, stranger?'

'God brings me.'

'God brings you, eh? Then He'll have given you papers. Let me see them.'

'I am John Sharpe, witch-finder, on God's errand.' I presented my papers for inspection. With luck, the oaf wouldn't be able to read.

The guard took the papers and ran a finger across the town seal. He frowned at me. 'These papers are from Newcastle. So what brings you to Berwick?'

'I've recently shown Newcastle a glorious sight and given them a spectacle that none will forget. Seventeen witches – foul servants of the devil – all hanged by the neck in a single day at my behest.'

The guard's eyebrows rose. 'Seventeen witches? In a single day?'

'Aye, man, seventeen.' I indicated my papers. 'And in several confessions, the town of Berwick was mentioned as a place thronged with sister witches.'

The guard shifted his feet. 'There are witches here? Behind these walls?'

'Indeed there are. Stone walls cannot hold the devil at bay, no matter how mighty. For that, you need my help. The Lowlands of Scotland are infested with witches. As is Newcastle. Berwick's proximity to both lands must mean that it is likewise infested.'

The man regarded me for a long whilst, then walked over to consult a fellow guard. Together, they pored over my papers.

These liminal counties and shires were prone to infestations – due to being neither flesh nor fish. People from the marches were typically untrustworthy, and so would need to be carefully watched. Their allegiance could shift in the blinking of an eye if it suited their need for survival. The lack of principles meant the women of this town would be highly immoral – maybe more so than the women of Newcastle. And who knew what evil this weakness might have allowed in. But it struck me that these men wouldn't suffer to hear ill of their kinfolk, and so I held my tongue.

Finally, the guard returned, holding up my papers. 'How long do you intend to stay here?'

'For as long as God needs me.' I plucked the papers from his hand and folded them back inside my jerkin. 'Now, delay me no more.'

He looked at his comrade, who nodded, and they stepped back to grant me entrance.

It was hard not to snort my contempt as I entered the town. Berwick's guards had required little convincing. At least the venal sergeants of Newcastle had possessed wit enough to demand silver. It spoke volumes that the very men who were charged with protecting the town had restored my liberty, albeit at a steep price. But my purse had been heavy with English silver, and I'd been pleased to purchase my freedom.

Once inside Berwick's walls, it became obvious that the streets were too narrow to ride through with a cart and a bellman. No matter. I would settle myself in the town and learn the lie of the land. Tales of witchcraft would reach my ears once word of my presence spread. And if none came, then it was short work to set people thinking. Folk were often ignorant of witches' practices until I brought them to light. It pleased me greatly to share my learning in the service of God. Now that I was back on my righteous path, nothing would deter me. As long as there was breath in my body, I would use it to find witches and bring them to justice. God needed my help, of that much I was certain. And it might yet be possible to return home with a heavy purse.

2

Jane

I Am for Hell

The sun had defeated my efforts at sleep once more, and I lay in bed, awake but exhausted. My nights were filled with dark dreams, and even in the sunlit hours, shadows came and went. But this darkness was something outside of me, and I couldn't face it yet. The best course was to pretend at living, for my daughter's sake, if not my own. It was only Rose who made me want to stay alive. It was wrong to feel this way, to wish away my life when Mam had lost hers, but it was impossible to change my feelings. Perhaps it was as well I must remain married to Andrew. It was a form of penance.

Rose was fast asleep in her basket, clutching her poppet, so I got up and went out to the kitchen garden. The back end of August was always busy, and there wasn't much time to gather all the herbs needed to keep everyone hale through the coming white months. For my remedies, I still relied on the woods and on the gardens at the manse. But there were the makings of a herb garden here at the back of the Drivers' kitchen. It was not as rich or varied as that at home, but it sufficed for the family's needs.

For now, I'd cut some rosemary. The spiky plant had started into its second bloom of the year and it was adorned with violet flowers. The rosemary in the manse garden only flowered once a year, it being high on the hill and exposed to the elements. Here in the valley, the sheltered garden allowed the more delicate plants to thrive.

I took the fragrant sprigs into the kitchen and sat at the table near the window to make the most of the weak morning light. The rosemary would make a fine wreath of remembrance. When Rose awoke, we'd go and lay it on the wooden cross in the graveyard. Mam's remains lay in Newcastle, and it would be a long time before I set foot in that town again. But Bill Verger had created a place to remember my mother, next to the memorial cross he'd created for Tom when we'd thought him lost at sea.

My heart skipped at the thought. Tom was alive and coming home! A strange thought entered me now. Despite seeing my mother's execution, somehow it might not have happened, and she might yet return as well . . . But this was madness. It couldn't possibly be so. It pained me to puzzle over it, and so my mind shifted back to Tom. What would he do when he got home and found me married to Andrew Driver? Surely, he wouldn't be able to bear living so close by, and I would lose him once again.

Rosemary was a difficult herb to work with sometimes. It was used for remembrance because it opened the memory and brought old feelings to the surface. But these feelings were too hard for me to face. I wondered whether it was the same for Reverend Foster . . . I'd not seen him in recent days, and we'd not spoken since returning from Newcastle. I should go and check on him and maybe ask him to come and lay the wreath with us later.

My musings were interrupted by a gentle tapping at the kitchen door. It was barely dawn, so such an early visitor must mean a birthing mother in trouble. I put down the wreath, shook away my thoughts and went to the door. It was May Green.

'May! What brings you before the sun's half up?'

'Oh, Jane. Sorry to trouble you so sharp in the day. And so soon after . . .'

Her gaze went to my shorn head and she put a hand to her own blonde curls. It sent a sharp feeling through my heart, and I drew my shawl tighter.

'Please, May, it's all right. Come, tell me what ails you. You're very pale and sweating far too much – even for a summer morning.'

She wiped her forehead with a trembling hand and cast down her eyes.

'May? You can tell me anything, you know that.'

But my oldest friend shook her head. I stepped outside, quietly shutting the door behind me, so as not to wake Rose or the Drivers.

She glanced quickly behind her, so I took her arm and drew her into the herb garden, but May put her hand to her mouth and shook her head.

'Sorry. I should have thought . . .' My own sickness had passed now, and it was easy to forget how overpowering some plants could be. 'Here, come to the barn, you should be all right there.' I drew her into the ivy-covered barn. 'No one will disturb us in here. Please tell me, May. Let me help you.'

She took my hand and pressed it to her belly. There was no curve there, nor yet any hardness, but her chin quivered and her blue eyes were glazed with tears.

'You have to help me, Jane. There's . . . well . . .' May slid down the wall and buried her face in her hands.

I crouched down beside her and put my arms around her. Poor May. It was terrible to see her so unhappy. I held her until her sobbing abated.

'Come, May. There's nothing in the world so bad that you cannot tell me.'

She rubbed the tears from her face and blew her nose on her pinny. 'I'm sorry to bother you when you . . . when you have so many problems of your own. It's just you're the only person who can help me.'

'It's all right, May. I'll help in any way you want me to.' It was clear to me now what she wanted, but it was best to let her find the words to tell me.

'I . . . I just can't have this child.'

'But whose is it?'

'I cannot say.' She wouldn't meet my eye. 'Please don't make me say.'

My mind raced. May seldom set foot outside. And since her youngest brother's birth, she'd hardly put her nose out the door. In fact, for some time before then, she'd scarcely left her house.

I hadn't stopped to consider what might have been going on. But now, it seemed all too clear. Oh, how could I have been so naïve?

'Don't worry, May. You needn't say another word. I'll mend what ails you. Now, tell me how many moons have passed.'

She looked up at me, her eyes reddened from crying. 'One moon. Not yet two.'

'So, no sign of the quickening yet?'

She shook her head. 'No, not yet.'

'Then that makes an easier task for us.' I placed my hand gently on her shoulder. 'Just sit there a whilst, and I'll be as fast as I can.'

I tiptoed back into the house to collect Mam's satchel. When I opened it, I breathed in the musk of old leather and herbs, the perfume of sweet summer roses and the tang of early autumn berries. My entire childhood had been spent gathering flowers, seeds, herbs and barks, drying them, pounding them into powders, preserving them in honey and brandy, and sealing them in beeswax. Now, the satchel bristled with the resulting linctus, unguent and tincture, and I ran my hand along the rows of crocks, bottles and vials.

Tears choked me as my eye rested on a bottle of elder linctus, tied with red thread. Mam's final batch. We'd picked the early elderberries and made syrup to sell to the apothecary. That was August. It was still August, yet so much had changed. How could something so innocent cause so much trouble? Of course, it wasn't the fault of the linctus. Nor was it the fault of my mother's vials and their contents. The apothecary's wife had almost certainly reported us to the witch-finder for sending babes to sleep in their mothers' wombs. A tremor passed through me and I forced my thoughts away from what had come next.

In my mother's old satchel were the mysterious vials. I took one and weighed it in the palm of my hand. These vials had come and gone all my life, changing hands from one cunning woman to another, without my ever truly knowing their contents. My poor mother. She'd tried to protect me from the darker practices of midwifery, maybe knowing how her work might be viewed in some quarters. She'd given me a gentle childhood, and one with no need to bear witness to life's terrors.

As thoughts began crowding into my mind, I shrank from them before they overwhelmed me. It was important to keep my mind on May, who'd suffered the hardest of childhoods without my ever realising. No longer was I a child. I was a woman. A mother. Someone capable of seeing life as it truly was. I would help May now. And others like her. This would be my life's work. But who would stop these men? I sighed. One ailment at a time. First, help May.

I opened a vial and inhaled the bitter notes of rue, the under-cutting mint from pennyroyal, the fresh notes of rosemary and the funereal sweetness of tansy. Although my own morning sickness had abated, the smell caused my gorge to rise. It was an ugly aroma for an ugly task.

When I returned to the barn, May was still slumped against the wall and weeping into her pinny.

'Don't weep, May.' I knelt down beside her and put an arm around her. 'All be will be well.'

'Do you promise?'

I nodded. 'Promise. Look, here's the remedy.'

She took the vial from me and held it up to the light. 'Will it make me bad?'

'It'll sicken you, but it will help you. Are you ready?'

She stared at the vial in her hand. 'Aye.'

'Come, then.'

May looked up at me with baleful eyes. 'I fear for my soul, Jane. This is a wrongful deed.'

'You've done naught wrong, May. It's you who's been wronged – much wronged.' I placed a bowl beside her in case she couldn't stomach the tincture. In that case, my task would become more difficult. I crossed my fingers behind my back. 'There's no wrong in this act we're about to do.'

I wished she'd told me or Mam last time. We might have helped her then and spared her suffering, although it was wrong to wish away little Henry Green.

'May, do you want me to help you take it?'

'There's no helping me.' She removed the stopper from the vial and tipped its contents into her mouth. At first, she gagged and wretched, but kept swallowing, wiping away her tears as she drank. 'I am for hell.'

'You're not for hell, May. None of this is your fault.'

She raised her head sharply. 'What do you mean?'

'I mean nothing. Only, don't blame yourself. Many girls – including me – end up in your position out of wedlock.' I crouched down and hugged her. 'You'll need to repeat the dose in a quarter hour, if you manage to keep it down. Then you can go home. You'll need to come back each day to repeat the dose until . . . until we know it's worked. Can you manage that?'

She nodded. 'What'll happen to me, Jane?'

This was a difficult question for I'd never administered these herbs. But I'd witnessed many women losing children at different stages. Now, I wondered how many of those had been accidental, and how many had been ordained by my mother's hand.

'You'll have cramping pains within a couple of days, or a week or so. Much like those you have at the time of the moon. Only stronger. There'll be more blood than usual, so I'll give you some extra rags to take away with you.'

She put her head in her hands and rocked herself. 'And what about the baby? I can't bear to see a tiny dead baby.'

'There won't be any tiny dead baby, May. It's much too early.' I took my suffering friend's hands in mine. 'Whatever passes from your body, you must burn. Burn your rags and burn them without looking too closely or thinking too hard. Or bring them to me and I'll do it for you.'

She nodded. 'And you're sure it'll work?'

'Yes, it'll work. Very soon, your womb will be empty.'

'But my heart will fill with guilt and anguish. Jane, I fear for my soul. I cannot go through this again. Can you stop my courses coming?'

'Well, you could take wild carrot seed, and that would disrupt your courses' I pondered a whilst. 'But really, it's your . . . it's the baby's father who needs to be prevented.'

'That would be better. But how could I bring that about?'

'Could you tell the sergeants about him?'

'No, never!' She stared into the empty manger. 'They wouldn't believe me. And even if they did believe me, what if they didn't stop him and just took him away and gaoled him. Or worse . . . What then? Who would provide for the little ones?'

I sighed. It was a problem that would not go away until she married. 'Get yourself away home for now. There's a plant to stop this, I'm certain of it.'

'Really?' She sat up and her hopeful face made me want to cry.

I nodded. 'Monk's pepper might be best.' There was a small amount in Mam's satchel and more in her pantry, but the dried berries would need grinding down to powder. 'It'll be ready for you the morrow.' It would take time to work, but May should be safe for a week or so. 'Now, here's the second dose. Can you stomach it?'

She nodded and drained the vial before hugging me. 'Thank you, Jane. Thank you.' She reached into her pinny and made to hand me some coins for my labour, but I waved away her offer.

'May, you're my oldest friend. You've no need to pay me.'

The Green family was troubled enough as it was. I had no real need of payment. Besides, Andrew would want to know how I'd earned it, and this was not something he should know about.

3

John

A Night of Succour

When I arrived at a coaching inn and dismounted, a groom took the reins of my sweating mare. The lowly youth eyed my slashed jerkin and obliged me to explain myself.

'A battle with the devil, laddie, only I came off worse that day. But a few nights of replenishment and my constitution will be fully strong again. Who's your master?'

'Mr Gillie, sire.' He pointed me towards the inn.

Once I was across the threshold, a stout man with a ruddy complexion appeared and he stared quite candidly at my jerkin.

'We want no troublemakers here, mind.'

His dialect was a curious mixture, ringing somewhere between the Lowlands of Scotland and the town of Newcastle. I took the Bible from my sack.

'My name is John Sharpe, and I am on God's errand, sire, only the devil has bested me of late. I need a night of succour to recover my spirits. Too much flesh has fallen from me.' I indicated my flanks. 'My sitting bones now dig into me with every step the horse takes.' A sure sign that I needed more nourishment to build myself up for the never-ending war against evil.

'Aye. Good enough.' The innkeeper leant on the door jamb and ran his eyes over me. 'There's a shared bed in the dormitory—'

'You must give me a chamber of my own – you cannot expect me to share with other travelling men.' A chamber of my own would deplete my dwindling silver, though, so I patted the Bible. 'You strike me as a pious man, Gillie, and one who would want to help God's servant.'

The man eyed the Bible and then nodded. 'Aye, well. It's a quiet enough week, so there's a chamber for you, but only if you have the silver. And if it's succour you're after, there's beef and kidney pie, plum duff and cream for sweet, with strong cheese for those that want it. Wine, ale and whisky aplenty. And a good, soft feather bed.'

'My habit is to eat and drink sparely and to sleep on hard floors whilst on God's errand.' But there was not strength left in me to protest. 'However, my spirit is weakened so one or two nights of softness will do no great harm, and might do much good.'

The innkeeper leered at me. 'You'll not be in need of a bed-warmer, then, you being on God's errand?'

Behind him stood a woman – most likely Goodwife Gillie – polishing an already spotless table. She was blonde-haired, plump and pert. The man's suggestion gave me pause – the devil tempting me even now! But he would not best me.

'As you say, man, there'll be no need to send up a bed-warmer. My goodwife was taken from me some years ago and there has been none since.' I dusted my cloak with one hand. 'Still, you might send up your woman to unfasten my boots and draw me a bath. The dust of the road is not to my liking.'

The stout man raised a brow but said no more. He tallied the bill and held out his hand. The price was steep. Clearly the innkeeper could read a man's hunger and charge him accordingly. When Gillie had taken my silver, he beckoned me to follow him down a dark passage where he showed me to my chamber. Once left alone, I found a hiding hole for my sack and left the ruined jerkin on the chair. Goodwife Gillie could mend it for me since her profiteering husband was charging me so dearly.

In the eating room, there was good cheer, and despite the sultry weather, travelling men devoured great steaming pies filled with collops of beef and offal. My mind was sickened by the mere thought of meat, but my traitorous flesh let me down when my belly growled and my mouth watered. Once replete, I would return to my sparing ways. God would forgive me this small slip

if I prayed hard enough afterwards. Tonight only, I would succumb to bodily temptation and slake my desire for strong drink,
blooded meat and a willing woman of the night.

Strangely, I had never once found a witch amongst the willing.
Assorted maids – faces too hard to be pretty, but soft of breast
and flank – often made themselves known to me on my travels.
Of course, they knew me weighted down by silver and wished to
relieve me of it. But it was more than that. In giving up their flesh
to me, they felt themselves brought nearer to God, and that was
something that I could do for them. A small sacrifice of my own
morals and these women could experience the Godhead. Afterwards, shame always washed through me, but God was forgiving,
and it was never long before my return to a spare life of cleanli-
ness and sparse living.

The pert goodwife approached me. Every man in the room
had his eyes on her, but I was only interested in the contents
of my platter. It bore a deep pie with golden pastry, mounds of
roasted tatties and parsnips, glazed carrots, pearl onions, broad
beans and a thick gravy. Goodwife Gillie filled my goblet with red
wine from a pitcher, which she left on the table. When I prised
the pastry lid from the dish of meat, savoury steam wet my face. I
speared a slab of beef on my eating knife and rammed it into my
mouth. The heat, the salt and the bloodiness overwhelmed my
senses. The beef fell apart in my mouth, which was just as well
for my jaws were unused to working on dead flesh. The bitter
kidneys – soft, tender and almost dry – crumbled on my tongue.
The heady wine filled my body with warmth, fetching the blood
up to my skin. Once sated, I wiped my mouth on a kerchief whilst
the goodwife cleared my platter and set down a plum duff and
a jug of cream. She came back with a great hunk of cheese and a
dish containing walnuts and almonds, which she set down before
refilling my pitcher. The rich duff swelled my belly, the spiced
currants perfumed my nostrils and the thick cream coated my
tongue. It almost put me in a reverie. My meal finished with a
sliver of savoury, sharp cheese, and my eyes closed after the final
mouthful.

A repast such as this was normally a sin, but it was needful
to bring up my blood and gather strength for the work that lay

ahead. The goodwife appeared to clear away my platters. Now that my belly was satisfied, my eyes roamed over her. Indeed, she was buxom and had a good rump.

'Mr Gillie tells me that you need your boots unfastened and a bath drawing.'

'Aye, he tells you right. Come.'

She bowed her head and followed me.

Once in my chamber, too full for prayer, I lay immediately on the bed. So thin were my flanks of late that my sharp bones showed through my flesh, and the softness and warmth of the feather bed were welcome. Wallowing in this unaccustomed luxury, and gorged from my feast, sleep threatened to take me. But the innkeeper's doxy scurried in after and looked to me for instruction.

'Undress me, woman. You can start with my boots.'

For such a plump creature, her fingers were nimble enough and she had me stripped bare in but a minute. Her bosom heaved beneath a tightly laced bodice, which conjured blissful dreams of unlacing it and biting her breasts. But even amidst these thoughts, when the woman unlaced my breeches, my flaccid member lay cold and pallid in the candlelight. The old curse was with me again. She reached for it with one hand.

'Leave it, harlot. Be done. Just draw my bath.'

'But I can help you, sire. Tis only a small matter.'

She gazed at me with wide, blue eyes. There was no sign that any jest lodged there, so I nodded my assent.

Goodwife Gillie took my member in one hand, where it stirred only a little. But she was not yet finished. She leant forward and covered it with her hot, wet mouth. Instantly, my senses sprang to life, blood raced through me, stiffening my member, and my back arched from the bed. What devil's trick was this? So much pleasure and such a stiffening! Already, my seed was making ready to surge forth and I'd not yet laid a hand on the wench, let alone sank my teeth into her. She sucked me hard, and just as my crisis approached, she took my member from her mouth, unhooked her bodice and stood up, allowing her breasts to spring free. She straddled me, plunging my member deep inside her. Such heat burnt through this woman! She rode me in much the same

15

way I rode my horse, all the whilst kneading her own burgeoning breasts and tantalising me by pushing them near my mouth. When I grabbed them and took my pleasure in biting them, the terror in her eyes and her squeals of pain caused the seed to surge within me. My eyes rolled back in my head, my organ pumping seed into her. I let it course from me with a great groan and lay back, limp and trembling, now drained of all goodness. She eased herself off me, and I was pleased to see a goodly amount of seed run down her thigh.

'Cover yourself, woman. You're not decent.'

She quickly pushed her breasts back into her bodice, wincing as she did so and then held out her hand for coin. It was in my mind to deprive her, but no doubt the hefty innkeeper would only seize the opportunity to come and beat it from me.

'Turn your back a whilst.' It wouldn't do to let her see my hiding hole. Although it struck me as unwise to leave my silver unguarded in the chamber as she'd know every cranny in the place. It might be wiser to carry my goods with me and take my chances with the cutpurses.

'Here's your ill-gotten gains.' I flung a coin at her and she stooped to retrieve it. 'And now draw my bath.'

'So, you don't need your bed warmed through the night then, sire?'

Was that hope in her voice? 'You've served your purpose, wench. Now draw me a bath and be gone. And take away my jerkin and mend it. In the morning, fetch me meat and drink, and then you may . . . attend to me again.'

Whilst she fetched hot water for my bath, I lay in bed fighting off sleep, thoughts whirling. Really, I should pray and seek forgiveness for my transgression. But the bed was so soft and the woman had left my bones like warm oil, so I was loath to press my bare knees to the cold flagstones. God knew full well what was truly in my heart, and the morrow, I would pray twice as hard.

The strumpet laboured over my bath and I enjoyed the spectacle. Really, she was a marvel. She'd brought life to my loins using only her mouth. To think that all those years ago, I'd half-killed myself trying to get a bairn on my goodwife. Hadn't I tried for some years to get a bairn on Lucy when her womb was found wanting? The humiliation had forced me – what folly – to put myself in the hands of the barber-surgeon and his so-called remedies. But MacBain's concoction had cost me dear. How had he taken me in so easily? His compound had worked. But Lucy and my son died at the hands of two hags, forcing me to rid the world of those particular servants of the devil.

But now, after only a few minutes with this woman, it was clear to me that MacBain's infernal potions and his assistance in the act of procreation were unnecessary, and I'd wasted my silver needlessly.

The whore interrupted my thoughts with a cough. 'Your bath is drawn, sire. Would you like me to help you bathe?'

'No. You can let me alone now.'

I must resist temptation for if she drained me of my seed again this night, it might weaken me to the extent that my flesh would be open to foul humours and my soul to malefic influence. I stood on shaky legs and slid into the hot water. Aye, that doxy was filled with sinful knowledge. But she struck me as a low woman of loose morals, rather than anything more sinister, and she had her uses.

The warm water soaked my muscles, which were sore from so much riding. The soft soap cleansed me of the stench and stain of the witches I had touched in Newcastle. As their taint left me, it floated in a scum on top of the water. The sight repulsed me. It wouldn't do to stew in tainted juices. And it wouldn't do to let my flesh and resolve soften too much. Once the water began to lose its heat, I eased myself out and scourged my skin dry with a rough cloth.

Aye, this inn would suffice. It would be a good place to rest and deal with the local coven. There was doubtless plenty of business for me in this town. I would hunt down the damned and prevent them multiplying and afflicting the innocent. Aye, my work was not yet done. In truth, it would never be done.

4

Jane

All the Permission He Needed

The sky had just started to redden. Andrew was tending the cattle in the top pasture and his father was away to the mart. His mother slept on, as did Rose, so I set off for the low meadows to gather rosehips to make a syrup. It would ease my mother-in-law's joint pains and Rose could have some on rice pudding as a treat. The remainder, I would put aside to keep away sniffles during the white months.

The last weeks of summer had been hot and dry, the air infused with the heady perfume of rose blooms that had now died back to make way for the fruit. The deer paths were dry, and even in the heart of the woods, the mud had almost dried. Most years, the canopy of leaves kept the sun out and the woods remained damp, so the unwary walker might easily lose a boot in a sucking bog. If this dry weather kept up, the fruit crops would do badly since apples needed a goodly amount of water.

The last rain had been on the day of my mother's execution and there'd not been a drop since. The memory left me faint and trembling. Mam's death was still too hard to take in. On busy days, my mind went blank and it was possible to pretend for a few hours that it had never happened. But at night, when my guard was down, the dreams came and left me shaking and soaked with sweat.

I came to a mighty beech and leant against her, drawing strength from the mother of the woods by wrapping my arms around her smooth trunk and gazing up into her huge canopy over a hundred feet away. I clung to the beech, whispering prayers for my mother, hoping the old tree might take my prayers and raise them up to heaven. In all the thousands of turns of the moon this tree had seen, what wisdom had she gained, and what protection might she give? Her silent strength slowed my heartbeat and ceased my tremors.

My peace was disturbed when a beech-mast hit me. I rubbed my head and looked up. Was the tree sending me on my way? At the top of the tree were some waving leaves. There, sat a cheeky squirrel, her red tail coiled prettily behind her, readying to pelt me with another nut. In spite of my sorrow, the little skugg's mischief made me laugh.

'Hello, shadow-tail. Have you brought me a message? Or are you protecting your dray? Fear not, your kitties are safe. I'm just doing the same as you and getting my pantry ready for winter.'

The squirrel reminded me of my task, so I embraced the tree and whispered my thanks before going on my way.

I came out of the woods and onto the low meadow next to the river. The hawthorn trees still sparkled with red berries. The elder trees drooped under the weight of purple berries, but the sight made me too sad, and I kept my distance from them.

I sighed and walked along the meadow to reach the old rose bushes. As I neared them, the air became sweetened with the music of song thrushes, and their singing was so agreeable, it almost made me turn back else I disturb them in their feeding. But the bushes were decked with hundreds of hips, so there was plenty for all. Even though the dry weather had rendered the hips at the manse much smaller than usual, these ones were plump and glossy.

'Clever girls to grow near the river. You must draw plenty of water and never get thirsty.'

As I plucked the hips, the risen sun began to beat down. There was none to see me, so I unwound my coif to feel the sun and air on my shorn head.

Picking hips required great concentration because of the vicious thorns and even though my fingers were nimble, by the

19

time my baskets were full, my fingers bled. There was always a price for sweetness. I wiped my hands, gnawed a stray thorn out of my thumb and then picked up my baskets. Rose would awaken shortly, and it would be good to get back before she missed me. But at that moment, I heard a shout. What was that? Someone was shouting my name. I looked towards the direction of the voice, squinting into the sun. I knew that voice! Outlined on the brow of the hill against the blue sky was a tall man. It was Tom! I dropped my baskets and ran towards him.

Tom raced down the hill towards me. Alive! My Tom really was alive! I blinked at him, hardly able to take in what was in front of me. Of course, I now knew him not lost at sea. But seeing was believing. He was so strong and vital. His burnt face made the green of his eyes and the red of his hair gleam ever more brightly.

'Jane! It's me. I'm back!'

He gazed at me with a face wearing so many emotions that it was impossible for me to say anything. It was clear that he didn't know. My whole body shivered and all my words stuck in my throat.

'Jane. Jane Chandler! Don't just stand there staring. Say something!'

He drew me into his arms and buried his face in my neck. Tom had a new smell, and I inhaled him, longing to keep him with me. No longer of woods and clay, but of air and sea. But he was as warm as ever and my blood surged. For this tiny moment in time – whilst Tom didn't know I'd wronged him – all was well in the world. For these few precious minutes, I let myself dream of all that might have been, but now could never be.

'Speak to me! Jane, it's me! Your Tom. Back from the sea.'

When he tried to kiss me, I turned my face away. There were no words. No words to tell him. How could I tell him that I was no longer his Jane Chandler? What would he say? Here he was, my own dear Tom, looking at me with so much trust. How could I tell him that I was now married to someone else? That my name was now Jane Driver. That I was the wife of his former friend. That I carried Andrew's child in my belly.

I was afraid to speak in case my tears betrayed me, and I had no right to tears after all that Tom was about to endure. How would I ever find the words to explain my betrayal? But it had to be done and it would be better coming from me.

'Tom . . . Oh, Tom.'

'Ah, Jane.' He took my face between his hands and searched my eyes with his own. 'You're treating me like a stranger. What's troubling you?'

'Tom, I can't–'

He shook his head. 'Of course, stupid me. Forgive me, please. How could I forget? I'm sorry about your mam, God rest her soul. This must be the worst of times for you, and I'm just thinking about meself, as usual.'

I stammered over the words. 'You know about Mam?'

'Aye, Jane, I heard the news when I got off the ship. And I'm sorrier than you can ever know. Annie was a good woman, and you must miss her so. And you've been in the wars yourself by the looks of you.'

At the mention of my mother's name, all my resolve was lost and I yielded to the tears that were welling in me. Tom swept me into his arms again. He held me close and pressed his face to my shorn head. I wept against his chest, for all that I'd lost. He held me quietly, letting me draw comfort and strength from him until my sobbing waned.

But then good sense returned. Could he feel my round belly pressing into him? This was not the way for him to find out, so I put my hands on his chest and gently pushed him away from me.

Tom frowned, perhaps puzzled by my rejection. 'I'm sorry for not being here to help you, but I'm back now to look after you and our bairn. Did you have a girl? Is she named Rose?'

'Yes. Yes, a girl. And she's called Rose . . . just as we planned. She's exactly like you – she has your colouring.'

He smiled. 'I cannot wait to meet her and see for meself. Ah, Jane, I'm sorrier than you can ever know for leaving you that night. But I'm back now, and all will be well. Now, I know this is not the proper place, but I made you a promise afore the navy took me.'

With that, he dropped to one knee and took my left hand.

21

As he raised it towards him, his gaze went straight to the gold on my finger.

'What's this? I didn't put that gold there.' He slowly got back to his feet. 'Jane, please tell me you put the ring there yourself, for the bairn's sake. It cannot have been easy for you . . .'

But it wasn't just the ring. He took hold of the laces at my neck. 'Your bodice is loosened.' His gaze dropped to the curve of my belly, and then the colour drained from his face. 'It cannot be. Oh, Jane . . . Please tell me it cannot be.'

I stepped back, my hands instinctively moving to my belly. Tom's face fell in dismay.

'Jane, how can you be with child again? I divvent understand.' He rubbed his hands across his face, shaking his head. 'Well, I didn't put that child there. So, who did?' He peered at me closely, until I had to look away.

'Jane, who? Please, you have to tell me.'

A cold feeling came over me. 'Tom. You have to go. You cannot remain here with me.'

'Who was it, Jane? Just tell me who it was. Did he take you against your will?' When no answer came from me, he picked up my left hand and scowled at the gold on my finger. 'I suppose this was all the permission he needed.'

I snatched my hand back and wondered how to tell him what had happened. Why could he not have seen his father or Reverend Foster first?

When he spoke again, his voice was barely a whisper. 'This is more than I can bear. You have to tell me why. And who.'

But my tongue was stilled as if by a stone pressing on it.

'If you won't tell me, then I'll sit here until I work it out for meself. It won't be too difficult, will it?' He sat on a fallen tree, pulled his knife from his belt and began hacking moss off the dead wood. 'There can only be one man, can't there? It could be no other . . . Driver. He always wanted you. Always.'

'I'm so sorry, Tom.'

He looked up at me then. 'What could ever possess you to marry Driver?'

'It wasn't done lightly–'

'Then why do it?'

'Because news came that you were lost at sea.' I looked down, as if searching for words in the earth, before speaking again. 'We held a service for you . . .' A dog barked in the distance and my heart raced. 'Tom, you must go – someone might be coming.'

'Aye, I will go. But first, you must answer me a question, which is plaguing me. How could you still think me dead? Did you get my message?'

'Yes. It came this month.'

'Only this month? That would be my second note. Did you not get my first one? I sent a letter and some golden coins.'

'A messenger delivered a pouch containing three golden angels, but there was no note . . .'

'But that makes no sense.' He frowned. 'Who would steal a letter, but not the gold?'

A sick feeling came over me. 'I don't know who might do such a thing.'

'Well, at least you received the coins. I trust they were useful?'

'You'd best ask your father that. He has them.'

'Why's me da got them? Those gold coins were for you and Rose.'

'Because I hurled them into the garden in a temper. And, well . . . Andrew fetched them and gave them to your father for safekeeping.'

Tom's face reddened. 'Driver? He was with you when the coins arrived?'

'Yes . . . Well, no. Not in the house. He'd taken to coming around – I sent him off every day, ignored. But when the messenger came, I hid myself on account of carrying Rose. Andrew was near the gate, and he took the message.' Hearing these words out loud, the sick feeling grew in my belly. 'He passed on the messenger's words and the pouch of coins.'

He leapt to his feet. 'And what words were they?'

'That you'd gone down with *The Durham* and that the coins were compensation from the navy. That's what caused my temper. The navy.'

'And did you not stop to consider that Driver might have lied? Clearly, he stole my letter to you. No doubt, he has it still!' A muscle in his cheek twitched, and it was clear to me that he was struggling to control his anger.

He walked to the riverbank and bent to pick up a handful of stones, which he threw into the river one after another before picking up a fresh handful. Poor Tom. He must be sick to the stomach. I loved him so much, but he must truly hate me now. How easy everything had seemed a year ago. And how impossible it all seemed now.

When Tom finally walked back to me, his jaw was set. 'This is hard, Jane. It's very hard for me to take in. It's not your fault, none of it. But it's hard to stomach. Even so, I love you, and in time, this anger will fade. I can care for your new bairn as me own. All is not lost. There has to be a way around this. There has to be.'

'Tom, you're such a good man. But Andrew won't let me and Rose go without a fight.' I smoothed my hands over my belly. 'And nothing in law could make him give up his legitimate child.'

My words clearly stung Tom, even though he must know there was no ill intent behind them.

'So, I have no claim on my bairn because she was . . . illegitimate? And Driver has full claim on his bairn because it'll be born in wedlock?'

I chose my next words carefully. 'Yes. But Rose was also born in wedlock—'

'You were married afore you even gave birth to Rose? So you're saying . . . what?' His voice cracked and he cleared his throat. 'That Rose belongs to Driver?'

I looked up at him. 'She has his name.'

Tom's breathing quickened. I moved towards him, but he brushed me away.

'So how long did it take my little widow to trot down the hill and set up home with my so-called good friend?'

It was too hard to meet his eyes when they were ablaze with so much anger.

'Not long . . . The wedding was not long before Rose's birth.'

'Not long? So, you thought me recently drowned and your next act was to marry Driver? Taking his name for yourself and for Rose.' He plucked a hip from the bush and caught his thumb

24

on a thorn. He didn't even notice the blood running down his hand. 'How could you do it, Jane?'

'Because I had no choice.'

'But you can't have wanted for anything between your mam and Reverend Foster. And what of me da? What did he have to say on the matter?'

'Your da encouraged me to do it. Bill gave his blessing.'

'Me own da? Was he touched in the head or something? Why would he do such a thing?'

'Because he had no choice either! If you ask him, he'll tell you.'

As soon as the words left my mouth, I regretted my sharpness. There was no reason for me to be angry at Tom.

'You tell me, Jane.' He looked at me steadily. 'At least give me that.'

'Very well. Something terrible befell me. A sergeant arrested me and took me to the House of Correction–'

'The House of Correction? You were in gaol? What could you possibly be imprisoned for? And with child?' He paused a whilst before the truth dawned on him. 'You were there *because* you were with child. You were an unwed mother.'

'We'd have died in there. Rose most certainly.'

He swallowed and his voice was gentle when he spoke again.

'Then why did no one set you free?'

'It wasn't possible. Your da was with me when the sergeant took me, and he went straight for Reverend Foster and my mother. They came to Durham to beg for my release. They tried everything in their power, but to no avail.' Poor Mam. She'd been turned away from the gaol holding me. How could I find the right words to say what had happened next? 'Andrew offered to marry me, and so the magistrate let me out. Andrew saved us both. There was no choice, do you see? Andrew offered himself as my saviour.'

'Saviour? And did none of you pause long enough to work out who might have put you in there in the first place?' He sank down on the fallen tree. 'Ah, how did none of you see through Driver's schemes?'

'You think Andrew told the sergeant of my condition?' My belly lurched at this thought. Had I remained there much longer,

Rose would have surely died. Andrew must have known this and not cared. 'You think he had me put away?'

'Aye, I do. And I'll prove it as well. But first, I'm going to find him and clash his brains out on the nearest boulder.'

'You cannot truly suppose Andrew capable of such malice.'

'Driver's shown himself more than capable. He'd stop at naught to have you – even if Rose died in the process.' He buried his face in his hands and shook his head. 'Well, that explains why you took him – you had no choice if you wanted to save our bairn! But that doesn't explain the new bairn growing in your belly.' He looked at me then and there was such a wounded look to him. 'This is not a question I rightly want to put to you, but it has to be asked.' He stood up and took both of my hands between his and drew me towards him. 'Does Driver force himself on you?'

'Tom . . . There's no way to answer that question in a way that won't break your heart even more than it already is.' I withdrew my hands from his. 'Andrew does not force himself on me, no.'

Tom blinked at this news, and it seemed he couldn't speak. He picked up a stone, turning it over and over in his hands.

'Even if he doesn't force himself on you, he's forced you into this marriage by underhand means. No true marriage can be based on such deceit, so even if you go to him willingly, he's forced the whole situation on you. He has forced you. Do you see?'

I nodded. 'Nothing would have made me marry another man if I'd known you were alive.'

'This is all wrong. It can be undone. I'll find a way, Jane. I promise you.'

'There's nothing to be done, Tom. I wish it were not so.'

He didn't reply and it felt as though his pain would stay with me forever. His fists were clenched so hard that his knuckles were white bones glowing under his skin. He would never raise a hand to me, but he would try to do serious harm to Andrew, who deserved it. Only, Andrew had a vicious streak in him that Tom lacked, and there was every likelihood that Andrew would take the chance to end Tom for good if given the slightest cause.

'Where is he? Where's Driver?'

I put a hand on his arm. 'Please, Tom.'

But he removed my hand carefully, this new coldness filling me with alarm.

'I divvent blame you for this, Jane. It's him I blame. That lad was always a conniver. He always wanted you for himself. I should never have left your side that night at the Town Moor. I can never forgive meself, and I'm truly sorry. But this is too much to bear. Even looking at you brings me pain. I have to go. I'm going to see the Reverend, to ask him to write to the Bishop on our behalf – and I'll go and see the Bishop meself if I have to. But first, I'm going to say me piece to Driver.'

There was real anger in him, something I'd never seen in Tom in all the years we'd known each other. He stood up and walked away on leaden legs towards the river. He must be bound for the top pasture. Leaving my baskets where they lay, I hurried after him in the hope of stopping whatever was about to unfold.

* * *

When I emerged from the shade of the woods and had a clear view up the valley towards the pastures, Tom had already set off up the hill, walking fast, but not running, which gave me half a chance to catch up with him.

Tom strode uphill directly towards Andrew, who was tending a calf. Once Andrew spotted Tom, he ceased his work. He stood, fists on hips, staring down the hill, eyes fixed on Tom. As I appeared behind Tom, breathless, Andrew's face darkened. He moved away from the calf and stepped into Tom's path.

'So, the dead man rises from the sea and returns to find life has gone on without him.'

Tom turned and saw me. 'Jane, go back. You shouldn't be here to see this.'

Andrew snorted. 'Verger. I'll tell Jane what to do, not you. She's my goodwife, not yours.'

'Come, Driver, let's have it. What excuse do you have for marrying Jane and taking me bairn?'

Andrew shrugged. 'No excuse at all. I always wanted her for myself, but she'd never spare me a second thought when you were anywhere near. So, I took matters into my own hands.'

'What? You had the hot press set on me?'

Andrew grinned. 'You credit me with more cunning than I possess. Mebbes it was just pure bad luck for you and a godsend for me. Still, no matter. With you gone, it was a simple matter to convince Jane to marry me, wasn't it, Jane?'

I said nothing, even though it would earn me trouble later.

'There's nothing on this earth that would have made her choose you over me, Driver, and you know it.'

Andrew's smirk made his features ugly. 'When your ship went down, we all thought you were on it. She'd already grieved, so when your letter came to tell her otherwise, I thought to spare her the excitement, given her fragile condition.'

'So then, she had no choice—'

Andrew's dark eyes glittered at me although he addressed Tom.

'She was still loyal to you, Verger, so she needed some persuading. That wasn't so easy, let me tell you. But she fell into line soon enough—'

Tom didn't let him finish the sentence.

5

John

Bitter as Wormwood

Crows scratching about on the roof disturbed my slumber, and I opened my eyes. A weak, grey light filtered through the window, and I groaned at being woken at such an early hour after so little sleep. Despite my godly intentions, I found myself still at the mercy of the innkeeper's goodwife, and she left me feeling drained of all vigour. At first, I thought this weakening of my moral core was due to being in such close proximity to the evil in Newcastle. But now, it seemed more likely that it was the lure of Goodwife Gillie's cunning mouth.

It might become necessary to leave the inn if this woman continued her nocturnal visits, because the combined temptations of her womanly flesh, the soft feather bed and the rich food were too great to resist. And they were taking a terrible toll on my purse. Goodwife Gillie had lured me with her devious ways and she would be my undoing. Thinking about her caused the hours to fall from my day. Why, this woman was stealing time from me! It was impossible to get on with my work without her pervading my thoughts. She left me with no choice but to return to her. Again and again. The urge was overpowering and just the memory of her mouth made my loins twitch.

As I pulled on my breeches, they chafed me. Already my flanks had become too sleek. Of course, my own greed hadn't helped matters – all this gorging on heavy wine, larded pastry and blooded meat. Well, there must be no more beef and kidney. They had inflamed the seat of my passions and ignited a fever in my blood. An immediate return to a bare life of prayer and a diet of plants that grew above ground would purify my blood and help me to deflect such powerful temptation. This purifying must commence today. It was time to stop my sensuous idling.

* * *

Innkeeper Gillie listened to my requirements, the man's greed chasing any trace of doubt from his features.

'This will be a matter best dealt with by my goodwife–'

'Really, Gillie, there's no need to interrupt her chores. It will be enough to pass on my requirements.'

'Hah! You afraid of blushing if you see my Patsy in front of me, eh?'

'What kind of man are you, Gillie, that you proffer your own goodwife as a bed-warmer?'

'No worse than the man who takes another man's woman into his bed.' He shrugged his meaty shoulders. 'Besides, she's my property, to do with as I will. She must do my bidding.'

Already, my cheeks were flaming, but the bold man was bent on seeing me squirm further, and he leant backwards into the kitchen to beckon his goodwife.

'Patsy, you're needed out here.'

She appeared in the doorway and gave me a saucy look. The doxy was even more brazen than her husband.

'What is it, Mr Gillie?'

'Mr Sharpe wishes to remain under our roof, Patsy. But it seems our fare is too rich for his appetite. From this day on, he wishes to dine only on leaves and the weakest of ales.'

The doxy nodded, as if she had any voice in a matter between men.

The innkeeper addressed me. 'Of course, there'll be no saving for you, Mr Sharpe, since these requirements will put Goodwife Gillie out of her way. The price will remain the same, whatever you choose to have . . .' he glanced at his goodwife, who pulled tight the laces of her bodice, '. . . or not have.'

Really, they were nothing more than a pair of swindlers! Leaves were served as an afterthought with every meal. But there was little to be gained by arguing my point, else I find myself without a roof over my head.

* * *

Although once again dining sparely on leaves, my blood must still be thickened by meat and wine, because I remained susceptible to the temptations of the flesh. Clearly the iniquitous innkeeper still wanted his pockets lined, because his goodwife continued to come to my chamber as before. When she was naked before me, it was impossible to keep a godly thought in my head, and my good intentions drained from me as quickly as my life-giving seed.

After giving in to the wench's ministrations once more, I'd dismissed her. As usual, she'd left me sated, but drained and with not enough strength to rise from my bed. Now I lay in a wash of guilt, pondering. Her mouth was moist and warm, as was her pocket. She made it impossible for me to summon sufficient moral strength to turn her away. Every time, I was too easily lost to her hot orifices. A thought struck me. Such warmth was surely unnatural. Where did that heat come from? Perhaps it came from the very fires of hell. She couldn't possibly be a natural woman, and certainly not a God-fearing one. My Lucy hadn't known tricks such as these. And even the common women I'd been forced to lie with over the years hadn't offered such pleasure. I considered this a whilst. What power did she wield over me? Was there some unnatural influence at work? A powerful magic?

The Bible was atop a table next to the bed. Its presence gave me great comfort and a suspicion began to grow in my mind. At first, Goodwife Gillie had struck me as just a low woman, and one with particularly loose morals. But it was impossible for me to resist her advances, even though my diet now contained no flesh, so there was something amiss. But what was it? Had I lingered in the coaching inn longer than intended because she held me in thrall? Did this woman have me under a spell so she could draw me to her again and again? That must be the answer! How had I not seen it before now? The woman was milking money from me, and at the same time, milking me of my blessed seed. That had the dual effect of weakening me and also removing me from my work. And for what purpose might she require my seed?

Why had these thoughts not struck me when I was first being drained of my manhood, of my very essence? The bitch was so strong and vital. And no wonder, emptying every drop of goodness from her night guests. If the English army passed through this inn, she could inflict more damage on its soldiers than the Scots ever could. And all under the nose of her husband.

Gillie felt himself in charge of her – of his property. But was he just misguided? Did she also have the poor cuckold in thrall so that she could have her way with me, deprive me of my vigour and distract me from my work? Sometimes, my own innocence amazed me. How easily I'd been taken in! But now her true purpose had been revealed to me, it would make it easier for me to see what Goodwife Gillie was really up to. Great resolution would be needed to deflect the ungodly urges she created in me. Like all forbidden women, her lips dripped honey, but truly, she was as bitter as wormwood.

I sighed, still weary, but knowing that there was work for me to do yet. My judgement had faltered in the face of her strange skills. How had I not realised it sooner? This woman must be a witch. She had never let me look in her eyes, because there I would see her true nature. And in my foolish lust, there'd been no opportunity to look over her hide for the devil's teat, but there was little doubt in my mind that she would bear his mark. I sat up in bed, newly strong, and took my pricker from its place next to the Bible, testing its point with my thumb.

Most certainly, I had inserted myself into flesh that the devil had infected. And now my flesh must be infected, too, making it meet to scourge myself. First, I would pray, which was the most cleansing act of all. And then I would scourge my body until it was as white as my soul. Once cleansed inside and out, it would be time to purify this whole village of its dark spirits, for how many others like her were living in my midst?

When I slid from the bed to pray, my knees touched the hard flags and the cold seeped into my joints, mercifully chasing away the taint of warm pleasure that had oozed through me only moments earlier.

'Oh, God, how weak is man, when in the hands of the devil's familiars. Please give me the strength necessary to combat this evil. And the strength not to be drawn into such darkness again. For a man with inflamed flesh is easily tempted from his righteous path. Please, Lord, give me strength and the will to defeat this darkness. Fill me with your love so that I can cleanse this town. So be it.'

A shudder moved through me as peace entered my soul once more. The floor was hard on my knees, but that was good. Cold and discomfort brought me nearer to God, whereas warmth and pleasure took me straight to the devil's lair. It would be unwise to bide at the inn any longer, so I must put up in new lodgings before making my accusation, and then I would prepare myself to test Goodwife Gillie. How could I not, now that the source of her body heat was known to me?

* * *

In the morning, I packed my belongings into a sack and went to settle my account.

The innkeeper raised his brows. 'You not staying for your meal? There's lamb's liver in onion gravy, and a treacle pudding for sweet—'

'No! I must go forth to seek more wholesome lodgings.'

The depraved man winked at me. 'My Patsy too much of a handful for you, then?'

It was best not to sport with this type of man, and so I busied myself counting out coins. Really, he deserved my pity, this cheerful cuckold, who sold his wife for the sake of silver. He seemed not evil himself, but only a victim of evil. It might be a kindness to warn him of what was coming, and so I laid a hand on the man's forearm.

'You're a good man, Gillie. Of that, I'm certain. But your slattern of a wife, of her, I'm much less certain. You must take heed and save your soul whilst you still can.'

The innkeeper's eyes widened and his mouth slackened. With that, I swept out of the inn. I would seek out a humble dwelling and ask for lodgings. There was bound to be a plain spinster here-abouts with a spare chamber. Then, with a clear mind, it would become easier to consider how to set about the cleansing of this town.

My plan to draw the townspeople to me hadn't worked. Evidently, this town had hidden corners where the light of God didn't shine as brightly as it might. But I was unafraid of the shadows and would root out evil wherever it might lie. It might require more investigation than Newcastle, which knew itself to be an infested town. But here, the townsmen were asleep, and they didn't know that evil lived and breathed in their midst. It was my duty to wake them from their spiritual slumber and save their souls from certain peril at the hands of unkempt women.

6

Jane

Avaricious Eyes

When I set off for church, the morning was already hot and my ears filled with the song of blackbirds. The Reverend had called the parish to attend a special sermon, but it was still early, so I paused at Tom's cross. Had it chilled Tom's blood when he saw the cross standing next to his mother's grave?

I cut some roses for Tom's mother and some for his former shipmates. Poor lads. All gone to the cold depths, never to see their loved ones again. Finally, I placed some for my mother, who'd lost her life, without so much as a prayer for her soul. If only she could be buried here instead of Newcastle. I sighed and wiped my eyes. Wishing was a ruinous way to waste time, and Mam would chide me for it if she were here. I only stood here breathing because she'd given up her life for me. The best way to honour her sacrifice would be to live a good life and make sure Rose grew up hale and happy.

Jim Driver appeared at the bottom of the hill, with Rose riding on his shoulders and Bett at his side, but with no sign of Andrew. I left the crosses and met them at the lych gate.

'Hello Rose. Do you want down?'

Rose climbed into my arms and then slid down onto the ground where she began to toddle around after a bumble bee.

'Hello Jim, Bett. Where's Andrew?'

Jim cast a suspicious look around the graveyard and eyed the roses on Tom's mother's grave.

'Thanks to young Verger, my lad's not fit to be seen in church. Besides, there's a cow in calf and she's struggling. You should be there helping him instead of dallying here amongst the dead.'

It wasn't the dead that he was worried about me dallying with, of course. But there was no sign of Tom, and so there was nothing for Jim Driver to complain about. If the cow was in a truly bad way, Jim would've stayed to help, and Andrew wouldn't thank me for interfering in his work. But it would be wise to hold my tongue.

Bett took up Jim's refrain. 'Aye, your place is by our Andrew's side. He saved your life and put a roof over your bairn's head. Never forget that you are in his debt. And ours. Always.'

'Of course.' I caught Rose's hand, drawing her into church with me so that the Drivers couldn't see the anger in my eyes.

We slipped quietly into the Drivers' pew. Tom was sitting with his father, so at least I couldn't be further accused of dallying with him. With my head bowed, I cast sidelong glances at him. The sight of his bright hair and his straight back made me ache for him. I wondered whether he'd spoken to Reverend Foster yet about writing to the Bishop. Hopefully, the Reverend had written already and we might have a response before too long. I would try to slip away from the Drivers and speak to the Reverend after the service.

Rose was restless and patted Bett's cheek, and she smiled fondly at my little girl. It was a comfort that Rose had another who loved her, even if it was Bett and her stern ways, but I wished with all my heart that my own mother might be sitting here holding her granddaughter.

Rose clambered off my knee. She stood on the pew and began singing a nonsense song that fractured the silence of the church. Tom started at the sound and turned round, his eyes locked onto Rose. A grin spread across his face at the sight of his daughter. But then Bett snatched Rose onto her lap and distracted her with a pretty thimble. Pain flashed across Tom's eyes. He swallowed and bowed his head. How I longed to take Rose to him, to sit with her true father and her grandfather. Rose belonged in the Vergers' pew, and so did I.

My thoughts were broken when the vestry door opened and Reverend Foster climbed up into the pulpit. He arrived there wheezing, gripping his lectern so hard that his hands trembled. He was grey-faced and drained of vigour, so gaunt he seemed barely able to raise his arm in benediction. Stubble silvered his chin and neck and his vestments hung limply. A light had gone out in him. It was sad seeing him so dishevelled in church. He needed something to lift him back up. A few doses of elder linctus would strengthen his lungs and give him vitality. But really, he needed something to mend his broken heart.

Finally, the Reverend caught his breath and pointed to a pile of paper on the lectern. 'Now, some of you will see these papers, and your hearts will sink, fearing that you're about to be subjected to a particularly lengthy sermon.'

Mild laughter filled the church.

'But no, you may rest easy, dear parishioners. These are letters addressed to men of God in the north of England and the south of Scotland. And I would ask any of you here who can write to lend his hand to the task.'

A few men nodded and raised their hands, Tom amongst them. He was no more able to write than I was, but my heart swelled at his willingness.

'And what am I writing about, you might ask? I am writing to anyone who will listen about John Sharpe, come amongst us lately from Scotland. He has taken from us our dearest Annie, and he almost took Jane, too. He has a taste for violence to women that will never be sated. There is something sick in his soul and he won't stop until forcibly stopped. Please believe me when I say that this threat is a very real one. I won't rest whilst there is a risk – however small – that he might return for our women and girls.'

Did his eye rest on Rose then? Bett held her close and buried her face in my daughter's mass of ringlets. My blood ran cold at the thought of any harm coming to her. Surely, surely, John Sharpe would never harm an innocent child. But then, he had harmed my innocent mother, and had he not been prevented, who knows how many more he'd have sent to the gallows. I shut my eyes in silent prayer but opened them when I heard Tom's voice.

'Will letters be enough, Reverend Foster?'

'Perhaps not, Tom. But we need to change the thinking man's mind. Mere words may not be enough, but they are a start.'

'Might it be better to hunt him down?' Tom stood up and faced the congregation. 'I'll go. I'm a good hunter. Not as good as Driver, of course, because I lack his cunning and instinct to kill.'

The barb missed its target because Andrew was not here, but Jim stiffened and Bett put a staying hand on his arm.

'I'll go after this Sharpe and make sure he doesn't get away again. I can hunt a deer. It cannot be much harder to hunt a man. I'll arm myself and track down this man. Then we'll see justice done.'

He looked at me, but I wouldn't meet his eye.

'No, Tom, lad. Your intentions are good, but you shouldn't track this man. No one should. There's too much danger. This man is filled with evil, and we cannot risk him spilling any more blood. Besides, he's most likely back in Scotland and you cannot follow him there, for Scotland is up in arms again, and you don't want to get tangled up in the wars.'

'And yet, he must be stopped.' Tom sat down heavily and pointed to the pile of paper. 'If we cannot run him to ground, how will writing letters stop him?'

'Sharpe will be plying his trade north of the border. Our task is to turn the tide against him. We must fight with words and ideas to change men's minds. You must trust in the rightness of this, Tom. It was kind of you to offer yourself. But you'll see that I am right.' The Reverend leant out of his pulpit. 'We must tell the world of John Sharpe. A madness has come upon England of late. Many in the Church are in the grip of a fervour so great that they murder innocents on the flimsiest of evidence. Women are being put to death in their droves on no more than the say-so of this Scottish man and his ilk. These hate-filled men must be stopped.'

This shook me. Would John Sharpe have the belly to come back for me? For Rose? Surely, he'd been frightened away back to his own country, and he'd be too afraid to set foot in England again. Perhaps the Reverend's words were just meant to put us on our guard. A precaution, that was all.

'These witch-finders cannot be truly inspired by God, but rather, Mammon, because they wish to empty a town's coffers into their own pouches. They charge sums of money that beggar belief. And their methods are deranged. They present women in ways that humiliate and demean them. These details are not suitable to share in the house of God, but suffice it to say, they must be designed to draw crowds of men and so turn their minds. This man, Sharpe, considers women guilty of all manner of transgressions, with witchcraft being only one of them. The witch-finder's hatred of womankind has infected people so that neighbour turns against neighbour, sister against sister, and friend against friend.'

But it hadn't turned mother against daughter. Mam had been strong, and she'd given up her life for me. I swallowed. Would I have the strength to do the same for Rose? I gazed at my little girl, snuggled in Bett's arms, thumb in mouth and eyelids drooping. She was so innocent and lovely. Of course I would lay down my life to save her. A mother's love for her child was the strongest bond in the world, and not even men like John Sharpe could break that.

'Ours is not the only parish to suffer. Up and down England, this scourge is carried. And in Scotland, it's like a fever. Though their population is scarcely a quarter of England's, the Scots are killing witches in their hundreds, if not thousands. If Sharpe and his terrible brethren are left to their own devices, there won't be a woman left in all of Scotland. And then we can be sure that Scotland's witch-finders will turn their avaricious eyes on England once again. We've already suffered great loss at the hands of John Sharpe. We must have no more of these fiends crossing the border. We must be on our guard for strangers in our midst.'

That shouldn't be too hard. Ours was such a small community, cut off from surrounding towns and villages. News of a stranger would spread quickly. But would John Sharpe bother himself to come all this way? Would any witch-finder come this way? In our quiet notch in the valley, we'd always been sheltered from the worst of everything, whether that be the elements, the Great Mortality, or the warring between king and parliament, catholic and protestant, Scotland and England. Surely, we'd be safe here.

'And I must caution you all against superstition – which might seem an innocent prop to lean on since we live so close to death. But the superstition surrounding so-called witches is not innocent – it is dangerous. People are blind to the real evil in their midst. There is evil abroad, but it is not witches – Annie was certainly none such.' A tear appeared in his eye, wobbled for an instant and then fell. He caught it on one finger and examined it with some surprise. 'And nor is Jane a witch. To my mind, there is no such thing as a witch.'

Mr Green's hand shot up. 'But, Reverend, how can you say such a thing. The Bible is filled with tales of witches. Denying God's word is surely blasphemy!'

The Reverend let out a long, juddering sigh. 'Ah, Green, the Bible is filled with many tales, and not all of them good or right.' He held up a hand to prevent Mr Green from interrupting him. 'This idea of witches has been concocted by angry men afraid of their own shadows.' He paused to cough and his chest rattled. 'They must be stopped. I should have tried harder to stop them before now. And then it might not have come to this terrible juncture. But it's a mighty trade, with much gold to be gained, and it may need more than a mere minister's words to halt it.'

'But, Reverend, the Bible–'

'Green, man! You must see sense. The very idea of a witch is nothing more than a phantom dreamt up by men so they can further punish women. Yes, the likes of Annie, Jane and Meg made remedies to cure various ills. But that's science and not magic. Does anyone point the finger at the apothecary or the physic or the barber-surgeon? No, they do not. Because they are, without exception, men. Make no mistake – this accusation of witchcraft is aimed squarely at our womenfolk.'

Mr Green was on his feet now, and May slunk down in the pew, her head bowed. 'But witches can fly abroad in the night on broomsticks. They say it's common happenstance at Riding Mill when the coven meets under the bridge. They say Meg Wetherby went there. They say the devil took her soul when she died.'

I put my hand over my mouth lest I be tempted to speak out. This terrible man, that he should be so addled of brain. It gave me a grain of satisfaction to know that it was Meg's teachings that had put paid to his wicked actions. Mr Green would never have dared speak such words within Meg's hearing.

Reverend Foster rested his gaze on Mr Green until the man began to fidget. 'Surely, even you, Green, cannot be so insensible as to believe a woman made of flesh and blood can fly through the air. Least of all alight something as slight as a broomstick. It is simply not possible. Use your brain, man. This idea of flying is something from an old faerie tale. It is not real.'

But nothing in the world felt real anymore. Everything had changed forever.

Reverend Foster paused, breathing heavily, looking around and putting his eye on men in the congregation, one after the other. 'I see you blink, some of you. I tell you, Green, what you say is not possible. Even a simpleton such as you can see this.'

Mr Green hung his head, his neck and ears scarlet. But then he raised his head again and started to speak, 'Aye, but–'

'But nothing, Green! Now sit down and be quiet, else you put me in an early grave.'

Mr Green opened his mouth to object, but there was steel in Reverend Foster's eyes now, and so he seemed to think better of it and sat down. I just hoped he wouldn't take out his anger and humiliation on his family.

'Good people of Mutton Clog, open your eyes and your minds. Ask yourselves why things happen. They happen because it is nature's way. God's way. If we have poor weather, then it follows that we will have poor crops. If anyone decrees poor weather, then it is God. Or the devil, if you must hold someone to blame. But no woman has a hand in this. Please join me in using your sense to unpick this threatening madness.'

But Mr Green had regathered himself and was back on his feet.

'Sorry, Reverend, but there can be no smoke without fire.' He looked around the congregation until his eyes rested on me. 'Since it's only women who are witches, these women must be doing something to warrant the suspicion.'

Reverend Foster drew in a deep breath, and when he spoke, his voice held some of its old fire.

'Green, listen to me. Women are held suspect because they bleed with the moon and do not die, so some unthinking men consider them creatures of the night. They bear life in their bellies, and often bringing forth this life costs them their own. God has made women for this purpose. It does not make them magic, nor does it make them belong to the devil or the night. Again, it is just nature at work – God's will. There is no enchantment in women, they do not hold sway over the natural world, they do not copulate with the devil. If any of you doubt the truth of this, then speak your mind now.'

The Reverend stared at Green for a long time until he sat down. There was some shuffling and fidgeting in the congregation, but no one else spoke up. The congregation respected Reverend Foster because he was a man of the cloth, and a good man. But there was more than that today, there was sympathy for his bereavement and his resulting fury.

'So, I am busy writing letters to tell the world of John Sharpe, who pretends to do God's work. I will put villages on their guard and beseech them to send news to me. I will ask them to consider, with properly critical minds, this question: do witches walk amongst us, or merely women? We must protect our women and girls.' He looked at me and Rose with rheumy eyes. 'I have failed in this regard once. I will not fail again.'

Even though I couldn't read, I was gripping a hymnal. My hands were shaking. I clenched the book hard, as if it were something real to hold on to. But it was only made of words, and what use were they?

7

John

Suckled on the Devil's Milk

The townspeople of Berwick had proven curiously tight-lipped during my interrogation of them and they'd shown considerable reluctance to turn over their womenfolk. Part of me wondered at this reluctance. Was it born from fear of losing their loved ones? Or was there a greater fear at play? So, I'd been forced to call a meeting in the town hall, and now I stood at the head of it, addressing a group of two-score men that included the magistrate, the minister and members of the guild.

To begin with, I listed the credentials that made me fit to carry out this work and then revealed my suspicions about the innkeeper's doxy before pausing to see the effect of my words. It pleased me to note the men take a step nearer to me, till they crowded around me, hanging on my every word, each of them sharing the same goggle-eyed expression. Eventually, the minister pushed his way to the front and spoke up, an impatient cast to his face.

'Continue, Sharpe, you must not keep us in suspense in this way. Is Goodwife Gillie the sole witch in our town?'

'She won't be alone, of that you may rest assured. If you will merely support me with the cost of bed and board for a few nights, and a small fee for my trouble, I will root out the evil in your midst.'

The village elders still seemed somewhat troubled and they stepped aside to let their magistrate to speak for them.

He stood before me and addressed me. 'But the innkeeper's goodwife? You are certain of this?' The old sap's jowls wobbled. 'After all, she's married to my brother, which makes her kin to me.'

The innkeeper stood behind the magistrate, and he appeared uncommonly upset. Both men were soft of face and belly, and clearly cut from the same cloth. A flicker of unease crept up my spine. That the innkeeper was the magistrate's brother hadn't occurred to me. How might such a slattern be kin to a man of high standing? This unfortunate turn caused me some dismay. But I might yet use it to my advantage.

'Why . . . being kin to a good man means nothing to the devil.' I peered closely at the magistrate. 'You see, unchecked, her evil could spread from one to another. Why, your own goodwife might already be afflicted by association.' I raised my Bible to make my point. 'For certainty, I will test your goodwife also.'

A sheen of sweat bloomed on the magistrate's face. 'But it cannot be . . . my goodwife is a God-fearing woman. She has duties in the church! The minister will tell you, will you not?'

He cast a desperate look the way of the minister, who closed his eyes, as if in prayer. The magistrate was an innocent fool – his friends were as untrue as his wife.

'Sire, do you now see how easy it is for evil to gain a foothold even in a Christian community? The devil doesn't go after his own. I've discovered this during my travels. He already owns their misbegotten souls.' I put an arm around his shoulders to bring him a measure of comfort. 'So, he goes after good women to ease his path to the heart of God's children.' I shook my head slowly. 'Don't be taken in, sire. This is what the devil wants. He will twist your minds. Weak hearts will make you want to save your womenfolk, but you must be strong in the face of the devil, or he will take us all . . .'

I paused for breath and gave them some time to confer, but not too long, else they talk themselves out of my bounty.

'Recently, I cleared Newcastle of a mighty coven. The devil was at work in every corner of that town. Why, there's so much money in its coffers, it's almost a sin in itself. The town has great riches from the filthy black coal it gouges from the earth's belly. You

44

know how easily coal takes the flame? And then it reeks of sulphur. Coal is governed by hell itself. No wonder Newcastle seethes with sin! In its many inns, women run as freely as strong drink. And a spirit is alive in the air of its people, who are far too ready to enjoy themselves. For the most part, they are already lost to God.'

At this, the minister nodded deeply. 'Aye, I've often heard it said that Newcastle is a town awash with sin. Your tale of its mighty coven is no surprise to me. We will hear you out.'

It was good to have the minister's support at last. People would seek spiritual guidance from him. Greatly encouraged, I continued.

'Seventeen witches were removed from Newcastle on a single day when I broke its coven. Yet seventeen are not enough. Such was the power of the coven that its mightiest witch escaped the hangman's noose. This witch still roams the earth and presents a danger to godly people everywhere. So, I must put down stores of money and strength before returning to remove her from this world.'

An overfed freeman, who had stared raptly at me throughout my speech, now blinked. 'Yes, we must do all in our power to help you. Why, Newcastle is our neighbour town. We cannot have its evil leaching into our own good people.'

By now, the magistrate's face was pale, and his lips had taken on a bluish tinge. Pleased at this effect, I looked from one man to the other, waiting for their response.

The magistrate swallowed before speaking. 'As the pastor suggests, Newcastle is a town not too far south of us. The affliction might well spread north if we don't stamp it out. Sharpe, you should return urgently to Newcastle and snuff out the contagion there, to prevent it—'

'No!' This transparent attempt to shift my attention had to be thwarted. 'Please be assured, sire, that the contagion has already spread. We must act now before Berwick becomes likewise infected. The contagion is already here, as shown amply in the case of the innkeeper's wife. I am a godly man of good standing, and I have witnessed the woman's lure first-hand. An unnatural fire burns in that woman's belly – it can be felt in her mouth, in her hands and in . . .'

This evidence inflamed several faces, and I wondered whether from guilt or desire. Only the magistrate seemed uncertain – clearly the man was concerned for his own goodwife. But would he be talked round by his brethren? Or would he dare stand against me? Perhaps they feared that my fee was too great. It might need to be reduced lest I leave this town empty-handed.

A white-haired man stepped forward then and cleared his throat. 'Neighbours, pay heed to me. This witch-finding man may be right. Our crops have fared badly this year. War rages around our ears. Evil stalks the land. We need to cleanse our town before it's too late. I say we employ John Sharpe and let him save us.' The elder looked from one man to another, until gradual nods came from the other men. 'Aye, John Sharpe, it is agreed. The town will take you on.'

It was hard not to smile, but I was practised in concealing my inner self. 'Very well. Now you should know my fee, which is three pounds per cleansing . . .' I considered the men's ample jowls, their bellies pushing out their waistcoats, their finely cut breeches and their snowy collars. Their crops might be sparse, but thanks to the bounty of the sea, there was silver aplenty here. And it could be mine. To think I had nearly reduced my fee! 'Three pounds per witch, that is.' I let this detail sink in. One or two men's eyes widened, but most of the men seemed accepting.

The white-haired man spoke for his neighbours. 'Aye, I suppose we cannot ask a man to imperil his immortal soul without proper reward. We have the coin, and we're prepared to use it to spare our souls.'

The minister frowned. 'But those funds are set by to finish the church. We need them.'

Had I overstretched myself by demanding three pounds per witch? Surely, they wouldn't put the kirk building before their eternal souls.

But the elder came to my aid once more. 'Aye, and little merit in having a church that our townsmen cannot set foot in because their souls belong to Satan. None of us are safe. None.'

They were on the brink of agreeing, but they still needed some persuasion. 'It's all the same to me, friends. Other villages also have great need of me.' I made ready to take my leave and began to gather my belongings. 'So, I'll take up no more of your valuable time.'

The minister frowned. 'Wait, John Sharpe! We'll pay. The church can wait. Stay and help us.'

'Very well, then.' I put down my Bible and my sack and paced about before them. 'Now, there will be a coven here. Thirteen witches in all. So, you must work with me to unveil them because they are sly and live amongst us as natural-appearing women. This is what we must do . . .'

In the end, it had taken a mere hour to convince the local worthies of the wanton evil in their midst. It never took long to make the case against witchcraft. In my mind, Berwick's thirty-nine pounds were already weighting my purse.

8

Jane

A Measure Spilt

I was at the Drivers' home, grinding up the last of the chasteberries to make monk's pepper. On my instruction, May had been lacing her father's early morning ale with it. More's the pity it hadn't occurred to me to lace Andrew's ale likewise. Then I might not be trapped in this marriage, carrying a bairn that ensured there could never be any escape. It was wrong to blame the bairn though. He was innocent in all this, and as much my child as Rose.

I sighed. There were enough berries to last May for a moon or two, but they wouldn't see her past the New Year. No chasteberries grew locally as they came only from warm climes. But there was bound to be some at Meg's dwelling place. Meg had been the green woman for Mutton Clog for as long as anyone could remember. She was now dead and buried, but her dwelling was still intact, and with it, her stores. If there were no berries there, then it would mean a journey to Newcastle. But any trade would have to be with the merchants on the Tyne, for I would never again set foot in the apothecary's shop.

When measuring out the pungent powder, my hands trembled a little, so I held my breath to steady them. Just then, there was a soft knock and the door opened, which caused me to flinch and spill my measure. I stared at the mess of berries and powder on the floor and then at my visitor.

'Tom! You cannot be here when I'm alone. The Drivers might return at any minute!'

'I'll take me chances with the Drivers. Besides, we'll not be disturbed. Jim and Andrew took the beasts to the mart early on. And Bett was away to the market by the looks of her. We'll be all right a whilst and I'll be away long afore anyone gets back. No one saw me. I promise you. Can I come in?'

'Tom, it's not wise . . .' Tom had left Andrew in an awful state and it had taken almost half my store of salves to mend him. 'He's still black and blue in places.'

But Tom laughed and rubbed his skinned knuckles. 'Still black and blue, eh? It's a great shame he's still breathing.'

'It's not funny, Tom. He raged at me for hours on end.'

His voice softened. 'I'm sorry you've borne the brunt of his temper, truly. He'd better not have hurt you, or . . .'

I shook my head. 'Please, Tom, promise me there'll be no more fighting. Andrew's after killing you as it is.'

'He's already half done that with his cattle prod. It knocked all the colour out of me vision. Look.' He lowered his head and parted his hair to reveal a large gash. 'I feel as though I've fallen under a horse.'

I sighed. 'Oh, that's bad. You're lucky to be alive.'

He looked steadily at me. 'I divvent feel lucky.'

'I suppose you don't. When did this happen?'

'Late last night. He crept up on me when I was digging a fresh grave. He must have knocked me out cold. Da found me lying half in the grave, bleeding from the wound.'

At least that explained Andrew's cheer last night. He'd come in late, wearing a look of grim satisfaction on his battered face. But he'd fly into a new rage if he knew I'd been in the same room as Tom, let alone touching him, but I couldn't see Tom in such a state and not help him.

'It's a bad wound and you'll have grave dirt in it. Let me put some salve on it before it starts to fester.'

He put his hand to his head and snorted. 'What, and cancel out the kindness from your loving husband?'

'I'm truly sorry, Tom. But I had no inkling of this.'

'Aye, well that was a great comfort to me as I lay in the grave.' He smiled at me. 'Aw, Jane. I'm sorry. Take no notice of me. None of this is your doing.'

He had every right to be bitter, and it grieved me that things couldn't be easy between us, but it couldn't be helped. 'Well, at least let me stop you losing your life through bad blood. Come, sit down.'

Tom brooded whilst I dipped muslin in a comfrey tincture and began to cleanse the wound. Although it must have stung, he didn't wince.

'There, that's the wound cleaned, so it won't fester. But let me apply some sage ointment to take down the swelling and the pain. What a state he's left you in.'

'It makes me wish for an axe to take to Driver's head!'

'You mustn't say such things! There's been too much fighting already. Tom, you must promise me that you won't fight Andrew again. Or one of you will end up dead.'

'Aye, and it'll be Driver. You can reckon on that.'

'And then you'd swing for it, and I'd be left with two bairns and no husband. You must stay your hand. Please, promise me, no more fighting.'

'No promises, Jane. Driver irks me. And he may pick yet another fight with me. There's no saying what he might do next time.'

'Please stop being so stubborn. If not for me, then think of Rose. You're still her father, and she'll come to know you one day. I promise.'

He hung his head for a whilst and then looked up at me. 'Aye, very well then. You have my word. But if Driver comes after me again, he can't just have at me.'

'Fair enough. Leave Andrew to me. Or his mother at least. He listens to her. Just as long as you don't start anything.'

'I won't start anything. You have my word.' He sighed. 'Have you anything for the thumping in me head? When I came to, the horizon seemed set at a fresh angle and me guts lurched when I tried to stand up. It was like being back at sea again.'

I rummaged in my mother's satchel. 'Here, chew on some birch bark. That'll soothe the pain and help with the swelling. Though it tastes so bitter, you may prefer the pain.'

Whilst Tom chewed, I dipped my ring finger into the soft unguent. Sage always felt cold to the touch. As softly as I could, I dabbed the cream over the wound and then moved round to dress his knuckles. Once in front of him, I became conscious of my belly, and tried not to brush against him. But he didn't once look at me as I tended him, staring straight ahead all the whilst. No longer was he my lovely Tom, but now a man with ice in his eyes.

I wiped my hands on my pinny. 'There. You're done. Now, you must go else someone finds you here. Please.'

He stood up. 'All right. But where's Rose? Can I see her afore you sling me out?'

'She's sleeping.'

'Oh.' His face fell.

My heart melted. 'Come, you can look at her whilst she sleeps. Just don't make a sound else you rouse her.'

I pushed open the door and we stepped through to where Rose slept in her basket at the foot of the bed. If the sight of that bed pained Tom, he showed no sign of it, and his eyes were only for Rose. She lay on her back, clutching her poppet. He gazed at her and swallowed, then gently moved a red tress and bent down to kiss her forehead. Her violet eyelids flickered and her tiny red lips curved in a gentle smile. I put my hand on his arm and drew him out of the room.

'Come, Tom, she looks set to waken and she mustn't see you here.' I closed the door and didn't add that she'd be frightened of a stranger in her room.

'I've got to see her properly, when she's awake. Look, I go to Meg's dwelling most mornings, to hunt and keep the paths clear. Can you bring Rose there sometimes to see me?'

'I'll try. But it won't be easy. Andrew might . . .'

He pointed at my belly and at the gold on my finger. 'And what else might Andrew do to you and my daughter?'

'Nothing. He would never hurt Rose. Please don't be angry with me, Tom.'

'I am angry, but not at you. It's not your fault you were taken in by Driver.' He put his hands on my shoulders. 'Listen, the Reverend has written to the Bishop, so it cannot be too long now afore we get an answer.'

'But the answer might not be the one we seek. And we'll be even more miserable once we know we cannot free me from my circumstances.'

He snorted. 'Nothing could make me more miserable than I already am. The Bishop must soon reply to the Reverend's letter, and you must have hope, Jane. Right is on our side. The Bishop must see sense and unchain you from this forced marriage.'

'Do you really think the Bishop might allow it?' I touched my belly and bit my lip. 'And even if he did, what of this child?'

'Like I said, it's no matter. I'll raise this child and Rose and love them both the same because I love you.'

'But Andrew will never let us go.' My eyes brimmed. 'Tom, please . . .'

'I cannot take Rose in me arms for fear of scaring her, but nothing can stop me taking you.'

He pulled me towards him and my heart filled with warring emotions. I wanted him so badly, but my belly was filled with Andrew's child.

'Jane, my lovely, lovely Jane. How I've missed you.'

'Tom, you mustn't hold me.' Despite my love, I was stiff in his arms, tree-like. Tears coursed down my face. 'You must go. Please, you cannot be here.'

'Then I'll go, to spare you further distress. But all this can be undone. Rose will know me in time. I'm good at waiting. She's young and children adapt. Please, Jane, this will soon be made right.'

'But, Tom, nothing can ever be right again. Everything stopped the night you were taken away.'

My head drooped and he raised my chin with his forefinger. 'It can start again, Jane. It can. As soon as the Bishop dissolves this mockery of a marriage.'

'Please don't give yourself false hope, Tom. Too much time has passed . . .'

'Such a marriage can be undone, no matter how much time's passed if it's been made on false pretences. The Bishop will have to pay heed.'

Oh, if only he was right! The thought was too tantalising, and it wouldn't do to let hope flare in my heart – or Tom's. I moved from him to put away my salves so he wouldn't see my face.

'Even if the Bishop will dissolve the marriage, Andrew wouldn't give me up lightly and you'd have to fight hard to prove it was false. Hearsay might not be enough.'

'My word against Driver's, you mean?'

'Yes, precisely that. You've no way to prove Andrew tricked me.'

'No, but Driver might prove it himself . . . The letter from me with the pouch of coins. If Driver stole it, he'll have kept it to gloat over. I know him.'

'You're right!' Oh, please let Andrew have kept the letter if it might end this marriage. 'But where would he hide it?'

'Same place he hid everything as a lad.' In front of the fire was a proggy mat. Tom knelt down and peeled it back. 'Watch.'

'Tom, don't look now!' I peeked out of the window, my heart thumping. 'When everyone's gone to bed tonight, I'll have a look. Andrew will be back at any time and—'

'And what? What can he possibly do to us that's worse than what he's already done?'

He took his knife from his belt and prised up the flagstone under the rug. In the earth beneath was a curved piece of metal.

'My fire steel? He had to have that and all.' He held it up, and it gleamed in the firelight. 'Well, you saved my life with it once, Jane.' He tucked it into his pouch. 'And one day, I'll give it to Rose.'

Beneath the fire steel was a waxed packet. He opened it and slid out a piece of paper with a broken seal.

'Is that it? Is that your letter?'

He ran his eyes down the paper. 'Aye. Aye, it is.'

'Then let me take it to the Reverend so he can tell me what it says.'

He shrugged. 'No need. I learnt to read a bit on the ships. And I remember most of it in any case.' He traced his finger across the message. 'But I might falter over some of the harder words and mebbes take a guess at some of them.' He started reading slowly. '"My dearest Jane, You might have heard by now that my ship, *The Durham*, went down. And you might suppose me lost with all the other poor souls when she went down—" What was that noise?'

'Ssh!' A dog was barking outside and I ran to the window. There was no one outside, and no sign of any dog, but my heart was thumping. 'Go on. But please hurry.'

'I've lost me place now.' He nodded and moved his finger along the page again. 'Ah, here we are. "But before she went down, I was moved to another ship as a volunteer, along with the physician who has written this note for me. Here's some money to keep you and little Rose." He stopped reading then. 'These next words, I remember by heart. "One day, I'll be home to see you both. And we'll be wed at last. I miss you and long to be home again. With all my love always, Your Tom." There, that's all of it.'

I took the letter from his hands. 'So these words . . . this letter . . . the sergeant would have accepted it as proof of a promise of marriage?'

Tom nodded. 'It's as clear as day we were to be wed on my return from sea.'

'And I need never have gone to the House of Correction?'

He took the paper from me and placed it on the table and then took my hands in his and searched my eyes. 'Aye. And this letter being hidden here proves you were only put in gaol because of Driver in the first place.'

'Then . . . he really did have me sent there. It's too terrible to believe.'

He pulled me to him and I inhaled him. The smell of happier times.

'Nothing's too terrible to believe of that man. We can take the letter to the magistrates now. We can show it to the Bishop.' He traced a thumb under my eye, caught a tear and tasted it. 'All will be well, Jane, I promise you. We have the proof now and–'

There were footsteps outside and my eyes flicked to the door. Andrew! I jumped back from Tom just as Andrew stormed in. He stamped straight through the mess of chasteberries on the floor and grabbed Tom by the throat. Tom's eyes flared, but he kept his hands by his sides.

'Come, Verger, what errand brings you to my home to tarry with my goodwife and daughter? Haven't you learnt your lesson yet? Now, let's get this settled–'

Tom shrugged him off and spoke in a low voice. 'I'll not fight you in a house where my bairn's asleep. We'll take this outside.'

Andrew snorted. 'Aye, right enough. You'd better not wake *my* bairn. Get outside and then you'll be left in no more doubt about who—'

His gaze fell on the upturned flagstone and then on the letter on the table.

Tom was quick and pinned Andrew's arms. But in his rage, Andrew was strong. He heaved Tom off, snatched the letter and flung it into the fire. Tom ran to the fire and put his hands into the flames to save the letter, but he wasn't fast enough. The flames devoured the paper, and with it, any hope of escaping from this marriage. It would cost me later, but I couldn't help my tears.

'Best place for that. Now, get out of my home, Verger.'

A howl came from behind me. Rose was awake. Oh, please let her not have heard this tumult. I turned to Tom, pleading with my eyes.

'I'll leave your dwelling, Driver.' Tom paused at the door. 'But this is not over.'

9

John

A Hardy Breed

Upon my entering the inn, Gillie raised hopeful eyes to me.

'Ah, Sharpe, so you've decided to come back to us. Your chamber's been taken, but there's another that might prove suitable, although it has a slightly higher price.'

He raised one hand to remove a large key from a hook behind him when the two sergeants stepped forward. He put down the key.

'You mistake my intent, Gillie. I'm not here as a paying guest, but to collect your goodwife.'

He paled. 'Patsy isn't here. She's away to stay with her sister.'

I leant on the counter and eyed him closely. 'And where might her sister live?'

'Down in York.' His eyes flicked left and right. 'But don't ask me the address, because I don't know it.'

'Don't lie to me – I'm no imbecile.' I reached over the counter and grabbed the front of his jerkin. 'There's evil in that woman and if you don't hand her over, then you'll find yourself on trial.'

Before the innkeeper could open his mouth to lie again, Goodwife Gillie appeared and walked up to her husband. She kissed him on the cheek but didn't say a word to him and then held her hands up before the sergeants. When they tied his goodwife's wrists with hemp rope and removed her from the inn, Gillie wept like a woman, tears rolling from his jowls as he begged for her return.

Goodwife Gillie didn't weep and she remained stony-faced as the sergeants walked her through the streets of Berwick. Citizens stopped to stare, and one man spat at her feet as she passed. But still, she held herself proud. I took her to the spinster's dwelling and into my chamber, which contained only a bed, a table and a stool. I sent the youngest sergeant to fetch some shears. The witch continued to hold her head up and was barefaced enough to meet my gaze.

When the sergeant came back with the shears, I dismissed him, barred the door and forced the witch to her knees. Her hair was bound in a coif and I unwound it, freeing her flaxen tresses.

'Now, Goodwife Gillie, you are much too proud.' Even though I brandished the shears, the woman didn't cringe. 'But that will change.'

Much of the witch's strength and beauty rested in her hair. Wanton tresses tumbling loose could unleash tawdry passions in the stoniest of men. It was just as well that modesty required goodwives to cover their hair. It might be undone by the man of the house as he saw fit, but it had no place being on show to inflame other men.

I fingered a lock of hair. 'How many men have let down your hair besides me and your gullible husband?' She continued to meet my gaze but held her tongue.

I snipped the first lock so close to her skull that the shears grazed her scalp, yet she didn't flinch or bow her head and continued to stare straight ahead. Every tress hacked made her less of a woman. As the floor filled with golden locks, she became more an object of pity than of lust. This treatment would stop any doubters being beguiled by her, and I sheared her remaining hair until the floor was covered with it.

Then I stood her up and cut her kirtle and bodice from her. Even without her tresses, this woman still had shapely parts, and enticing eyes and lips. I would cover them all if I could – temptation should not be allowed to walk amongst decent men to deter us from our true path. When her breasts tumbled free, they still bore the marks from my teeth. But now was the time for duty and not for indulgence.

For all her fleshly softness, Goodwife Gillie had a core of iron, and she remained mute, refusing to say a word and speaking her rage only with her eyes. She was a powerful witch this one, to keep her lips sealed so, and her will was strong, but no woman's flesh could hold out forever. Her hide was plush and when I moved her body towards the window for examination, the sunlight revealed none of the silver lines caused by child-bearing.

'How have you borne no issue, witch? What satanic force interferes with your body's natural courses?'

Still she was mute, her eyes sullen, and she mocked me with her silence.

I examined her from head to foot, but this initial examination showed no obvious marks, so she would need a more thorough probing.

When I laid her back on the table, and pressed open her thighs, the sunlight revealed a livid teat. The sight of it caused me to tremble. How had this teat not been apparent to me in all my dealings with the woman so far? The devious bitch had hidden it in the shadowy chamber of the inn.

I clutched my Bible to my heart for protection. 'Here, here is the devil's teat!' A shudder ran through me at the thought that my own flesh might have touched a teat suckled by the devil's imps.

Finally, the woman spoke. 'That's no devil's teat. You ask how many men have let down my hair?' She stood up and gathered an armful of her shorn locks before pouring it onto the floor. 'You should know that the answer is nearly every travelling man who ever entered the inn. Mr Gillie likes to watch, you see.'

I swallowed. She'd lain with other men? That could hardly be a surprise. But Gillie had watched me coupling with his goodwife? This was an abhorrence, a crime against God. What was wrong with the man? More likely, she had made up this untruth to disturb my mission.

'Don't try to distract me from my work with tales of your debauchery.'

She lifted her chin. 'They bring me everything, these men: their tales, their woes, their–'

I backhanded her then and she fell to the floor, blood oozing from her nose, and began rolling amongst her shorn hair, naked and laughing at me. It would have been the work of a minute to stamp on her head, but instead, I left the room in an effort to still my heart. This was Satan at work, tempting me into a rage that would only release her from this life and put my own neck in the noose. I fell to my knees outside the closed door.

'Dear God, please help me ensure this woman receives her just punishment. Give me strength enough to resist her baiting. And to resist her womanly wiles. Help me to uncover her sister witches so that I might protect this town from Satan. So be it.'

So far, Goodwife Gillie had proved nearly impossible to break. No doubt, she planned on turning mute and refusing to give up the names of any other women. But we would see. We would see. She would prove no match for my most persuasive methods.

* * *

It took three long days and nights of waking and walking, but in the hour before dawn, when the soul is at its weakest, Goodwife Gillie finally broke. But even then, she gave up only two women: her sister-in-law and a mute who lived off the kirk. It was not much, but it was something to work with, a beginning. Once the trial got underway, the people of Berwick would start to see the evil in their midst and be better able to identify it. More names would be revealed to me then until I captured the entire coven.

The sergeants had a devil of a job fetching the sister-in-law, and some force had to be used, but the mute came quietly. When the sergeants fetched in the two named women, I spent the night trying to elicit other names from them. But they proved resilient to my probing and no names issued forth. These Berwick women were a hardy breed.

My mistake had been in keeping the women together, hoping they'd feed off each other's terror. But instead, the vixens had each drawn power from the other women's presence and it had strengthened their resolve. My efforts to turn one against the other failed, and the two women named by Goodwife Gillie refused to point the finger at others, and neither did they turn on the innkeeper's wife. Instead, all three women regarded one another with gentle eyes filled only with pity.

This stubborn silence frustrated me. A few more nights of being forced awake and endless walking on hard stone floors would milk names from them. It never failed. Eventually, they must give others up – it was only a matter of time. But time was against me now. The longer I tarried here, the more silver it would cost me. These three women would just have to be used as my proving ground. If I failed to reveal any more witches, then nine pounds would have to do for now.

10

Jane

A Wolf Disguised

I was walking back from the village after delivering a first-time mother. It had gone well, and both mother and infant thrived. Even so, the toil had exhausted me. Mam's satchel was bulky and it weighed on me. But before going to the Drivers', I must call at the manse and collect Rose from the Reverend's care. I would ask him whether he'd heard from the Bishop yet. For now, though, all that was on my mind was my heavy belly, my aching back and my sore feet. But all aches and tiredness left me when I heard a shout and saw May staggering towards me, her blonde curls wild and uncovered, her face tearstained and Henry cradled in her arms.

'Jane! Jane! There you are! Thank goodness!'

'May! What's happened?' I ran towards her, my heart in my mouth. 'What's the matter?'

'It's Henry. Something's wrong with him, Jane, very wrong. I found him asleep in the woods amongst the flowers and he won't wake up. Can you help him?'

'Asleep? That cannot be right. Here, let me take a look at him. He's very white.' All the shape had left his face, which now resembled a round, flat plate. There was foam at his lips, he shone with sweat and yet the backs of his hands were like ice. I stripped off my shawl and wrapped it about him.

'Come. I have Mam's satchel. Best you take him home and we can see to him there. What happened to him? Why was he in the woods alone?'

'Everyone's away to the mart and I was meant to be minding him, only he was naughty and ran off when my back was turned. I won't be able to forgive myself if something happens to him.' She looked at me, desperation in her eyes. 'It's a punishment from God.'

'Nothing will happen to Henry, and it's not a punishment from God, so you needn't torture yourself. Come, fetch him indoors and put him on the table near the window so I can see him properly.'

May was trembling from head to foot and I wondered if her state left her fit to help me.

She touched Henry's face. 'Do you know what ails him?'

'Not yet.'

I placed my hand over the little boy's heart and counted the beats. His heartbeat was so faint that it was barely there, and it was much, much too slow. I looked at his hands. His left hand was clenched over something. May followed my gaze and moved to open Henry's little fist.

'No! Don't touch it.'

She stepped back, shocked. I took a spoon from my belt and gently prised open Henry's plump little fingers. In his hand was a flower with a sapphire hood. Aconite! From the side, a stand of them resembled a swarm of blue butterflies and children often picked them, mistaking them for the pretty insects. The bloom's beauty gave lie to its deadliness.

'It's monkshood.' I unfolded the hood with the spoon to reveal the sinister clutch of stamens inside. 'So, he must have aconite poisoning. Though, he cannot have swallowed any, otherwise he . . . well, it doesn't look as though he's swallowed any. The poison must have seeped through his skin. He'll have a tiny cut somewhere.' I blew the bloom out of his hand and onto the floor and began searching his skin for cuts.

'Monkshood! Will he die?' Tears flooded May's eyes. 'Oh, Henry, why did you have to run away from me?'

My friend seemed as though she might collapse in a flood of tears. It would do her more good to be kept busy.

'May, can you fetch some water and cleanse his hands? Quickly, so no more poison seeps into him.'

Obediently, she fetched a cloth and a bowl of water and began gently rinsing the little lad's hands, her own trembling all the whilst.

I examined Henry's palms and fingers. 'There aren't any obvious cuts, so that might mean not much poison has entered him. But then his small frame wouldn't need much—'

'Please, Jane, can you save my little Henry?'

'I hope so. But we must act quickly.'

In Mam's satchel was an array of vials, crocks and jars. The most beautiful bottles were the poisons as they were cut in intricate patterns to make sure they weren't confused with the less dangerous remedies. All poisons had both deadly properties and healing properties – it was simply a question of dose. It was impossible to tell them apart by looking, so I would have to open each vial and smell it, careful not to touch the contents. As I unsealed each bottle, I murmured its name and healing properties to make sure I chose the right remedy. Larkspur to give courage, foxglove to steady fluttering hearts, mandrake to soothe mania, hemlock to cool hot humours, snowdrop to slow senility, ivy to take down inflammation. Finally, I found the tincture of belladonna and gave the vial to May.

'Deadly nightshade. To speed up the heart.'

May started at these words. 'Deadly nightshade? Jane, are you certain?'

I nodded. 'One poison to cure another. It'll make his heart beat more robustly. But dose is all. Too little, and it will slow his heart more . . . too much and he will convulse. To calculate the right dose, I must weigh him.'

I pushed my hands underneath the sleeping boy's oxters and hefted him, raising and lowering him a couple of times to estimate his weight.

'About two stone. May, can you get a finger between his teeth? He might bite you hard, mind.'

May put her littlest finger between the boy's lips. His milk teeth were small, but sharp. She eased the child's jaw slowly open and pushed a thumb between his teeth to give me room to work.

'Henry can bite off my whole hand if it'll only save him.'

Carefully, I counted in drops of the belladonna tincture, then sealed the vial and stowed it away again.

'Now, we must wait and watch for symptoms of too much belladonna.'

May looked sharply at me. 'And what are they?'

'Rising heat. A dry mouth. A flushed face.'

After a little whilst, I pulled up Henry's eyelids and watched his eyes darken and the black begin to swallow the blue. I placed my other hand on his chest and counted, nodding with each slow, faint beat of the little boy's heart.

'It's working, his heart is quickening.'

'But will our Henry live?'

'He will be well . . .' It was hard to look at May for fear of what she might see in my eyes. 'Most probably he will live.'

'I cannot forgive myself for letting him out of my sight. He's too little to go to the woods alone.' May pointed at the blue flower lying on the ground. 'When I think of the times I've wished him away, and now he was nearly taken. I tell you, it's a punishment from God.'

'It's no such thing, May. You mustn't distress yourself with such thoughts. It was an accident, that's all. Now, we must wait. It'll help Henry if you hold him as he loves you so. The comfort of your arms will give strength to his heart for the battle he faces.'

May took Henry in her arms and cradled him, rocking the boy gently whilst I checked his heartbeat and his temperature.

'See, having you hold him has given little Henry great comfort. There, his breathing is steadying and he's not too warm. These are good signs. Place your hand on his brow and feel for yourself.'

May felt Henry's brow and gave me a watery smile. 'I can never thank you enough, Jane. You've been a true friend to me.'

I shook my head. 'Not a good enough friend, May.'

'More than good enough. I'm fortunate to have you.'

Henry began to stir. His eyes fluttered and opened now of their own accord. The darkness had started to leave them. I placed my hand over his heart. It retained its rhythm.

I smiled at May. 'He'll live. I'm certain of it now.'

'Thank you for saving him, Jane!' She cradled Henry close. 'I shudder to think what might have happened–'

'He's going to be all right, so don't torment yourself with what might have been.'

'Oh, Henry, I'll never take my eye off you again.'

'And don't blame yourself – little lads are full of mischief, even when you do have your eye on them all day long.' I yawned and covered my mouth. 'Sorry, May, but today has left me dog-tired. Andrew will be out looking for me if he learns the baby I set out to deliver arrived hours ago, so I'd better go and get Rose now. But please come and fetch me if there's any change for the worse. In any case, I'll come by in the morning to check on him.'

I kissed Henry on the forehead. He was cool and dry and his eyes had returned to their usual blue.

'Thank you, Jane. I'm truly grateful to you.' May kissed me and held me close.

I bent to scoop up the monkshood bloom in a cloth.

May frowned. 'What will you do with the flower, Jane?'

'It's going onto the fire, where it can do no more harm.'

11

John

A Man in Shadow

Whilst travelling to the hearing, my innards churned, and it took a good draught of whisky to settle them. Last night, when I'd paused to take a piss, I saw that a devil's teat had appeared on me. There was no soreness, yet it was red-raw. The sight had filled me with horror, and no amount of praying had made it go away. It was the witch's doing, no doubt. She'd set Satan on me. I'd not dared sleep all night for fear of what might come to prey on me. So I'd stayed awake to pray, and God had protected me, for no imps had visited. The effort had exhausted me and it was hard to think straight, but I had to concentrate on the trial before me.

When I entered the hall, it was lined with the men of the town, and a good many women too. They must be hard-pressed for amusement in these remote parts. Still, given the cunning nature of Goodwife Gillie's tongue, more than a few goodwives might be keen to see the back of her.

The sergeants fetched in the three accused women and a hush fell across the room. How different these women appeared once they'd lost the artifice of their silken tresses, their slatternly bodices and their colourful kirtles. Now shorn and clad in thin shifts, they were as one lumpen mass and barely human at all. Amongst them stood Goodwife Gillie, no longer filled with fire and verve, her head finally bowed in admittance of the shame she carried.

The magistrate showed no sign of starting the proceedings, doubtless hoping for a last-minute reprieve for his wife. Trying a woman of high standing was somewhat daunting. By naming her own sister, Goodwife Gillie had proved that she possessed more wit than I'd credited her with. But high standing or not, a magistrate was only a man and it would be unwise to forget that. The magistrate himself paid me no heed and instead kept glancing towards the door. No matter. Let the man amuse himself however he might. God would help me win over the townspeople. A ripple of muttering spread across the room as I approached Goodwife Gillie, but she didn't whimper or cry. Instead, she lifted her head and levelled her gaze at me. I seized my Bible in both hands and raised it high above my head.

'People of Berwick, the devil has moved amongst you these past years, and you have slept through his presence. But I am here to wake you up to this evil infestation before it devours the souls of every man, woman and child amongst you.'

The innkeeper began to weep and the magistrate wound an arm around him. It was little wonder Gillie's goodwife was so wanton when the cuckold was so weak.

'I give you the leader of the coven, Patricia Gillie. See for yourselves how the witch stares me out: she does not move, nor does she blink, because the devil has steadied her gaze. What natural woman could look a man of God so brazenly in the eye? Eve herself might have been a little cowed by the gaze of Scotland's foremost witch-finder.'

I paused, but still the bitch didn't blink. What was her game?

'Goodwife Gillie is preparing herself, because she has been granted the gift of prescience by her master. She knows that I can tell a witch merely by looking into her eyes, but she won't fool me by setting her eyes like glass. Her fiendish efforts won't stall me in my righteous work because God has granted me the means to see into her soul if I only look hard enough.'

This statement brought forth a general hubbub, and it pleased me to note that many in the room dropped their gaze. Their fear was real, and no one wanted me looking into their souls.

'It gives me no pleasure to find that this town is riddled with witches. Oh, there are those amongst you who have wagged your

long tongues and said it was the thought of gold that drove me.'
I held my Bible out towards them and patted its cover. 'But you
are wrong, for it is only my godly fervour that drives me. The low
country of England is rotten with witches – and no wonder as it
is so populous.'

This news seemed to cheer many in the room, but I would
quickly lay waste to their false cheer.

'But Scotland, too, is infested. At first, this might appear to be
a puzzle as so few souls live there. But as it is such a godly nation,
it poses a greater challenge for the dark saint. It must offend him
that little Scotland is so very close to God.' I turned on my heel
to address the other side of the room. 'So much so, that it fills
Satan's belly with black bile and causes him to lust after innocent
people and sully their souls in his own image. This can be the only
explanation for so many of my countrywomen turning their back
on God.' I spread my arms wide, as if to embrace the townsmen.
'And Berwick is a liminal place, set in the marches between England and Scotland, wavering between two countries, and so your
people are at particular risk.'

I walked across the room to stand in front of the three accused
women.

'Already, the dark one has intruded in your lives, by choosing
these three weak vessels to spread his evil. Take a long look at
them, good folk of Berwick. Look deep into their eyes, and there
you will see the devil resides.'

Some of the men nearest to me shuddered, but a few of the
more common-looking men did then approach the three women
and begin peering into their eyes and muttering to one another.
The innkeeper's wife was brazen as ever and didn't blink. The
magistrate's goodwife held her chin high, making it difficult for
the men to look into her eyes. Even without her blue gown and
her chestnut mane, she was a haughty bitch and felt herself above
these men. But she was above no man, and she would learn that
very soon. The mute sobbed and trembled and wouldn't meet
any man's eye. Her sister witches took her hands between their
own. I watched them, seeing how close they were. But despite
their closeness, three was not a full coven, and I let my eye
rove over the townspeople. The other ten were hidden here

somewhere. Indeed, there might well be more than one coven. It was important then, that all three witches were found guilty so that their proving might encourage other names to be called out.

When the men had finished their examination of the witches, I made to address the room again, but was interrupted when the door opened and three young military men entered. What was their business? They didn't state it but took up positions surrounding the magistrate. This gave me pause. Were they here to arrest him? Or had he summoned them? But their eyes softened when they rested upon the magistrate's goodwife. Surely, these tall and angular men couldn't be the magistrate's sons. My guts roiled at the realisation. But it was no matter, for God was at my side, and I must continue.

'Even though these three hags know they face death, they still turn their faces away from God. The devil's grip must be strong to prise these goodwives away from the Lord.' I addressed the magistrate and his sons now. 'And the devil must surely lie with them and fill their bellies with his issue. Why, sire, your own babes might be to the devil born, and I urge you to look to your offspring.'

But the magistrate didn't respond and only narrowed his eyes at me. Although I did notice some of the elders next to him shifting awkwardly, doubt written on their faces, and looking from one to the other.

'Oh, he is wily, and you won't know that your children are not your own. Even the most upstanding goodwives can find themselves abused in this way.'

This statement bordered on being too florid because, of the three accused women, only the magistrate's goodwife bore the signs of childbirth on her body. The magistrate rubbed at his throat, casting anxious glances towards his sons, and then he spoke up.

'No! You cannot make me believe it. My sons are in my own image. And they are good men, all of them. Delivered safely into the world by the same midwife who delivered me.' He glared at the minister until that reluctant man returned his gaze. 'And baptised shortly thereafter.'

I seized on this. 'Of course! That is why Satan's most loyal slaves are so often midwives. Who better to usher his spawn into an unsuspecting world, but his own handmaidens?' I walked up to the magistrate and touched his sleeve. 'I myself have suffered at the hands of these dread hags.'

But the magistrate's sons had a hardness in their eyes, and their stares bored into me. The tallest one put his hand on his father's shoulder. And the magistrate covered his son's hand with his own. The three sons surrounded their father closely. They were not soft-looking like their father but had the same bearing and gimlet eyes as their mother. These were military men and would have the support of other armed men, so it wouldn't pay to force that particular issue.

It might well be that their mother was innocent after all. It wouldn't much harm my purse to let one woman go, and it might then keep the magistrate and his sons on my side. The innkeeper's wife and the mute would line my pocket decently enough for now, before turning my attention to the wider town.

I approached the three women and studied the magistrate's goodwife. If I freed her, would it appease her sons? Whilst they might not stand for their mother being taken from them, none would care much for the fate of the innkeeper's wife or the mute. I grasped Patricia Gillie by the arm and drew her to the centre of the room. Here was a basic platform where I would examine each woman in turn. Sunlight shone on the platform, making Goodwife Gillie's womanly form visible through her shift. But she cared not and her eyes were filled with contempt. That would leave her soon enough. I approached her and took hold of the shift in my bare hands. This was a task usually given to the sergeants, but I braced my arms and wrenched, tearing the fabric so that it hung to either side of her naked body. This act of humiliation was designed to humble witches so that they would be hard put to speak in their own defence. Bitemarks showed clearly on her breasts and my loins surged at the sight.

But the innkeeper had noticed the marks as well, for he pointed.

'What's this? What have you done to my poor Patsy?'

When I spoke, it was a struggle to keep my voice steady. 'Why, sire, what can you mean? If this is not your own doing, then it must be the work of the devil. Clearly, your goodwife has been suckling the devil's imps.' I appealed to the guild men. 'These imps are remarkable for their greed. And their sharp teeth. I will show you her devil's teat. It has been suckled so often that it is livid. So evidently, the hag has begun to feed the imps with her ample breasts.'

Goodwife Gillie laughed in my face and spoke to the room, unashamed of her nakedness. 'If this is the devil's teat, then John Sharpe must also have one. If I am to be tried on these grounds, then he should be tried likewise.'

I backhanded the slattern to silence her and blood flowed from her nose. A wave of noise erupted and the innkeeper made to run to his goodwife, but the sergeants held him back. This blow was injudicious of me – not just because many in the room began to complain about it, but because the presence of blood worked against the whole principle of the pricker and the dry wound. The mute began to sob copiously, and the magistrate's wife comforted her. Goodwife Gillie didn't attempt to staunch the flow of blood, and it dripped from her face and ran down her breasts. She had guile, this witch, perhaps knowing that blood made her appear human.

The innkeeper railed against his captors. 'Please, Sharpe! My own goodwife. I let you take her, but she is no witch. She has loose ways, but . . . I . . . I encouraged her.' The man mopped his eyes with a large and grubby kerchief. 'Greed for gold, you see. I should have put an end to it. She is a wanton woman, yes, but not a witch. Never a witch. You must set her free. I'll amend her ways. Please. I'll see to it myself.' He wrenched himself free of the sergeants and grasped the front of my jerkin until I feared for the stitching. 'I curse the day you came to our town, John Sharpe.'

I plucked his hands free of my jerkin, despising the man for his weakness. 'Cease your weeping upon the instant, for a man who wails for a witch may draw suspicion to himself. You've been under her spell for too long, Gillie. Perhaps you should be tried yourself . . .'

The innkeeper wiped his face again and peered at me. 'You're a demon, Sharpe. You should swing. To think I let you stay at my inn, eat my food and . . . and . . .'

I sneered at him. 'The cuckold cannot bring himself to say it. That he let me lie with his woman.' I backed away from Gillie to address the crowd. 'My flesh was weak and she overcame me when I was most prone to temptation. No doubt every travelling man who ever came through Berwick has lain with this she-devil.'

The minister looked aghast at this remark and the magistrate's sons began to talk urgently amongst themselves. This made me wonder whether I had overstepped a boundary as many of the men in the room wore ugly expressions on their faces.

The tallest of the magistrate's sons stepped forward, removed his cloak and placed it gently around the harlot's shoulders, covering her, and then handed her a clean kerchief. This shifting of sympathy spelt disaster. It must be put down quickly.

'Clearly, this man has also fallen under the witch's thrall. She is a powerful witch and no man here is safe from her.' I swept out an arm to indicate the tallest son. 'Not even her own nephew.'

This might appeal to the women in the room and gain their support, lest their own men be taken by Goodwife Gillie. But the women had mutinous faces and the magistrate's son stepped up to me.

'I am under the thrall of no witch, and nor am I under the thrall of any woman. This has gone far enough, Sharpe. You will turn every woman in the north into a witch in return for gold if you're not stopped.' His brothers came and stood next to him, and newly strengthened, he addressed the minister.

'This cannot continue. These women don't have magical powers.' He pointed at Goodwife Gillie. 'My aunt is a woman whose conscience has much cause to be troubled, but a witch she is not.' He towered over me. 'This man, Sharpe, is naught but a rogue, out to line his pockets at our expense. Our gold will be better spent on completing our church.'

There were some shouts of 'Aye' at this remark and I sensed that the trial was starting to slip from my control. The magistrate's son had the floor now and he kept going.

'Neighbours, we must throw this stranger out of our town. Or better yet, hold him until he can face the quarter sessions . . .'

Cheers rang out around the room, and the magistrate's son had the temerity to grip my neck with his big hand. 'We will put you before the justices, John Sharpe, and let them decide whether or not you tell the truth.'

I blinked, hardly able to believe the rising cries of support for the insolent pup. What had happened? What was wrong with the English? Why did these people not just accept my word as so many before had? But the mention of the quarter sessions and justices caused my innards to shrivel and I eyed the men in the room, my mind racing.

The turmoil of war made the quarter sessions less regular than they might be. If they held me, I could post bond and then breach it. But that would put me foul of the law. And my purse would be light. Oh, these men of law were too clever for their own good! I might argue my way through, but was this a risk worth taking? I'd been fortunate to escape Newcastle. Might fortune fail me in Berwick? Would it be best to leave now on my own terms, with my dignity intact – and my remaining silver?

I shrugged myself free of the man's grip and raised my Bible over my head to attract all eyes to me and to command silence.

'Very well, people of Berwick.' My voice wavered, and I took a deep breath to steady it before speaking again. 'It is clear my services are not appreciated in this town. So, I will take my leave and return to Scotland, where people understand the true danger of the devil and his ilk, and where my services are required.'

The magistrate went to his wife and took her in his arms. 'Aye, get going, Sharpe, and don't curse our town with your presence again. Or else you will face justice and swing.'

I walked from the room as slowly as I could. The room was weighted with a grey silence as all eyes watched me. My heart pounded, but I was determined not to run as I left this town, a man in shadow once again.

12

Jane

Harvest Moon

I'd spent the morning baking pies, with Rose balanced on one hip. Great, tall crusts, bursting with collops of jugged hare, roasted lamb and stewed beef. Just as I set the final pie on the sill to cool alongside three others, Andrew came in and put down the first sheaf of the morning before lurching towards the pies.

'Ah, the savoury smell!'

'Hands off. They're for the kern supper and well you know it.'

His face crumpled, and he gave me the boyish smile that May had once so loved. But it held no charm for me.

'Go on, Jane. You can easily make another.'

'On any other day, yes, but there's no more time for baking as there's so much still to do. Look, there's plenty of cold meat and jelly left over, so you and Rose can share that.'

He sat down heavily at the table and drew Rose onto his lap.

'See this, Rosie, we're reduced to scraps.'

'Hardly scraps, Andrew. There's the best part of a lamb on that platter.'

He chose the tenderest morsels and picked off the fat before giving them to Rose, and I smiled in spite of myself.

He took my hand and pulled me down next to him. 'Come, Jane. Sit by me. You have to eat something.' He took a half leg of lamb for himself and then pushed the platter towards me. 'My bairn needs feeding up as well.'

'I'm not hungry, Andrew.' The lamb was succulent, but my appetite had left me of late. 'I've been picking on and off all morning whilst doing the baking.'

I made to stand, but he pulled me back down. 'Well, you can still sit and keep me company. You're here little enough as it is.' There was menace in his eyes, but his voice was lilting so that Rose would have no sign that trouble might be afoot. 'Always gadding here and there, up to who knows what . . .'

'Very well.' I gave in and remained sitting so he couldn't draw me into a sing-song argument in front of Rose.

'Look, Rosie, more for me and you.' He drew the platter back. 'Make you grow nice and plump – ready for market.'

He joggled Rose on his knee and made her giggle. The hint of her being sent to market sickened me and I lifted her off his knee.

'Here, sit by me, Rose, before you bring your dinner back up.'

He frowned. 'I meant nothing by it, and she knows it's only play. Don't you, Rosie?'

But Rose had picked up her poppet and was rocking her to sleep so she paid him no heed.

Once Andrew had finished eating, I stood to clear the platters away, but he hooked an arm around my waist and pulled me onto his lap.

'Put Rosie down for her nap so we can spend some time together.'

He pushed his hand under my bodice and squeezed hard. When he kissed me, his lips were greasy with lamb fat and it was hard not to shudder.

'Rose isn't the least bit tired. Look at her, busy making her poppet dance.' I pushed him away and straightened my bodice. 'Besides, there's no time. I've a hundred tasks ahead of me.'

His dark brows knitted together and he glowered at me. 'See, Rosie. Your dada's not good enough for Lady Jane.' Rose hugged her poppet close to her. 'But she never turned away Tom Verger. Aye, and I wager she wouldn't turn him away yet.'

I put down a pot of ale before him and hissed in his ear. 'That's not true, Andrew. And it's not fair, either. And not in front of Rose. Please.'

He snorted. 'Never fear, Jane, you'll keep.' He nodded at Rose. 'She'll have to sleep sooner or later.'

At this, my heart sank. If Rose would only stay awake a little longer, then he'd have to get back to the fields before it was time for her nap.

'Rose, do you want to come and help me make the rowan crosses?' She popped a thumb into her mouth. Her eyes were drooping at the corners. 'All right, then, I'll make them myself.'

At the door was a pile of young rowan branches I'd cut the day before. All the twigs, leaves and berries were stripped off, leaving only bare wood. It was the work of a few moments to bind them into crosses with red twine to hold them fast. Before long, I held the final cross up to check it was even.

Andrew glanced at Rose. 'Time for me to get back to the fields.' He drained his pot and stood up. 'I'll nail those crosses up afore I go.'

'There's no need, Andrew. I can easily put them up if I stand on the cracket. You get yourself back to work.'

'You'll not go clambering about with my bairn in your belly.' He picked up a cross. 'Anyhow, hammers and nails are man's work—'

'Wait!'

'What? Do you not want me to get back to work?' He stepped closer to me. 'Is Rosie ready for her nap, after all?'

'No, she's nowhere near ready.' I glanced at my sleepy girl. 'She's far too giddy. Let me say the charm over the crosses first.'

'Charm?' He raised his brows. 'Haven't you and yours had enough trouble from charms?'

Was Andrew threatening me? It wouldn't do to underestimate him again. 'Well, not so much a charm ... more of a wish. A prayer. For protection against evil.'

He pondered this for a whilst. 'Go on then, but be quick about it.'

It felt wrong somehow, with Andrew standing over me. But it had to be done.

'Red thread and rowan wood.' I picked up each cross in turn and shook it. 'Out evil, in good.'

He frowned. 'Why are there seven crosses?'

'Two for here. Two for the manse. And one each for both church doors.'

He eyed me closely. 'And the seventh?'

'To hang over the barn.' Heat rose up my neck. 'To protect the beasts.'

'Is that usual? You've never done that afore.'

'No. Because . . . well, this wasn't my home before.' I forced a smile. 'And now it is.'

'Aye, well, just so long as that's all it is.' He looked up the hill towards the church. 'Our beasts have survived this long without any rowan cross. But if it keeps your face straight, then it'll get done.'

He took his hammer and tapped in five nails to hold the first two crosses, and then he picked up the remaining five crosses. At last, he left, and I closed the door behind him and leant on it. It was hard not to yawn. Harvest was a long day, with everyone up before dawn to cut the first sheaf. But it was no good resting, and so I set to, stripping the sheaf and then separating the wheat from the chaff.

'Rose, do you want to come with me to the mill?' I walked my fingers along the table. 'A walk?'

She nodded, but she was half-hearted. If she would only stay awake long enough to get the wheat ground. 'And then you can help me knead the dough. Would you like that?'

She smiled and held out her arms to me for a carry. 'Come then, let's go and see the miller.'

Whilst Rose napped, there would be time enough to prove the dough and bake the ceremonial loaf for the kern supper. Providing Andrew didn't return. With any luck, he might be kept at the fields.

As the Drivers owned most of the arable land in the quarter, it fell to them to make the supper preparations. And now that I was married to Andrew, these preparations fell to me. It was still impossible to think of myself as his goodwife, even though that's what I was now. With all my heart, I wished the world might turn widdershins a whilst and take me back to the time before Tom was taken from me, before my wedding to Andrew and before Mam's death. Yet, I still lived and breathed. My child was hale.

There was much to be thankful for. And this was the day of all days to be thankful for life's bounty. I sighed, folded away my sorrow and went back to my work.

* * *

Finally, Andrew left after delivering the last sheaf of the day. Mercifully, he'd shown no interest in me and instead went off carousing with the field lads. My final task was to make the corn dolly and its kern baby. It was fiddlesome work with all the bending and plaiting of straw, which kept slipping and cracking even though I kept damping it down. No wonder Bett was so pleased to pass the task on to me. By the time the dollies were finally complete, there was more straw on the floor than anywhere else.

'Rose, put your finger here, please, so I can tie the ribbons.'

I pointed and she obliged with her chubby thumb. Then I stood my strange creations up to dress them in white shifts made from old sacking. The corn dolly was much smaller than me, but still taller than Rose, and my little girl seemed afraid of it now, hiding behind the curtain and peeking out at it. But she loved the kern baby, and took it from me, cradling it in her arms and rocking it. When she lay down for her nap, I had to ease the kern baby from her arms and replace it with her poppet. I kissed her smooth cheek and watched her eyes flutter. Convinced she was sound asleep, I tiptoed away to tuck the kern baby inside its mother's womb. Then I stood the dolly upright once more and stepped back to check my handiwork.

The door opened and Bett came in. She set down some flagons of cider and examined the dolly closely.

'Well, she's bonny enough, and not a bad job for a first attempt. In all honesty, it never was my favourite task! Now, is the kern baby in its proper place like I told you?'

'Yes, Bett, it is.'

'Good, we need to do everything possible to make sure the harvest is a good one next year. We cannot afford another one like this year. We need some decent rainfall. Now, you finish off here and I'll fetch some more cider up from the barn. Is Rosie still sleeping?'

'Yes, she is.'

'I've never known a bairn nap so much. Though I doubt you'll be so lucky with the second one.'

I smiled at her back as she bustled out of the door. Bett had been a difficult enough woman at first, but for all her sternness, she loved Rose. She was fair to me, although it sometimes felt as though her eyes were always on me, watching for any hint that I might betray her son. I swept up all the stalks from the floor and flung them onto the fire, where they gave off an awful smoke. I coughed and wiped my eyes, squinting at the dolly.

'You're missing something, aren't you?'

I went outside to find some late roses and returned with an armful of white blooms, only to find that Rose had risen from her nap and was standing near the dolly. She started when I entered and ran to her basket, huddling under her blanket and refusing to get out of bed again.

'Come, Rose. Help me make a garland for the dolly's hair.'

But she sat in her basket, sucking her thumb and refusing to look at me.

'What have you been up to, little maid?'

My daughter had naughtiness all over her face, but there was no time to find out what she'd done. So, I bent to my job and fashioned the roses into a garland for the dolly. It was a smaller version of the garland that had graced my hair at Beltane, the night Rose was made. The memory of that night made me smile for a moment. But Bett came back in then, carrying more flagons of cider, and I set the finished dolly to face her.

'Oh! The garland sets her off very nicely. Can you manage to carry her down to the dell, or will you need Andrew to lift her?'

I hefted the dolly. 'No, she's not too weighty. She should be all right for me to carry.'

'Grand. I'll bear the loaf, and Andrew and Jim can fetch the cider and the game pies. Although it might be best if Andrew doesn't touch them, or they'll not survive the journey to the kern supper!'

'You're not wrong. It's almost killed him not taking a slice. He's had his eye on them all day.'

And that was not all he'd had his eye on, although it seemed he'd found something – or someone – else to amuse him for the day and he'd left me alone. But there was still the night to come. My belly heaved at the thought.

'Well, my lad can eat his fill soon enough. Come, bring the dolly, for we cannot let down the harvest lads. Rosie, get out of that bed at once and help your mother.'

* * *

I lugged the corn dolly to the dell where the kern supper would take place. Rose and Bett were at my side and following behind us were the field lasses – all in fine fettle and singing. The harvest decorating must have taken them the best part of the evening. The woodland had been transformed into a magical labyrinth. Tiny torches glowed, marking the woodland paths, and the night sky obliged by being dark and starry, with a yellow moon perched quiet and low in the sky. A huge bonfire burnt brightly. The pond absorbed the light from the fire, the moon and the stars, and then reflected it back in gentle ripples. The trees were hung with corn dollies and lanterns made by the children. But the centrepiece hung from an oak. It was a great chandelier with a dozen or more tiny forms swinging from it in the soft breeze. When I realised what they represented, the shock caused me to drop the corn dolly.

Tom emerged from the woods and walked towards me. He picked up the dolly and stood her upright next to the table, then he frowned at the tree. He shinned up and unhooked the chandelier, before climbing higher in the tree and hanging it somewhere out of my sight.

When he leapt down from the tree, I mouthed thank you to him. His gaze moved to Rose, who was toddling to and fro in front of the corn dolly. On seeing Tom, my little girl looked at her true father through eyes that belonged to him. Tom smiled down at her before wandering over to adjust the dolly's slipped flower garland. My heart skipped and I yearned for his touch. But until we had news from the Bishop, my marriage and the child in my belly weighted me down, and the ring on my finger might as well be a metal cuff around my ankle. When I moved away from Tom, Bett was watching me closely, and even when she placed the massive loaf on the table, her eyes never left me.

The field lads began appearing, carrying contributions towards the autumnal feast. Before long, every flat surface – whether stone or tree-stump – groaned with apple pies, sheaves of bread, barrels of cider, casks of ale and pitchers of mead. Cauldrons of ham broth bubbled over the fire and a boar turned on a spit. May Green sat in the shadows with an elderly looking fiddle. She was so lithe and pretty, with her cheeks flushed and her eyes sparkling, and she was much more like her old self again. I went to her side and touched the back of her hand.

'How are you keeping, May?'

She beamed at me. The first such smile in many moons. 'Very well, Jane. All thanks to you.' She fidgeted with her fiddle. After a loud screech, she managed to draw out the sound she was seeking and started playing a reel.

Mr Green sat near the fire drinking from a flagon of ale. He was red in the face but seemed harmless enough. Long may it last. Young Tilly played with Henry. Hopefully, she might be spared her older sister's suffering. I sighed. May's life had been terrible, but with luck, it might start to get better from now on.

By now, the glade was heaving with people clutching tankards in one hand and spearing meat on their eating knives with the other. So, it was here, Harvest, with the full moon overhead. Music and laughter filled the dell, and the huge bonfire released crackling red and orange dragons into the black sky. The men's faces were reddened by cider, mead and ale. But not Tom, who sat to one side with his father and Reverend Foster, talking quietly, his eyes never far from me or Rose.

When Andrew lurched into the clearing, a flagon of cider in his hand, it was clear from his eyes that he'd already drunk at least one flagon. He waved to Rose and beckoned her to him. Tom's jaw tightened, and it was all I could do not to snatch Rose and run to Tom. The combination of rage and love did battle in my heart whilst Tom's daughter sidled to Andrew's side and put her hand in his. She raised her sweet little face to him and he hoisted her into the air.

'Dada.'

The name that belonged to Tom by rights. The blood surged to Tom's face, but he made no move. Rose buried her head in

Andrew's neck, but then she turned her fiery head and gazed at Tom through clear green eyes. She blinked. Did she see herself there when she looked at him? My lovely Tom swallowed and looked away, but not before I saw that his eyes were bright with tears.

Andrew drew me to his side. He raised his voice. 'Come away, Jane, there's no need to rub poor Verger's nose in it. Him with no sweetheart, goodwife or bairn to call his own.'

How could he! Making sure Tom heard his jibe. I bit my lip to stop myself speaking out, or it would go worse for me later.

Reverend Foster touched Tom's shoulder and then got up and walked towards us, frowning deeply. I looked up at him, the question written in my eyes, but he gave a minute shake of his head. So there was no news yet from the Bishop. I sighed. I would have to learn patience, but how much longer would it take?

The Reverend prodded the corn dolly and scowled at the revels around the bonfire. He peered into the woods, as if expecting something to appear from the trees. Then he raised his eyes heavenwards and held out a hand.

'Come, young Driver. If we must indulge in this old festival, then better to get it over with before the rain comes.'

Andrew set Rose down and she tottered over to me. 'There'll be no rain this night, Reverend. Leave the elements to those that know the lie of the land, why don't you?'

The Reverend shrugged. Jim Driver laughed harshly from his seat on a tree-stump where he was picking his teeth with a piece of straw. Then he snorked up a batch of phlegm and shot it into the heart of the fire. Reverend Foster shuddered at the hissing stench, but he said nothing.

Jim Driver stood up on unsteady legs. 'Come, lads, come one and all. It's time to burn the dolly and her infant.'

A roar went up from the field lads. Led by Andrew, they snatched up the corn dolly. Reverend Foster closed his eyes. Was he hiding or praying? Tom stared at Andrew, and there was a hardness in his eyes I'd never seen before.

The lads formed a long snake, with Andrew at the head of it. They ran circles sunwise around the bonfire, bearing the corn dolly above their heads. As they ran, they chanted ancient words.

'By the light, by the light, by the light. Of Litha, of Lammas, of Mabon. By the moon, by the moon, by the moon.'

After they'd made three rings, they let out a loud cheer and hurled the dolly into the centre of the flames. The smoke from the burning dolly made my eyes water and forced me to turn away.

* * *

It had begun to drizzle and the fire was dying out now. Most people had left for home, but Jim stayed nearby as my chaperon even though Tom was long gone. Only the more raucous of the field lads and lasses remained. The corn dolly and her baby had been sacrificed to the fire. The smoke had gone to the sky. The feast had been devoured. The rain became heavier and raindrops fizzled into steam as they neared the fire. I pulled my cloak around me and looked at the moon. It was mostly covered with cloud, so it was now no more than a scrape of yellow butter in the sky. We were desperate for rainfall. But it was a bad sign, raining on harvest. Still, the crop was safely in for the year and the next one hopefully assured – thankfully, the corn dolly and her child had burnt away entirely. The rain grew heavier now, bejewelling the flame-coloured leaves still clinging to the trees. Finally, the rain put the fire out, and it was time for me to leave as well.

* * *

At home, Jim went straight to his bed. Everyone else was already asleep. Soft snores came from Bett, and Andrew was collapsed on the bed, dead drunk, arms and legs askew. Rose was in her basket, sound asleep, but her poppet lay on the floor and her arms were wrapped around something else. I peered closer in the moonlit room and saw that she was cradling the kern baby. Whilst my back was turned, the minx must have plucked the babe from its mother's womb, leaving her dry belly empty. I held my breath as I prised the kern baby free from my daughter's arms and replaced it with her poppet. Rose stirred a little, but then her breathing slowed again.

By rights, the kern baby should have burnt with its mother. It was only an old superstition, but I still found myself wondering what harm it might do to the harvest. It would have to be burnt, but the rain had put out the bonfire in the dell. I crept into the kitchen, where a low fire burnt at all times. Surely, any fire would do. The smoke would still go to the sky and the infant would join its mother there. I thrust the kern baby onto the fire and watched the red embers flare into yellow flames, which began to lick the baby and then devour the tiny form. The smoke made me cough, and I tried to smother the sound in case it woke anyone. Rose would bawl at the cruel end to her new poppet and that risked waking Andrew.

Once the kern baby was reduced to ash, I stood over the fire as it returned to being embers, watching out for any stray sparks. Now the harvest should fare well. Rose taking the kern baby was a small act, and one done without malice, yet it troubled me a little. Although not witting of her wrong, had Rose gone against the local lore and risked the village harvest? I supposed none need know what had passed, but if the next harvest was a bad one, it would grieve me.

13

John

The Seeds of Destruction

Once free of the Berwick trial, I looked towards the knowe. Today, three female forms should have swung from a gallows there. But it was not to be, and now a second town had forced me out in disgrace. My flask of whisky offered some comfort, but it was dry before the mare had gone more than a mile. My throat craved more to put out the fire of humiliation that raged in my guts. But there was more than humiliation raging in me. There was fever also. The witch's contagion was upon me, and in my weakened state it would sweep through me. I must be purged and blessed the very instant I set foot back in Scotland.

To add to my woes, the rains had returned and it was bad weather for riding. The mare's footing was poor and my cloak was already drenched, causing me to shiver, even whilst my flesh burnt. And my purse felt the lack of the nine pounds that were rightly mine. All the silver spent on bed and board and on hiring the sergeants was now wasted. Newcastle's silver was dwindling fast. My fortunes had gone bad of late. And the blame could only rest in one quarter.

Misfortune had dogged me ever since the English bitch, Jane Driver, escaped justice in Newcastle. My own eyes had witnessed her call the rain from the sky with her silent scream. No doubt, she'd had a hand in the rain now making my way so difficult. Clearly, the young hag had set a curse upon me. It was the only explanation for the terrible fortune that tailed me. But how to set about reversing this? There was only one sure way to undo a witch's curse: sacrifice the witch and her progeny. It grieved me that she'd escaped so neatly and that she still lived and breathed, carrying a new witch in her belly. Why should she bear a bairn when I'd struggled so hard for one, and my goodwife had died in the attempt? Well, no more! Jane Driver would be made to pay for what she'd done to me. Once I'd finished her, the curse would be lifted and the world set aright. Her death would let me continue God's errand.

* * *

Once over the border into the Lowlands of Scotland, the dark skies had released ever more rain, causing my flesh to run hot and cold, so I'd put up at an inn to wait out the weather. Although this innkeeper didn't keep a slattern for a goodwife, I was careful not to indulge in rich food and kept only to leaves.

Despite my meagre diet, fever washed through my body and I writhed all night in the serpentine sheets that wound themselves around me. From the depths of the darkness, an owl screeched and there came the dread vision of it rising, great wings outspread, its claws gripping an inverted black lamb by its feet. The lamb made no sound, as if dead already. Would the great owl – that harbinger of death – come for me next?

But God showed mercy and I awoke bathed in sweat, heart pounding. Even awake, this vision troubled me. What could such a dream mean? Outside, the screech of a real owl reached my ears and my heartbeat slowed. So, the owl had reached into my sleep and pulled me out of it. But what of the black lamb? What did that signify?

I fumbled for the tinder box, lit a candle and leafed through my Bible, searching for an answer. It was there in the Gospels! *Behold the lamb of God who takes away the sin of the world.* If the white lamb was the son of God, then this black lamb must be the son of Satan. Why had God shown me this strange vision now? Why did He speak to me in riddles? But it was God's wont to be mysterious – it would be my task to deliberate and work out the message.

The night was cold, and so I got out of bed and perched next to the fire whilst considering the puzzle. God had lost His only son, as had I. The solution must lie there, with my boy, who was born still. But he was my own progeny and not the son of Satan. So what could God possibly mean? My thoughts moved again to my son, thinking again about how he had been gotten, and a revelation struck me about the magic of his birth. When my goodwife's womb remained resolutely dry, I'd innocently submitted myself to MacBain and his potions.

The foul barber-surgeon had given me known poisons to light a fire in me and create a child. Had MacBain knowingly set my child up for destruction? Would he be capable of such wickedness? Why had I not suspected him before? Of course, he was a man, which had immediately set him above women and beyond suspicion. Men were closer to God, made in His image and therefore stronger vessels. It would take more to corrupt a man than a woman. Yet, a man could still be a witch. Wasn't this proven at Newcastle with Matthew Bulmer? For there was a weak vessel given over to the dark arts. Had Newcastle let me continue my work, other men might very well have been revealed as witches.

My innards burnt, and I dragged myself away from the fire to piss in the pot. In the firelight, it appeared that the devil's teat was no more. Could my own eyes have deceived me? Had God taken the teat away in the night during my vision? These revelations left me faint and I staggered back into bed. My aching head was grateful for the bolster, no matter how dank with night-sweat.

My head swam thinking of MacBain and what he'd done to me. It hadn't struck me before just how close to the devil he was. Hadn't the man knowingly helped at least one witch escape justice? And right under my very nose! The evil of women had so blinded me that I'd scarce considered that the worm of evil could embed itself in a man's heart. Yet, the likes of MacBain, tinkering with herbs and potions, were really no better than these midwives. It was clear to me now – MacBain was a cunning man and no better.

In my most desperate hour of need, he'd concocted a witch's brew, telling me, 'This compound will fetch a bairn from a stone if there's one to be had.' How could any man have such certainty over a matter that only God should know about? And hadn't the spurious surgeon been proven right, after all? The compound had worked. Of course it had worked, as the devil's cures always worked, and my goodwife's dry belly had been filled. The barber-surgeon had sown the seeds of destruction in my child before I'd even made him. And he'd robbed me of a silver coin for his reward.

My head throbbed, and I reached for my flask of whisky. The burning fluid made me cough, and I sat up in bed, my head beset by old memories. Ah, but once with child, hadn't my goodwife taken a queer turn? Yet, I mustn't blame Lucy. She'd been a good woman, and one who only needed moderate chastisement to keep her within the bounds of God's law. No, the fault most surely lay with MacBain. By his hand, the devil must have possessed me, and through me, entered Lucy's womb and left his satanic princeling there.

A few moons into her term, Lucy had bled so mightily that she'd almost lost the child on a tide of blood. This must have been God's attempt to loosen the demonic infant's grip on his mother's womb. But the devil's midwives had nursed her tenderly and their herbs and queer practice had prevented the child from being expelled.

At the time, this bleeding had seemed only a weakness typical of women's wombs, a sign that Lucy's organ was not strong enough to hold my boy's life. A sob rose in my throat at the memory of his tiny, still form, but I choked back the tears, forcing myself to remember that this was God trying to vanquish his adversary's spawn. And God had won. He'd taken Lucy and her son. At the time, the grief had almost killed me. But now . . . now it was just as well. My past sorrow was locked away from me at last. For I had been cuckolded by none other than the devil. I bit down on the inside of my cheek in rage and then spat out blood upon the realisation.

In a hellish parody of the immaculate conception, my own wife had been chosen as the receptacle for this unholy issue. The dark saint's child was to be born of woman, to suckle at her breast, so that he might live amongst men and spread his lies and hatred on God's sweet earth. How innocent I'd been – lying in my marriage bed, ignorant of the spawn that made my goodwife's belly big – but God had prevented the birth of the devil's scion.

My eyes blazed now with the vision of the inverted black lamb. It was the son of Satan, deposited in my goodwife's womb. Even now, the changeling rested in hallowed ground, asleep in his mother's arms. He would pollute the sanctity of the church as long as he lay there. God was telling me to remove the pollution. That was the message in the dream! It was clear to me now and I crawled from the bed onto my knees.

'Dear Lord, thank you for opening my eyes. Hear my pledge. Give me strength enough to disinter the black lamb. Please help me sanctify my goodwife's grave once more. Aid me to remove the pollution from your hallowed ground so that it might be holy once again. So be it.'

14

Jane

Another Man's Flesh

I was at the manse with Rose, in my mother's pantry. After some persuasion on my part, Andrew had finally relented and permitted me to come and help the Reverend. Although the moon had turned three times since my mother's death, he was ailing and his health concerned me. But in spite of my worry, it filled me with joy to be here again because Mam was never more alive to me than in this room.

Now that harvest had passed, the colours and scents had changed from the bright colours and heady perfumes of summer to the muted tones and pungent odours of autumn. Berries in dull reds and glowing rusts. Seeds in all shades of earth from golden sand to wet mud. The richness of the season surrounded us, the earth's bounty filling the pantry in readiness for the coming white months, when the earth would become frugal and autumn's plenty just a distant memory.

But for now, the days were still warm, Gyb was curled up on a sunny sill and purring loudly, and Rose was helping me make a hawthorn tincture. A flat basket of red haws sat on the table and Rose stood on a high stool trying to reach the berries. I held out a haw to Rose and she took it.

'No, don't eat it, Rose.' I steered her hand away from her mouth. The berry itself would do no harm, and in a year or two, I would show her that she could eat the nourishing berries and leaves, but just now, she might choke on the stone. 'Look at the end of the haw. Can you see the tiny star? Star?'

I rubbed her fingertip over the five-pointed star and she tried to say the word, but it came out as 'Tar'. I smiled and kissed her nose. 'That's right, Rose. Star. Just like the ones in the sky.'

The star was from where the blossom had died back to make way for the haw, but when I was a girl, Mam had told me it was a blessing from the heavens. I ran my thumb over the star and smiled to myself. When Rose was a little older, I'd tell her the same.

My eyes watered at the memory of learning like this at my mother's side – all the syrups, powders and tinctures we'd made over the years – and I had to swallow before speaking again.

'Rose, can you sprinkle the haws into the flagon, please?'

I watched as my little girl dutifully added the red berries until the flagon was a third full and then I topped it up with brandy. The Reverend, of course, would prefer the brandy on its own. But his heart could use the healing cheer afforded by the haws.

I stoppered the flagon. 'Now, Rose, we need to turn the flagon upside down – just the once. Can you help?'

I placed her hands on the flagon and together, we inverted it and I then set it in the cupboard where my mother used to store her mead.

'The Reverend must come and turn the flagon every day for one moon and then it'll be ready to use.' I dropped a kiss on the top of her head and rubbed my thumb across her cheek. 'It'll make Reverend Foster hale and it might help him smile once again.'

It would take more than the sacred hawthorn to bring cheer to the poor man, but its healing properties might mend his broken heart a little. I swept stray haws and twigs from the floor and when I was satisfied that it was clean, I took a final look around the pantry and filled my memory with all the sights and smells, for who knew when I'd be allowed back here. 'Come, Rose, let's go and find Reverend Foster.'

This house had once been filled with so much warmth and joy. Every day, I'd gathered plants with my mother, and the hearth fire had always warmed pots of nourishing stew. The kitchen had been alive with savoury smells and with warmth and light. Now, though, it was cold and dark, and the only smell came from the dark spirits the Reverend was drinking. He was a mere shadow these days, and since my mother's death, he had very little cheer in him, except the hollow kind that came from a bottle. He sat, hunched over his breviary in the corner, his sunken eyes skimming listlessly over its pages. It was as though he'd stopped living and was only waiting for death to claim him.

I indicated a mutton pie cooling on a wide sill. 'There's something savoury for you, Reverend. Please see if you can eat some of it.'

Grey-faced, he eyed the dish. He nodded but made no move towards it. Once over, my mother would have had to stop him devouring the whole pie before dinner. There was a knock at the door. He raised his head towards the sound and began to get up from his desk.

'Stay there, Reverend, I'll go. Come, Rose.'

At the door was a messenger, and he gave me a letter. The seal was an almond of brown wax. My heart lurched at the sight of it. I ran my nail over the embossed pattern and showed it to my daughter. The shape of the seal told me it was clerical.

When we returned, Reverend Foster looked up. I brandished the letter, but there was no excitement in his expression. 'Is it from the Bishop?'

'I think so! Please, open it, Reverend, and tell me what it says.'

The Reverend began looking about for his letter knife. Just as my exasperation was about to overwhelm me, there was another knock at the door. It must be Tom – he would have seen the messenger! My heart raced at this unexpected chance to spend a moment with him. Andrew wouldn't be happy, of course, but the Reverend was here, so there was nothing improper, except what went on in my heart. But that was between me and God. And if the Bishop had sent good news, we would be together again before very long.

I opened the door and Tom stood before me, breathless, eyes gleaming.

'Jane! Was that the messenger? Did he bring it?' He grinned, and his dimples winked at me. 'Is it a reply from the Bishop?'

The questions tumbled out one after the other. This was the old Tom. My Tom.

'Yes, it is! Reverend Foster's opening it now.' I pulled the door wide. 'Come in, Tom. Come in.'

He followed me in and went straight to Rose, his arms open, and he bent as if to swing her into the air, but when Rose just stared at him, open-mouthed, he seemed to change his mind and knelt down to speak to her instead. 'Hello, Rose. Are you helping your mammy?'

Rose covered her face with her hands and scurried over to the Reverend. Tom frowned and sat on the cracket but didn't remark on her behaviour.

I took down a jar and held it out to my daughter. 'Rose, do you want some sugared rose petals?'

My coaxing worked and Rose toddled over to me, her eyes on Tom the whole time. She stuck her hand into the jar and pulled out a handful of petals. I lifted her onto the settle and she snuggled up with her poppet, delicately nibbling the calming blossoms, her eyes fixed on Tom.

The Reverend opened the letter and held it to the window whilst he read it.

Tom sat, one leg joggling. 'Reverend? Please put us out of our misery!'

Reverend Foster sighed and his finger paused halfway down the page. 'Well, the new baby complicates matters.' He pointed at me with his paper knife and my hands crept over my belly. 'It complicates matters greatly.'

Tom leapt to his feet. 'So flesh is what matters? And Jane is full of another man's flesh. Is that what you're saying?'

The Reverend nodded. 'I'm afraid so, Tom.'

Keeping one eye on Rose, Tom paced back and forth, and then crossed over to the Reverend.

'Well. What about Rose? I've lost Jane, but I needn't lose Rose, I'm still her father, no matter what else has passed.'

The Reverend held up a hand. 'Wait, there's more . . .' He ran his finger down the letter until near the end. 'Ah, here we are. The Bishop says that Rose was born within the marriage, so–'

'So Rose belongs to Driver? My own daughter belongs to another man? And with her, Jane?'

The Reverend nodded. 'That's right, Tom. The Bishop says that even though Rose isn't Driver's flesh and blood, her being born within the marriage is what counts.'

The Reverend passed me the letter and I sat down on the cracket, my eyes running uselessly over the fine hand. 'So, what does that mean for us?' My voice was barely a croak. 'For Tom and me? And Rose?'

Tom took the letter and pored over it for some time. 'The Bishop says you're married to Driver for good or ill.'

When he raised his eyes, there was a film of tears over them. He looked at me and then to Rose. At the family he knew was no longer his.

I felt my heart tear as surely as if a knife had been inserted.

'Then there's no hope for us?'

Reverend Foster shook his head. 'I'm sorry, Jane, but there's naught to be done.'

I looked at Tom, but he was rubbing his brow and staring right through me. 'I cannot believe it. The Bishop doesn't understand. How can he?'

'He understands all too well. It's a terrible blow for you, but his word is final.' Reverend Foster folded the letter and placed it in a box before locking it. 'The letter will be safe here. There's no need to give young Driver any more power over you than he already possesses.'

I stood up but had to grip the edge of the table when my head began to swim. 'So, with these few words, the Bishop has condemned me to a life lived as Andrew Driver's wife?'

Tom came to my side. 'Come, Jane, sit back down, you're distressed and it's not good for you and the bairn. Look, we'll find a way round this. We'll make a way.'

The Reverend sighed – it was a juddering sound that made me wonder about his lungs again. He picked up his hourglass, examined it carefully and then stared out of the window at the Pennines. 'You mustn't dwell on matters you cannot change, Jane. Let Rose be your comfort. And let the fact that Tom is alive be another.' He set down the hourglass. 'But the Bishop won't permit you to have him.'

I walked over to the window and stared out at the darkening line of the horizon. Cold came in waves from the glass. Night would fall before long and Andrew would come looking for me. I pressed my forehead to the cold glass. 'God will not permit me to have you, Tom, because you are joy and love, and because you are from my old life. I don't deserve happiness. I deserve the penance of marriage to Andrew.'

Tom came and drew me away from the window. 'You've gone to a dark place in your soul, Jane. But there's a way back to the light. There is another way.'

'What other way? You heard what the Bishop said.'

He took my hands and looked at me, all the shades of green alive and dancing in his eyes.

'We can leave Mutton Clog. You, me and Rose. We can make a new life.'

My mind raced. 'Tom, what are you saying? I cannot leave . . . Andrew would never permit it.'

He shook his head. 'You don't need his permission. We'd leave this land and go overseas. To the New World.'

'But what about the Reverend? What about your father? They've lost enough people already. They can't lose us as well.'

The Reverend smiled. 'Jane, I will miss you and Bill will certainly break his heart at losing Tom.' He looked upon Rose and his eyes glazed. 'And the thought of never seeing little Rose again will be the most terrible pain of all for both of us. But do you think it makes either of us happy seeing you here like this?' He tapped the back of his Bible. 'Now, as a man of God, I cannot give my blessing for this. But I won't condemn you for it either. Tom, you must plan carefully, for if Driver learns of it, he will put Jane and Rose under lock and key. Now, I'm away to the church to pray for your souls. Don't dwell here too long, Tom, else Driver come and find you with Jane and Rose.'

I hugged the Reverend and pressed my wet face to his thin chest. 'How will I ever face life without you?'

'You will face it, Jane, because it's the best course for you, and Tom will take care of you.' He blinked and pushed me away from him. 'Now, don't detain me further.'

He opened the door and left, and I watched him walking away into the dusk. How many more times would I see Reverend Foster? Must I lose everyone? I thought of Mam's grave. 'But leaving here would mean . . . leaving Mam behind. Forever.' I blinked at the enormity of what Tom had suggested. 'I could never visit her again.'

'You carry your mother here, Jane.' He pressed my hands to his heart, and its slow, steady rhythm flowed into me. 'She's *in* you. And in Rose. Just as my own mother is in Rose.'

How could I forget Tom's mother? He'd be leaving behind her grave. I brushed my lips against his knuckles and looked up at him.

'If you're willing to make that sacrifice, Tom, then so am I. We'll make a new life together away from here.'

15

John

All the Hordes of the Night

On waking, it took a whilst to remember that I was back in my own home. My guts were awash with acid and sweat drenched my body. The blanket was on the floor, and the thick air pressed down on me, making it hard to breathe. Someone had put the hex on me, that much was clear. On my homeward journey, and since arriving home, I'd eaten little more than leaves, so a rich diet was not to blame. My dreams had been haunted with hags, imps and demons, and even my waking hours were troubled by visions.

Praying would help, but my voice had deserted me and my hands were too limp to press together in prayer, so in my mind, I began asking God to cast out any evil presence from me. As the familiar words started to form in my mind, the fog began to lift, and with it, the constriction to my throat. Finally, words emerged from my mouth, croaking at first, and then the strength returned to my hands, making it possible to clasp them before me and push myself from the bed and down onto the flagstones. The cold against my bare knees sent sweet pain flashing through my body and my humours seemed to be reviving at last.

'Dear God, give me strength to fight the powers of darkness, and all the hordes of the night – those who haunt decent people and steal their souls whilst they slumber. Give me the means to dispose of the wickedness that walks the earth, bearing the name of your adversary, whether disguised as woman, child or man. In your name, dear Lord, help me to pluck these evil souls as though they were but freakish flowers. Help me deliver them unto you. So be it.'

In the half-light, the familiar shapes of the table and the settle emerged from the gloom of the night. The sweat chilling on my back caused me to shiver. The sight of my rumpled bed filled me with regret. A weaker soul would tumble back in, but God had work for me to do and there was no time to waste idling. Still, God would want me to build up enough strength to fight the dark legions, and so a few more minutes in bed would do no harm.

It was so cold that I allowed myself a slug of whisky from my flask. It scorched my throat and chest, warming my insides. The drink gave me no pleasure, which meant it was an acceptable weakness on this occasion. I drained the flask and retched slightly. The cleansing liquid would purify any lingering miasma from my nose and throat. I eased myself back on the straw mattress and closed my eyes against the spinning room. This was the spirit of the grain cleansing the contagion from me and it released me back to sleep once more.

* * *

Pale sunlight seeped into the room. Pulling the rug over my eyes was useless, and now I was fully awake for the second time. Apart from a sore head and a belly full of bile, my body and soul were refreshed. My manhood was vigorous and I slid my hand beneath my linings. A thorough examination revealed that the devil's teat had not returned. Soon, it would be time to carry out God's instructions on ridding His holy kirk of the black lamb. It sickened me that the devil could infect the soul of infants. But what better way for demons to slip unnoticed into the world? Attended at birth by their evil midwives. How had I been so blind for so long? The devil must be sleeping in cradles the length and breadth of the country! The mask of infant beauty beguiling unsuspecting fathers, who were ignorant of being cuckolded by the dark saint himself.

My first errand would be to remove the tainted child from hallowed ground and inter him far away from the kirk. This infernal task must be carried out under the mantle of the night. It would be best to do it before Uncle James knew of my return, as this would avoid suspicion falling on me. He would understand once he heard of my vision and of how God had spoken to me, but that could wait until the infant had been moved. My stomach was not strong and my limbs were weak from all the travelling, so part of me dreaded the horrible unearthing that would be necessary. Of course, the child's mother also lay in that grave, and she'd been an unwitting receptacle for the devil's spawn. It would be impossible to remove the infant from the grave without disturbing the mother's rest, but she would forgive me.

But what of all those children who had survived childbirth – and there must be many – how would it be possible to tell a demonic child from a godly one? How might I tell which child was infected? Pricking might work, but children yowled at the merest touch, or even from being looked at in the wrong way. My pricker would only result in a great many screaming infants and might let the guilty escape their just punishment. This problem required much consideration.

Of course, there was one child due to enter this world, and that child was certainly tainted. No test would be needed to prove the wickedness of the infant lodging in Jane Driver's belly. It was certainly infected by the devil. Her womb protected the infant for now, but it would face God's vengeance once born. Yet, Driver was the most powerful witch in the north of England and a mighty adversary. The vixen was so important to the Newcastle coven that her dam had laid aside her own life. But this was no act of maternal sacrifice. Women were not born to be so noble – why had I not questioned this at the time? Instead, this was merely the older witch ensuring the beast residing within her daughter might see birth. Aye, this mistress of the elements had enslaved her elders in the service of birthing a demon, but it wouldn't draw breath – I would see to that.

16

Jane

The Saviour Caul

Some of my remedies were running low and the monk's pepper had run out altogether. The Tyne was too far a walk now and the idea of entering Newcastle terrified me. So, the need for supplies provided the perfect excuse to follow the deer paths through the woods to Meg Wetherby's dwelling. With luck, Tom would be there.

Meg's dwelling was in the woods, where she'd lived like an anchoress, drawing solace from the natural world. Not very much time had elapsed since her passing, but already the woods were reclaiming what was rightfully theirs. If left alone, nature would swallow her home and with it, Meg's memory.

Above my head, the vegetation was bent and twigs had been newly snapped. This was not the work of a deer. Had Tom come this way just before me? A wisp of wood smoke in the air hinted at the answer. My heart skipped a beat, my step became lighter and I hurried towards Meg's dwelling. A spire of smoke from the chimney told me Tom was there for certain! But then my child began kicking and my step slowed.

I put my hands on my belly and felt my son. Through the trees was Meg's home. Tom would meet me in secret, but there was always a risk of being seen, especially since Tom had lit a fire. And though I'd been tricked into this marriage, I was still another man's wife and carried his child. Should I turn back?

What would Tom expect from me? But before I could turn back, Tom came out of Meg's dwelling, picked up an axe and began chopping wood. When I took a step, he heard me and looked up, grinning.

'Jane? Finally, you came!' He put down the axe and wiped his hands on his breeches. 'Does Driver know of your whereabouts?'

'He knows I've come to check Meg's stores as some of mine are low. I don't think he's followed me . . . You've lit a fire.'

'Aye, every day, I light one, just in case you come. To keep the damp off you.

'Thank you, Tom. That's very thoughtful.' I hurried through the door lest anyone be watching from the woods.

Tom came in after me and began stacking logs next to the fire. He lifted a cauldron of water onto the tripod.

'This is your first time here since . . . well, Meg. And your Mam. Is it hard for you?'

I nodded. 'At the time, Meg's death was the saddest moment in my life.' She'd left this earth with me and Tom at her bedside, and she was old, so it was easier to accept. But my mother's death was still a dark sack that I was afraid to put my hand into, and so my thoughts drifted back to Meg. 'But you know, Meg was old and her death a kind one . . .'

'Sorry, Jane.' He took my hands. 'Mebbes this wasn't the best place to meet.'

'No, Tom. It's the best place to meet.' I smiled and pulled my hands away to wipe my eyes on my pinny. 'Meg still makes me smile. She was a terrible old woman, really.'

Tom smiled. 'Aye, always brimming with gossip and old saws.' He pointed to the settle. 'Here, sit down. You look flushed. Are you too warm?'

'A little. Let me take off my cloak and unwind my shawl.'

At the sight of my belly, Tom looked away and began to rummage on a rough-hewn plank that served as a table.

'Do you need some light?' He held up a fistful of tallow candles.

'Please don't – my eyes are watering enough already!' Besides, there was light enough from the fire.

I sat down on a settle hewn from an oak trunk. Tom paused between the fireside cracket and the pallet bed. Eventually, he perched on the cracket, his knees up to his ears, legs joggling. He wasn't built for sitting still.

'It's good to see you, Jane.'

I smiled at him. 'It is good.'

'Do you want some tea?' He indicated Meg's larder. Against one wall were rows of shelves, and on them rested crocks containing remedies, stored according to season and potency. 'They're not labelled. You might have to help me find something that won't kill us.'

'It's all right, Tom. Meg kept everything in order so she could put her hand to a crock in the dark and know its contents by sight and smell. Anything beneath the top shelf should be fine – she kept her poisons there. Unless you want some warming spice – they're on the second-highest shelf.'

He frowned. 'Why? Are spices poisonous?'

'Sometimes, if you have too much. Dose is all.' She kept them up a height because she was suspicious of anything that didn't grow locally. But the eastern spices alone held fire, and their warming properties were much needed in our climes. 'Meg fancied the hot sun was contained in these fiery seeds and that their warmth seeped into a sickening body, no matter how suspect they might be.' I stood and gazed up at the jars containing aromatic pepper, cinnamon, saffron, turmeric, anise and cloves. 'We could try some ginger. There, that one there, I think.'

Tom lifted down the crock and opened it. He blinked at the smell. 'Aye, but something so startling to so many senses at the same time must carry great power.'

'You and your ways, Tom! You sound just like Meg. You know, she told me once that everything necessary to feed and heal a body grew within a mile of where they were born.'

'Is that right? So mebbes it's not good for a person to uproot themselves.' Tom looked at me carefully. 'Moving too far from native roots might unsettle a body and weaken it . . .'

So, Tom was worried about leaving home as well. Had Bill been trying to dissuade him? It was understandable. Bill had lost his wife, and now he would lose his son and granddaughter. But staying here, married to Andrew and not being able to have Tom would be unendurable.

'But you went to sea, Tom, and you came back full of life. Look at you – stronger than ever.'

'Aye, but only because it wasn't such a long journey. Half the old salts had no teeth in their heads.' He put down the crock before taking my hands and drawing me towards him. 'Jane, you know I would do nothing to cause ill to you and Rose. But taking you overseas might do you both harm. And the new baby. Mebbes–'

'No! We cannot think like that. We'll sharp settle in a new land. We just need to meld with the earth and sky. Eat the local roots and berries, drink the spring water, bathe in the rivers. Go skyclad . . .'

'Go skyclad?' He raised a brow at me, and the blood rushed to my face.

'Tea, Tom!' It was best to keep him busy so he didn't start worrying about the future and change his mind. 'Make the tea, please.'

'All right, but mebbes we should stick with what we know. What's the best tea to have from these parts?'

Tom, for all his time at sea, still craved simple fare. 'Mam loved lemon balm and Meg loved mugwort. But neither is too good for me . . . right now.' I took down a jar, opened it and sniffed the contents. 'Shall we have mint? It's soothing.'

'Aye, all right then.' He took down two bowls. 'How much? A pinch each?

'A small pinch for me – dried mint can be overpowering and not so good for a woman carrying a baby.'

He frowned at this. 'What do you mean?'

I shrugged. 'Well, too much can cause a mother to miscarry . . . Why do you ask?'

He sighed. 'Jane, this will pain you, and it's not a good time, but can I ask something about your ma?'

What on earth did he need to know, at the cost of my tears? But it would be better to answer his questions. 'Go on, Tom. You can ask anything of me.'

'Was Annie really put to death just for boiling up a few plants to bring down milk fever and the like?'

103

I sighed. 'Would that it were it only that.'

'What do you mean?'

'Well, there were charges of . . . of sending children to sleep in their mother's wombs.'

'Sending children to sleep in their mother's wombs?' His brow furrowed as if solving a riddle. 'Is that a kind way of saying she was murdering infants afore they were born?'

'Well . . . it cannot properly be called murder until a child is a child and has drawn breath.'

This idea troubled me, though, and I thought back to when I'd first learnt of Rose. She was barely a tickle in my belly, but she'd seemed real enough to me and Tom. And she'd certainly been real enough to the sergeant and the magistrate.

A hard look crossed Tom's face then. 'And Rose? Did neither you nor your mother try to, well, rid you of your burden?'

It was hateful to hear Tom speak of our daughter with such words. 'No, Tom.' I placed my hand on his forearm, but he snatched it away. 'I would never have considered such a thing. Never. Not even to save myself from the House of Correction. And the horror of that place lives within me to this day.'

'Sorry, Jane. But I had to ask.' He seemed uncertain but kept digging. 'Will you continue to do your mother's work? And will Rose be brought up in these ways, learning of midwifery – deciding which children should live and which should not?'

His questions set a cold feeling flickering up my spine. I thought of Rose plucking buttercups and daisies and laying them in her tiny basket. Playing at being mother with her poppet. Such innocent play, but now Tom made me wonder where it might lead.

'I'm sorry, Jane. Please don't look so downcast.'

'It's a feeling I cannot help. It overtakes me daily, but it's not surprising after spending time in gaol, being tortured and then watching my own mother hanged by the neck. And now I'm living in a sham marriage to a man who deliberately set out to dupe me.' Tom looked miserable at my outburst, but my blood was up now and it was too late to stop myself, even if my words hurt him. 'You cannot begin to imagine the thoughts that whirl in my mind. And now you've come back from the dead, to remind me of my old life and all that I've lost, and then you start picking over my mother's life in such a harsh way.'

This rant left me breathless.

Tom placed his hands on my shoulders. 'I'm sorry, Jane. I meant no harm, but I'm just afraid for you and Rose, that's all.'

There was so much anger and hurt in his eyes, and so much love. But what was I to do? Fall into his arms and risk being caught by Andrew? He would lock me up better than any gaoler if he knew what was afoot.

'Come, Jane, here's peace. Have some tea.'

He ladled out hot water and passed me a wooden bowl, smoothed through years of use. I blew on the surface to send the refreshing steam into my face. Outside, there was a loud crack and my heart started thumping.

'Andrew! If he finds us here—'

Tom held up a hand to quieten me. He put down his bowl and crept outside, pulling the door closed behind him. Quickly, I drew my shawl around me. Was Andrew outside? Had he heard our plans?

The door opened. I held my breath and let it out when Tom appeared alone, closing the door behind him.

'There's nobody there. Mebbes just a deer or a fox disturbed in the day . . . Jane, you've gone very pale, what troubles you?'

'Nothing. Only this has made me worry that Andrew might learn of our plans. We need to take more care. If he finds us together, he'll have me put under lock and key, and then there'll be no escape. Bett already has her sergeant's eye on me half the day. I'd better go, Tom.' I stood up and drew my cloak around me. 'And we mustn't meet again before we leave.'

Tom's shoulders drooped. 'You're right. Typical me, thinking only of meself. It'll be hard not seeing you, but it won't be for long.' He pulled me into his arms, and for a moment, I leant on him, feeling safe and happy. But it wasn't safe. Nothing was safe here anymore and I peeled myself away from him.

'Tom, I have to go now.'

'Aye. Go on. But you'd best take some remedies with you in case you meet Driver or his mother coming back out of the woods. Then you'll not be caught out in a plain lie. What's best to take?'

'A few things – Mam's supplies are running low. First, monk's pepper.' I'd need to show May how to make her own remedies so she could look after herself once we'd gone. I pointed to the second-highest shelf. 'Could you help me, please? Only I'm not steady enough on my feet to climb.'

'Show me where.'

'Up there, please. The spices. Same shelf as the ginger.'

'Which crock do you want me to get down?'

'All of them, as I'll have to sniff each pot till I find what I'm looking for.'

Tom reached up to the shelf, passing down tiny pots of jewel-coloured hard berries, seeds and barks, and jars of poppy milk.

Tom was so tall that he needed no step to reach the highest shelves, and he moved easily. Every part of him was dear to me, and I longed to reach out and touch him. If only we could fetch Rose and live happily here in the woods until it was time to go to sea.

Tom suddenly stopped lifting down crocks and reached behind them. He drew out a small chest and rested it against his heart before handing it to me.

'Da made this for me – many moons ago.'

'What's inside it?'

'See if you can guess what's inside it.' He didn't smile, but some of his old mischief danced in his eyes. 'Open it and find out.'

I held onto the box, wanting the moment to last. But Tom was watching me keenly, and so I opened it. Inside was a dry and fragile scrap, waxen, but as fine and yellowed as old lace. I touched it with equal amounts of care and curiosity.

'Do you know what it is?'

I nodded. 'A caul. A rare happening.' This would have covered an infant's face and head like a snug cap at birth. 'I've delivered a couple of babies born with one. Whose is this?'

'Mine. Meg removed it at me birth and kept it for me. She said as long as it was kept safe, it would keep me safe over water.' He smiled a crooked smile. 'Well, something did keep me safe.'

I smiled back and passed him the box. 'Indeed, something did.'

'When Meg showed it to me, it seemed daft because there was no likelihood of me going to sea, what with living so far inland, and me having life as a verger mapped out from the day of me birth. But Meg argued that it was a special grace to be born with a caul. And she said a man could never tell when the sea might call him.'

'Do you think Meg knew that the sea would try and take you one day?'

'Mebbes.' He shrugged. 'Meg had her strange inklings, didn't she? And the sea very nearly did have me.'

'The thought of *The Durham* sinking and taking all souls down with her makes me shiver.'

'Aye, me and all. Most of them were young lads like me who'd been pressed into service . . .'

Tom's eyes glazed over and he seemed to go somewhere else for a time.

A thought struck me. 'Tom, are you afraid to cross water again?'

He shook his head and held up his caul. 'Not with this to keep me safe. And with it, you, Rose and the bairn.'

My heart lightened then. It was a sign from Meg! We did right to go, and we'd have a safe passage. 'Tom, you must take the caul home for safekeeping – as a natural charm.'

His face darkened. 'Me da won't like that, you know what he's like.'

Same old Tom, afraid of anything that might hint at the other world. 'Well then, take it as a grace straight from God.'

'Aye, a grace from God. Me da won't mind that so much.' Tom placed the box inside his jerkin. 'It'll be good to take it away with us – it being a connection to me ma.'

I nodded. 'And to Meg.' She'd severed the cord so he could breathe his own air and so his mother could succumb to the long rest that had – according to Meg – been calling her since she was a babe herself. 'Tom, you'll have your caul and I'll have Mam's satchel. Our mothers will protect us and live on in our hearts. And in our children.'

'Aye. All our children. Whether born of my blood or not.' His eyes shone. 'They'll all be my bairns.'

'Oh, Tom . . .' I stepped towards him.

'You should go, Jane. If Driver finds you here alone with me, it won't go well for you. Will it?' He moved aside to examine the shelves again. 'Quick, tell me the other remedies you need, and let's get you out of here. What are you short of?'

'Oh . . . chasteberries, rue, pennyroyal, parsley, wild carrot seed, angelica root.'

Tom frowned and began passing me crocks. I opened each one and sniffed until I found the necessary herbs and placed them in my sack.

'They're not an everyday sort of plant, are they? So why the need for those particular herbs?'

I paused. 'Sometimes, girls need help with . . . their monthly courses, or they need a way to . . . prevent further issue . . .'

Tom looked as pained as if an arrow had lanced him. If only I'd left sooner, all this could have been avoided.

'What is it, Tom? What's the matter?'

When he spoke, there was no kindness in his eyes or his voice. He pointed at my belly. 'I've spared my feelings by telling myself you had no choice but to bear this child. But now I know different. You had the means to prevent it and you chose not to.' He bit his lip. 'You must have wanted to have this child. And so, despite the ill fortune Andrew Driver has brought on you and me, you must love him yet.'

He turned his head away from me.

'Tom, please don't turn away from me. You don't understand.'

He snorted. 'Mebbes I do wrong to take you away from Driver. Mebbes you belong here with him, and you can have a long life together, filled with good cheer and many bairns—'

'Tom, how can you say that? It's not . . . it's not . . .' How could I explain and make him understand? My mind wasn't right at the time. Andrew never expected me to lie with him when I was carrying Rose, and then when he did, I was still nursing her and should have been safe from falling.

'Tom, this baby took me by surprise—'

'Aye, me and all!'

'Tom, once the baby was there, it wasn't . . . I couldn't . . . To me, it doesn't matter who his father is.' I placed a hand on his arm, but he flinched and drew it away. 'Only, this baby is my baby as much as Rose is. I couldn't bring myself to . . .'

'Yet you can bring yourself to do it to other bairns?'

'Tom, please, this is hard enough. Some bairns are not meant to be – through no fault of their own – or their mothers. Or their mothers might not have the means to keep them. It's a mercy sometimes.'

'Aye, well it's a strange form of mercy to me. But then I only have a narrow understanding of life.'

He handed me my sack. His eyes welled and I wanted to hold him, but there was a look in his eyes that warded me off.

'It's time you were not here, Jane. You'd better get back to your husband.'

17

John

That Putrid Child

Since returning home, I'd reverted to my old eating habits, so my stomach had shrunken and the hunger no longer pained me. Instead, it was a source of joy, as if a silver light were illuminating me from within. No flesh had passed my lips in weeks. I ate sparely – only bitter leaves that grew above ground. Not even bread had passed my lips for it was sinful. Its softness on my tongue – surely the most sensuous and unholy organ – might lead me back into sybaritic ways. If held on the tongue like the forbidden host, bread dissolved with sweetness so akin to honey that it must invite impure thoughts.

Uncle James had taught me that papists gorged themselves on bread, believing they devoured the flesh of God's son. To see a priest place the soft bread on a man's tongue was a sacrilege. They greedily supped what they believed to be His blood, when it was merely fragrant and seductive wines from countries too near the sun, where men are naturally overheated and prone to sinning. Above all, for the bread and wine to transmogrify into the flesh and blood of Jesus Christ was a monstrous act of magic, brought about by unnatural practices such as incantations in strange tongues, perfumed smoke, ringing bells and burning candles.

There was more ritual and magic on a priest's altar than ever there was from a witches' moot. There was so much witchcraft around us that we could no longer see it for what it was. Even the slaughter of dumb beasts was nothing short of a pagan sacrifice designed to appease the demon gods and in so doing, bring plenty to satiate men. God cautioned against the sin of gluttony, so I eschewed blooded meat, soft bread and perfumed wines. I'd never been a voluptuary, but following my appetite was a sure way to slide back into gross bodily appetites. Only water and weeds for me from this day forward. Even so, I'd permit myself a tot of whisky to steel me for what lay ahead. No ordinary man would have the belly for such a task.

* * *

Once night fell, I stole into the kirkyard, my way lit only by the moon. Lucy and her child had been interred in one grave so they might spend eternity together, waiting for the time I joined them. In my hand was a spade. My stomach clenched at the prospect of the hideous work ahead. But I crept along the headstones until Lucy's grave was before me. After quaffing from my flask, I fell to my knees, tears running freely as I begged for strength. Then I stood up and began to dig by dint of a frenzied hacking at the cold earth. They had been buried a full six feet. My extra coin had seen to that so no creatures would devour their remains. The thought of what might be unearthed made me shiver. Death and all its terrible sights and smells were no stranger to me, but this deed chilled my blood.

The kirk and Uncle James' house loomed over me. Years of living under his roof told me he slept soundly at night, but his dog didn't, so it was important to work quickly and quietly. When the hole was deep enough, I slid down into the grave, trying not to think about the dank clay walls surrounding me, and the sly creatures that lived there, just waiting to feast on human flesh. The air was heavy with water and its dampness made me shiver, yet sweat still haled from me. Undeterred, I kept digging.

When I finally reached wood, I scraped the top part of the coffin free of soil. But as I used the spade to smite the wood, a volley of barks issued from inside the house. Curse my uncle's affection for dogs! I kept my head down and held my breath, eyes flicking towards the manse door, watching for a light appearing.

Eventually, the dog quietened down, and no lanterns were lit. No angry face appeared at the door to search the night for an intruder. I remained silent a whilst longer to let the dog and my uncle fall back to their slumbers. Uncle James was fond of his bed and might be sufficiently sleep-addled to ignore one bout of barking, but he wouldn't let another pass.

After a time, I resumed my breach of the coffin, but more carefully now, to avoid rousing the vile beast again. Once the wood was split, I prised it away with the spade and then continued with my bare hands, wincing at the sharp spelks. Finally, the coffin was open, and a suffocating miasma bloomed from beneath me. I held my breath and lifted a small bundle from the grave. It would be mostly bones by now, but the swaddling binding the tiny form stank with the juices of putrefaction and they made me retch. The child's body had the fetor of Lucifer on it – here was certain proof that it was vital to continue my quest.

I reached up and placed the infant remains on the graveside, clambered out of the pit and set off, clutching the corpse. After squeezing through some old bushes, I started running, causing a terrible stitch in my side. The pain left me sick and once I'd made it through the woods and across the river, I collapsed to the ground, sobbing and still clutching the rancid bundle.

By now, the sun was with me and the golden dawn started to leach the grey from my eyes. There was not much time. It was almost fully light and who knew what folks might be abroad. My chosen burial spot was outside my father's old dwelling.

This had been an unhappy home, and one with no mother. My sole comfort had been my dog, Jinny, who was buried under a small cairn just outside. At the memory of her, I touched my pouch to check my milk teeth were still safe. The cairn was well away from sacred ground, and it had been here for so many years that no one would notice if it was suddenly a little larger. This was a quiet area, although hunters might come by, which would increase the chance of being caught. With luck, the task would be finished before sun-up. I put down the infant and began moving the stone cairn.

The digging was heavy going as my clothes impeded me, and I had to remove my upper garments. When I paused to mop sweat from my brow, I heard a tiny snap. My heart raced, and I held my breath, the better to hear. My eyes scanned left and right, but there was nothing to see. After several minutes, no further sound came. It might have been a deer. Yet, it hadn't sounded like a deer . . .

I was standing in the pit, up to my knees, when there came a loud snapping of twigs and a large man emerged from the undergrowth and stood before me. He was grey of hair and beard, big, but thin, and he was swathed in his usual mangy jerkin of rabbit fur. The foul barber-surgeon grimaced at me.

'What heinous practice are you about, John Sharpe? What has fetched you back to your father's home? No good, I'll warrant, since naught comes from you but badness.' MacBain peered into the pit and snorted. 'Scrabbling about and burying a corpse by the looks of you.' His gazed rested upon the bundle of rags near the lip of the grave and his tone changed. 'Whose bairn is this?'

'It's of no concern to anyone but myself, MacBain. Be off and get about your own business.'

'It is my business if it means stopping fiends murdering infants and burying them. Perhaps this is a matter for the bailies.'

'No need for the bailies. No infant has been murdered.' I sighed. 'This is the child borne by my late goodwife – Lucy. He is contaminated and will pollute the sacred earth of the kirkyard.'

'You've dug up the remains of your own infant?' MacBain's eyes bulged. 'Sharpe, you've always been a curious creature, but now you're surely missing something vital in your mind. Come, I'll take you to the pastor, and he can deal with you.'

'No! Not Uncle James. I beseech you.'

'Get going, Sharpe.' He pointed to the thick club that swung from his belt. 'Unless you wish to join your son in this shallow grave.'

'Don't threaten me, MacBain.' But my words were hollow. This man could break my skull and bury me without anyone missing me since Uncle James thought me still in England. 'Oh, very well. But you cannot make me touch that putrid child again. You must take him.'

MacBain frowned, but picked up the bundle, closing his eyes against the sight, and I climbed out of the pit. It would be as well to explain myself to my uncle. He was a man of learning, as well as a man of God. He had taught me the Lord's ways himself and would understand my mission once the whole terrible tale was explained to him.

18

Jane

The Promise of Snow

All night, I'd dozed fitfully and now sleep evaded me even though my eyes were closed. My dreams were haunted by longings to slip away to Tom. By day, my heart was lighter now that we were going to be together. But at night, my soul was troubled. Andrew had married me in the eyes of God and the Bishop said we were married for good or ill. But Andrew had tricked me. So, surely God would understand that this was not a true marriage, even if the Bishop refused to see sense. The prospect of living in a new country filled me with terror. I'd never been further than the mouth of the sea. The thought of sailing into it created a void in my heart. But it was the only way and then Tom would be with me all the days of my life.

Now there was a plan, it gave me hope. Every time I visited the Reverend, it was a small matter to secrete a few items about my person. We couldn't take everything with us, but we would need warm clothes and Rose would need her poppet. Most important of all was my mother's satchel. The preparations made my heart lurch with guilt every time one of the Drivers looked at me. I lay with these thoughts whirling in my mind until Rose crawled into bed and began kissing my nose. My eyes were bleary and I struggled to open them.

'Oh, Rose, if only I wasn't so tired.' But looking at her and seeing her so bright lent me energy. And now the terrible weight of an endless marriage to Andrew had been lifted from me, my spirits were raised for the first time in months. I was hungry and my mouth watered at the thought of earthy mushrooms cooked in salted butter. There were none in the house, so I would need to go and pick some, and the early morning air would wake me up and staunch my tiredness.

'Come, Rose, I have a curious craving for mushrooms. Shall we go and find some for breakfast? Mushrooms?'

She nodded, and I wrapped her in a little green cloak and pulled the hood over her red curls. A creaking door startled me and I looked up to see Andrew standing before me.

'So! Sneaking off again? And where are you thinking of escaping to at this time of the morn?'

My heart started racing. He'd used the word 'escape'. How had he guessed at our plans? My face flushed and he must have noticed it.

'What are you up to, Jane?'

'Nothing, Andrew. We're not up to anything – just going to pick some mushrooms. Now the sickness has left me, my appetite's back and it's making me crave mushrooms.'

'Aye well, you can just get yourself back to bed. If you've energy enough in the morning, there are better uses for it. And if you've still energy after, then you may go and pick some mushrooms for my breakfast.'

'But Rose is awake now–'

'No matter. She'll fall back to sleep easily enough.' He grabbed the front of my cloak and pulled me towards him, causing me to stumble. 'Now get moving when I tell you!'

Rose began to whimper at the sound of his raised voice. It wouldn't do for her to be so afraid.

'Andrew, please let go of me. There's no need for force. I'll go back to bed. Come, Rose. Sleepy time again. Get your poppet.'

* * *

Finally, we set out in the cold, damp morning. Guilt surged through me at my latest betrayal of Tom. But there was no helping it. And it would not last forever. Tom was taking us away and our lives would be filled only with hope and joy.

Rose rode on my hip, and as we walked, she tickled my ears, and her antics and the earthy smell of the woods soothed me. The first frosts were yet to come, but there was a sharp bite of winter in the air. The morning dew had drenched the bottom of my cloak. We should turn back – it wouldn't do for Rose to catch a chill from the damp air and fall ill. But she wriggled in my arms, intent on getting down to run about.

'Come, little one, down you go. You can help me. See if you can find me some mushrooms.'

Rose toddled about, pointing each time she found a clump of mushrooms, and I walked over to cut them. I passed each fungus to Rose, so she could sniff it and run a tiny finger over the black gills before placing it in my basket. Mushroom gathering was fraught with danger, and it was all too easy to pick something that might destroy life rather than sustain it. So it was important that Rose learnt to identify plants from an early age. I showed her red toadstools and mushrooms with white gills, stem rings and bulbous sacs. Each time, I screwed up my face so she would learn they weren't safe to eat. It still made me shudder to think of Henry Green and how close he'd come to death with the monkshood. Next summer, when it bloomed again, we'd be long gone. But there would be different plants in the New World, and it would take me time to learn them. Some of them were familiar to me, thanks to Meg bartering with merchants over the years, but there might be thousands that were unknown to me.

For now, I plucked a late-flowering sprig of white blossoms with golden eyes. 'So then, Rose. What's this flower?'

I crushed it under her nose so she could inhale its spicy aroma. She screwed up her face.

'This is yarrow. Sometimes we call it woundwort because it's good for healing wounds.' I didn't add that yarrow had once saved her father from bleeding to death.

Rose nodded, but the nods weren't deep, and her brow was furrowed. Her eyes took on a faraway look for a moment. She was too young for such learning – no doubt my mother had often seen this look on my own face. But in time, her young mind would absorb the remedies and she would reach for them without having to think about it.

On the other side of the clearing, I spotted Reverend Foster walking down the hill. I waved an arm in the air and he waved back.

'Rose, look, there's the Reverend.' I pointed so that Rose could follow my finger. She raised her hands in the air and scrunched her fingers open and closed in greeting as he picked his way towards us.

He grinned at Rose and ruffled her curls. 'Jane, what are you doing out so early?'

I raised a basket with my free hand. 'Gathering breakfast. And you?'

'On my way home from blessing the dear departed.'

I raised a brow and he shook his head.

'The elder Smith. Just old age, I think. Nothing to concern yourself about. Hello, Rose, what have you been picking?' He crouched down to her level, but she hid behind my skirts. 'Have you been gathering mushrooms for breakfast?'

Rose peeked out, her face solemn. She held up a tiny mushroom. 'Dada.'

He smiled at her and slowly stood up, groaning as his joints cracked. 'Speaking of Dada, Tom tells me there's news of a ship.'

'Really?' My heart leapt at this news. 'When?'

'You'll need to leave here the morning after Candlemas to journey to the docks. It's not the best time of year to set sail, but you'll need to take the first chance you get. Are you still certain of this venture?'

'More than ever, Reverend. And the sooner, the better.'

'Very well. You'll need to leave in darkness and on foot, so you're to meet Tom in the church in the early hours – long before sun-up on the third day of February. Can you remember that?'

I nodded. 'Yes, of course. I'll be there as soon as possible after midnight to give us the best chance of getting away unseen.'

'Then you must start fetching more clothing in readiness for your departure. It's reckoned to be devilish cold in the New World, so you'll need plenty of warm clothes for the three of you.'

I touched him on the arm. 'Oh, Reverend, whatever will we do–' A faint sound distracted me, and I tilted my ear towards it. A piteous noise, halfway between a mew and a bleat. Rose tugged at my skirts and I gathered her into my arms. 'There it is again.'

Reverend Foster held up a hand. 'Stay there and I'll see who's abroad.'

'I've no fear of the woods, Reverend, that's not what's to be feared these days.'

He shrugged and we kept walking, following the sound until we came across a spindly ewe-lamb, bleating next to her dead mother. There was a dead lamb on the ground next to the mother. Twins. But only one had survived and it was newborn as its coat was not yet fully clean. Rose trembled and buried her face in my neck.

'Hush, little one. There's nothing here to harm you, but we must help the lamb.' I kissed her and rocked her and she began sucking her thumb, nuzzling against my shoulder. 'Shh, baby, shh. The mother's beyond our help now, but the lamb will get better. You'll see.'

I feared the lamb might run off in terror and die alone in the woods. But the Reverend crept slowly towards her, speaking soft words all the whilst to calm the frightened creature. Then he scooped her up and placed her around his neck, the lamb protesting loudly all the whilst.

'Now, I'll carry this one back to the flock, and then I'll get away home to my bed.'

'But, Reverend, you're gasping dreadfully and you're covered in dew. It cannot be good for you, especially when you've been out all night.'

But he laughed. 'I'm made of sterner stuff than you think, Jane. And if a priest cannot fetch home an orphaned lamb, then who can?'

I smiled. 'Thank you. There's sure to be a ewe without a lamb who can mother this one.'

The Reverend set off along the deer path that led to the meadow, and I walked after him, carrying Rose.

'I think that was Andrew's prized ewe.'

He replied without turning to look at me. 'Then how did she get out?'

'Perhaps Andrew let her out so he could blame Tom for sheep stealing. It's a hanging offence, and a sure way to be rid of him.'

'Ah, surely not, Jane. More likely an accident. I doubt Andrew would sacrifice his own ewe to be rid of Tom. He cannot be all bad. Few of us are.'

'Well he nearly finished us off in the House of Correction–'

'True enough, Jane, true enough. Although, I think he put you there to force your hand. And I'm not defending the man, but that struck me as a ruse, not a real attempt to hurt you or Rose. And for all his faults, he does love Rose, and he wouldn't hurt her.'

'Yet he would hurt Tom. He has a look in his eyes when he sees him. He burns with something. I wonder how he got to be so bad?'

'Hard to say. Love will make men do strange things.' He shrugged and when he spoke again, there was a catch in his voice. 'It's for the best that you're going to sea. You'll all be out of harm's way before spring comes.'

As we approached the meadow, Rose began wriggling in my arms and pointing to the lambs.

The Reverend climbed the gate and set down the orphan. Whilst he straightened up and caught his breath, she huddled against his legs, trembling and bleating until he climbed back over the gate.

He leant against it, panting heavily. 'Now, Jane and Rose, my bed is calling me, so I'd better go. And now that you have a date, start bringing as many warm clothes as you can in readiness for your journey, because you don't have very long left.'

He placed his hand on my head and then kissed Rose. It felt like a blessing. I watched him slowly make his way uphill until he vanished over the brow.

'Come, Rose, let's go and find a mother for this orphaned lamb. And then, we have lots of knitting to do.'

19

John

Desecration

Uncle James appeared from the mist as we approached the kirk. He was holding back a huge, growling dog, its teeth flashing.

'Holdfast – friend, not foe! Now cease your growling.' He forced the dog to sit and held it still. 'John, thank goodness you've come back home. An atrocity has taken place whilst I slept. Holdfast discovered it this morning. The poor hound has been out of his mind ever since.' He put his hand on my forearm. 'John, lad, I'm so sorry. I scarce know how to tell you this, but someone has desecrated Lucy's grave.'

MacBain stepped forward holding the corpse. 'He knows it already, Pastor. It was your own nephew that desecrated the grave and stole the bairn.'

Uncle looked from MacBain to me, his gaze resting on my breeches and jerkin, which were covered in grave dirt.

'What in the name of God has happened to you, John?' He took a step back and pointed at the infant's remains. 'And what is this, MacBain?'

'I thought your nephew was burying a murdered bairn. But it seems he's plucked it from his own goodwife's grave.' MacBain thrust the child into Uncle James' arms. 'Here, take it. The child's corpse was taken by your John in the night.'

Uncle James shuddered. 'Well, this cannot be. John is . . . well, he is on the side of God. Why would he indulge in such practices?

121

Why on earth would anyone plunder his own goodwife's grave and snatch his son?' He glared at MacBain. 'Now, why should I believe you are not the grave robber?'

MacBain snorted. 'Because I'm sound of mind and your nephew is not. I watched him outside his father's old dwelling. He'd pulled down the little cairn and was digging the child a shallow grave until I stopped him.'

'Well, it seems an act fit only for witches and ghouls, and it's hard to believe this act of depravity has been committed by my own kin.' He narrowed his eyes at me. 'What have you to say for yourself, John?'

But the barber interrupted before any words had a chance to form on my tongue.

'First, let's get this child decently covered and prayed for, and then we can argue over what's to be done about your nephew.'

MacBain walked towards the kirkyard and my uncle turned to me. 'Tell me, John, what has excited your humours this time?'

I lowered my voice so the barber-surgeon wouldn't hear. 'Uncle, this is a terrible thing to have to tell you. Lately, I've been made to see that Lucy was not bearing my child, but one spawned by the devil.' My uncle had no goodwife and no child, so he might not understand what had happened. 'Lucy was an unwitting receptacle for something quite hellish. Please don't make me tell you how I came by this knowledge.'

'Are you certain of this?' He frowned. 'Lucy struck me as a pious woman, and one no nearer to the devil than any other woman.'

'More certain than I've ever been.'

'John, in the name of God, what ails you, man?'

'Naught ails me, Uncle.' I snatched the bundle from his arms and sniffed it. 'See, see. He has the stench of Lucifer on him. I must continue upon my quest.'

I tore off through the elder bushes, sending tiny berries showering to the earth. But before I had gone far, I heard Holdfast crashing after me. I kept running, my heart fit to burst. There was no way of outrunning a dog, but with providence, it might put a foot down a rabbit hole and break its wretched leg. But then I heard it panting and barking and felt its fangs sink deep into my leg. The pain left me sick and I collapsed to the ground, sobbing and still clutching the bundle, the dog latched onto my flesh and growling.

By the time Uncle reached me, I was half-crazed with pain, and he roared at his dog.

'Holdfast! Cease at once. Heel! Heel, I say!'

Finally, the dog unlocked its jaws and I rubbed at the wound.

Uncle James softened his tone. 'John, please come with me and let us rebury this child with his mother. I will bless the grave and MacBain can replace the earth. The verger will tamp it down when he comes in the morning. We mustn't disturb the dead from their eternal sleep. It goes against God. You know this, John, better than most.'

The dog began growling and it lunged at me again. 'Uncle, your dog!'

'Holdfast! Good dog.' He seized the brute and rubbed its ears as if it were a lapdog. 'John, I am an old man. I shouldn't have to race about the glen like this. Come now, it's clear to me that you've some terrible sickness of the soul.'

MacBain appeared. He gripped my arm, dragged me to my feet and removed the infant from my clutches, carrying it almost tenderly as he marched me back to the kirkyard.

Uncle James led the way to the ruined grave and shook his head when he saw it. He didn't want to touch the demon child, and nor did I, but MacBain thrust the parcel of bones into my arms. Uncle James tied his dog to a yew tree, then held out his hand and made the sign of the cross in the air above the corpse's head.

MacBain dropped to one knee at the side of the open grave and then lowered himself carefully over the breached coffin. I shivered. Was it the cold, or the brush with demonic influence? MacBain was no stranger to the dark arts, I was now convinced, and it was unwise to allow him near any malefic influence. A fragile form lay in the coffin. Lucy, my poor goodwife. MacBain wedged his feet either side of the coffin and held up his hands for the bundle. My uncle glared at me until I handed it down. The thought of what this being might unleash in hallowed ground made me tremble.

'You will rue this, MacBain, we will all rue this!'

But the big man steadily ignored me and placed the bundle on top of Lucy. Then he unfastened his rabbit-skin jerkin and tucked it over the child as a blanket. What curious behaviour – surely this sealed his fate as one of Satan's own. Then he replaced the pieces of wood over the coffin. Was this to prevent the soil from seeping in? It gladdened me. Although Lucy was dead, I didn't like to think of the wet clay pressing against her face. The barber-surgeon hauled himself out of the pit and he began filling it as Uncle walked away and bade me follow him through the mist.

We entered his sparse room where a meagre fire burnt, and the beast sprawled before it as if asleep, sucking up most of the heat. When I approached, it opened one eye at me and showed its teeth, so I took a seat far away from the fire, even though my bones were frozen to their very marrow. MacBain had deserted his burial duties and followed us in and Uncle James eyed him.

'Yes, what is it now, MacBain? Haven't you a grave to fill?'

MacBain shrugged. 'They're both decently covered. Your verger can finish up after your nephew's kirkyard pillage. We need to talk, Pastor. This cannot continue.'

Uncle sighed loudly. 'Very well, if you must. But be quick about it.'

MacBain occupied the settle. The dog opened one eye and then resumed its feigned sleep. MacBain rubbed his hands together and glanced at the pitcher of whisky.

'Keep your eyes to yourself, MacBain; there will be no tot for you this time.'

'We need to discuss your nephew. His behaviour of late.'

The audacity of the man – he spoke of me as if I were not present! I shivered and wished the beast would move from the fire so I might hold my hands before the weak flames.

'Aye, go on man, but don't be all day about it.'

'You know, there's something deeply wrong in a man's head when he digs up the corpse of his own child and then buries it far from the church. What does that suggest to you, Pastor?'

My uncle patted his knees and the dog got up and slumped its head on its master's knee, and he fondled its big ears.

'I hardly know. His long contact with so many witches may have weakened his defences. The evil has begun to seep into him—'

'No, Pastor, that won't wash with me. He's been putting innocent women to their deaths.' He held up a big hand to silence my protest. 'No, don't try to defend yourself, Sharpe. You have madness howling in you. And cruelty.'

I leapt to my feet. 'No, no. It isn't true—'

But Uncle waved me down. 'Sit down, John, and be quiet. Leave this to me. Look, MacBain, you know that my nephew was once possessed by witches after coming into contact with their blood. I sent him to you because he was beyond my help at that time.'

'Aye, you did. I recall that day all too well. He was possessed by no more than an infection of the blood after cutting himself over and over with a dirty knife. Now, Pastor, what kind of man does that to himself?'

I bit my lip. There was much I wanted to say but felt it wise to keep my own counsel and let Uncle speak since he knew MacBain of old.

'He is somewhat overworked. There are so many witches. He sleeps little and barely eats.'

'Pastor, you mustn't make excuses for your own flesh and blood. He's broken into a grave and taken a body. Had this act been carried out by a woman, she'd be on trial for witchcraft at first light and reduced to ashes come the gloaming.'

My uncle stirred the fire with an iron poker before replying.

'Well, you must consider motive. A witch removing a corpse from hallowed soil must have heinous plans for it. Whereas John—'

MacBain shook his head slowly. 'No. You cannot have one rule for women and one for men. There's no such thing as a witch. Innocent women are being put to death on the say-so of your nephew. Good women, kind women. And when your nephew is caught in a terrible act, excuses are made for him. He must be stopped.' He took the club from his belt and pointed at me with it. 'And he must be punished.'

I ran my eye up and down MacBain. His ragged appearance was made worse by the addition of grave dirt. Without his fur

125

jerkin, he was quite scrawny. But his belt was hung with knives and various pouches, and he had the big club.

'So, I must be punished? And who will take your word, MacBain? A man who dabbles in dubious practices himself. One who takes the power of life and death into his own hands, when such a task should belong only to God.'

'John, don't be so hasty. MacBain is a barber-surgeon, and above all, a man.' Uncle sounded troubled. 'There's no suggestion of ill-will from him, let alone sorcery.'

MacBain stood. 'And the people hereabouts will take my word. Because it's the truth. They know me for a good man. And one of sound mind and high standing.'

Uncle James snorted. 'A mere barber-surgeon? I hardly think so.'

MacBain brandished the club at my uncle, Holdfast growled and Uncle James stood up.

'Silence, Holdfast. MacBain will not harm me. See, I have the protection of God and my dog.'

'Maybe so, man, maybe so. But your nephew doesn't. I'll take this matter to the bailies if you yourself will not. Your nephew is a danger. Think on, because he'll only try to repeat the action once your back is turned.'

It startled me that the man had such a clear insight into my mind. My plan was to wait for my uncle to fall asleep and then get to the grave before the verger finished filling it in. The soil would be quite loose this time and with quick work I could remove the devil's spawn and dispose of it properly. A heavy hammer would pound the bones to dust. Then the ashes could be scattered. No one would be able to find the child once the wind had taken him.

I shivered, yet sweat still ran freely from me. Uncle stared at me and took a loud breath.

'MacBain, my nephew clearly has the fever on him. You can fettle this, can you not?'

'Aye, Pastor, I can. But I won't.'

'As a man of healing, you have a duty before God.'

'I have no duty to this wretch. You're both so keen to quote God, so let Him decide your nephew's fate. But Sharpe should be punished for what he's done to his bairn. Disturbing the child from his burial place is a sin.'

'You have no say in this, MacBain, and you will say naught of what you have seen, unless you wish to feel the judgement of God on you.'

'Trust me on this, Pastor. If you fail to do something about your nephew, you'll feel the judgement of God on you, to say nothing of the bailies. He cannot go on as he is. Think what wickedness he might be brewing in his mind now.'

Uncle James paled at this and held out a trembling hand. 'But look at him. He is so sick, my dead sister's only son.'

'Thank you, Uncle.' I was grateful for his intervention. He'd saved me before, and he'd save me now. 'But you must help me get that child from its grave. I must pound its bones to dust and then scatter the—'

'John! Whatever is the matter with you? To speak of your own son in such a way.'

I shook my head, beads of sweat flying from me. 'No, you're mistaken. It was never my child. I was cuckolded by Satan — MacBain put the devil's potion in me and so he should burn for a witch.'

Uncle James started. 'Is this right, MacBain?'

MacBain nodded, weariness beginning to mark his old face.

'Aye, he came to me for help for his supposedly barren wife. Yet, the problem lay in his own loins. I gave him a stiffener, that's all. And it worked. It brought forth a child.'

'No, you opened my goodwife up to the devil and the beast planted his own seed in her belly.' I lurched to my feet, eyes bulging. 'That is why this child must be destroyed. It must not lie in hallowed ground, infecting the innocent dead.'

Uncle James frowned. 'John, this is hard for me to say, but even as a boy, you were given to fancies and you were known to be something of a romancer . . .'

'This is no lie, Uncle. You're much mistaken. You're leaving our village wide open to evil influence. It is no lie. Please, you must believe me.' Tears ran freely with the sweat on my face, and I wiped a filthy sleeve over them, smearing my own face with grave dirt. 'It's no lie.'

'No, John, not quite a lie, since I suppose you believe it to be true. But you are the one who is mistaken. Perhaps you've been touched in the head by something and need to take some rest. A long rest. A spell in the infirmary would let you take proper nourishment and help keep you off the whisky. And then you will be safe from these . . . inspirations.'

I staggered slightly. 'They are not inspirations . . . or lies. You just refuse to see what's before your own eyes.'

MacBain gripped me with his bony fingers. 'You're not mad. You're evil. And you should answer for your crimes. You cannot be allowed to continue.'

I struggled, trying to free myself, but the man had a grip like death as he removed a length of twine from his belt.

'Here, I'll bind his hands until his humours settle. Pastor, your nephew is naught more than a common lunatic. If you don't want to risk being accused as his protector, put him away for a spell. It might be kinder than letting him loose with such a fever in his brain.'

Uncle James nodded. 'Very well, man. Name your price. He is my kin, and I cannot see him in such a dire condition. If you can heal him, MacBain, then do it. John will pay.'

20

Jane

Yuletide

At last, the snow had come, and with it, Yuletide, which meant the lengthy preparations for the constant feasting would soon be over. It was an exhausting time, and it filled me with longing for the Yules of yesteryear, which were all filled with good cheer, with the Reverend and Mam at the table, and Tom and his father joining us. My cruel memory recalled this happy day and added Rose to the table, and for a moment, it was easy to believe that all was well and that the last year hadn't happened. But then Andrew's harsh words reached my ears, and it was impossible to imagine myself anywhere else but under the Drivers' roof.

'You might try to smile, goodwife, it's meant to be a time of great cheer.'

'It's hard to be festive, Andrew, when there's so little cheer in my heart.'

Andrew's face purpled at this reply. 'Still mooning after Verger? Am I never to know peace in my own home? Well, you're mine now, Jane Driver, and you must make the best of it. Don't make me have to remind you again.'

My face became warm. 'Truly, I'm not . . . not mooning.'

'Your mouth might lie most convincingly. But your eyes have yet to manage the art, so you do well to look down. I must work harder on Verger to convince him that he must leave. Or, must I work on you again?' He ran his thumb along my jawbone. It was still tender and his touch made me wince.

I blinked. 'No. There is no need to work on me again.'

'Tread carefully, Jane. Your insolence needs to be checked. And you cannot be trusted. Every time my back's turned, you're to be found in Verger's presence. Tell me what other man would put up with such humiliating behaviour?'

'None. No man.'

'Exactly. No man. Keep away from Verger, or it'll go bad for you. Very bad. Do you hear me, Jane?'

I nodded, but kept my eyes cast down.

'Look at me when I speak to you!' He grasped my chin and forced my head up until our eyes met. 'Give me your firm promise that you will see Verger no more. On Rose's life.'

It was hard to speak between his thick fingers on my chin and the tears clogging my throat, but silence would only earn me further pain. I gently prised his fingers away from my jaw.

'You cannot ask me to swear on Rose's life. I won't see Tom again. You have my word, on my own life. But nothing on this earth will make me swear on Rose's life.'

'Hah, so Verger means that much to you?'

'No. Rose means that much to me. It would be wrong to tempt fate by offering up her life. You cannot make me swear such a thing . . . it would be unchristian.'

He thought about this. 'Very well then, on your own life. But show me your hands. I want no crossed fingers.'

I held out my hands and Andrew grasped them. 'They tremble. What are you afraid of? Not being able to keep your word?'

'I will keep my word. But you're scaring me.'

He snorted. 'Scaring you? You're scaring yourself. Now take heed of me, Jane. It's for your own good.'

Bett opened the door, with Rose on her hip. 'Jane? There you are. Stop dawdling and come to the table.'

For once, her sharp tones were welcome, giving me good reason to leave. I followed her out, guarding my eyes from Andrew. It was a relief to walk away from him and into a room filled with the stife of woodsmoke, lard and goose fat.

At the table, Jim carved great slices of pork and crackling from the boar Andrew had slain. There were mounds of roasted potatoes and parsnips, with buttered carrots, and redcurrant and rosemary jelly. Rose dipped a finger in the jelly and sucked it. She pulled such a face on tasting its sourness that we all laughed, and she must have enjoyed our reactions greatly because she did it again.

'Oh, Rose, you must think it's sweet like strawberry conserve.'

Seeing my daughter's happy face made me determined to stay cheerful for her sake. There were scarce forty nights from Yule to Imbolc – or Candlemas as Reverend Foster would insist – and from there to a life of freedom with Tom. The thought made me joyful and it was hard to hide my smile.

Andrew banged his eating knife on the table and gloated.

'That's more like it, goodwife! You'll see how happy you can be with a tribe of little Drivers to busy you. There'll be no time for mooning about then, so enjoy your freedom whilst it lasts.'

At the thought of freedom, a great hunger swept down on me. Now was the time to eat, to build up my strength and reserves for the coming voyage.

'Rose, come, eat up.' She was so pretty and plump now, but our long journey would strip that from her. 'Here, take some more potatoes and some of this fat.'

When Bett carried in the great pudding, Rose stood up on her chair and clapped her hands. She'd been excited about the pudding since stir-up Sunday. Although too young to make a wish, Bett had allowed her to stir the silver thimble into the pudding mixture. Advent had been a long month, with Rose going every day to inspect the pudding in hope of gaining the thimble. But Andrew was not amused by her excitement and gave her a hard look. It would be better for any chiding to come from me.

'Come, naughty maid. You have to sit down for this part.' I patted my legs. 'Come, sit in my lap.'

Once Rose was settled, Jim raised a flask of rum and drenched the pudding with it before touching it with a lighted taper. Blue flames shot out of the pudding and Rose shrieked, covering her face with her hands. She writhed on my lap, and I had to hold her firmly so she didn't slip off. Eventually, she peered out from behind her hands and watched the flames dance and then subside. The flames had frightened her so much that she couldn't be persuaded to eat a bite of the pudding, not even when Bett showed her the shining silver thimble in her portion.

Andrew shovelled pudding into his mouth and spoke with his mouth full. 'Afraid of her own shadow, that girl. She'll need to grow out of that sharp enough.' I longed to lean over the table and push his face into his food. It would aid his shovelling if nothing else. Rose would grow out of her fears once she was out from under this roof and with her true father.

After I cleared away the platters, we sat around the fire to share our gifts. I'd knitted stockings for everyone, and in my days of non-stop knitting, had managed to make extra stockings and vests for Rose and the baby. They were hidden in Mam's satchel, ready to take to the manse at the first opportunity. Rose's Yuletide stockings were scarlet. She insisted on wearing them straight away and gambolled about the room in them.

Andrew had whittled a wooden top for her and painted robin redbreasts around it. When he span the top on the floor, the robins blurred into a streak of red. Rose danced up and down and then whirled about in excitement, her eyes sparkling, her cheeks flushed and her red tresses streaming around her.

My heart swelled at the sight of her happiness. And in a few months, she would be happy all the time. When she was so lit up with joy, she was the image of her father and her grin mirrored his exactly. Andrew banged down his tankard. Had he seen this for himself?

'Come, Rose, you're getting too giddy, and you'll never sleep. Settle yourself down.'

But she kept whirling and when the top stopped spinning, she held it up again to Andrew. When he shook his head and took it from her, she put on a pet lip.

But Andrew was adamant. 'No, no more today. It's bedtime for you.'

I picked her up. 'Come, Rose. The robins are tired too and they need to rest. Let them sleep, and they'll be ready to play again in the morning.'

When she wailed and held out her hands for the top, Andrew made to throw it into the fire. I gasped and Rose burst into tears, howling and struggling to be down.

'Andrew, please! There was no need for that. Now she'll never sleep. It's all right, Rose, Dada was just playing. See, the robins are there, safe and sound.'

But my words brought her no comfort and she continued to flail in my arms, howling and snot-covered.

'Too spoilt for her own good. She's becoming a brat. I'll knock it out of her when she's bigger.'

I held Rose close to me, sick at the thought of him raising a hand to her. Imbolc couldn't come soon enough.

'There'll be no comforting her now, Andrew. So, I'll have to lie with her till she sleeps.'

'Aye, well don't get any ideas of sleep yourself. I'll be in afore long.'

Once Rose was tucked up with her poppet, thumb in mouth, she settled down to sleep. I tucked her in tightly and then lay on the bed, hands over my belly. I closed my eyes. If only sleep would take me before Andrew came to bed. But it was futile wishing for sleep because it had never spared me in the past. Still, I kept my eyes shut to sweep away the pain of the real world and escape into my own private world for a whilst. This life wouldn't be forever. The end would come soon.

* * *

In the morning, I was woken by a furious kicking. So, the little soul was getting ready for life. I placed my hands over my belly, trying to soothe my child. Andrew snored next to me, and it wouldn't do to wake him. Carefully, I slid from the bed. Rose was still curled in her blankets, but she would wake before long and insist on playing with her spinning top.

It worried me that there were so many clothes hidden in Mam's satchel. But there was no way of taking it out of the house without arousing suspicion amongst the Drivers. There were no expectant mothers in the quarter apart from me. It seemed wrong to hope for someone to fall ill, but that would be my best chance. Or, I could say I was going to check on the Reverend. There again, maybe Henry Green would be a more believable excuse and let me out of the house. He was a sickly child at the best of times, and he'd ailed ever since touching the monkshood.

My stomach rumbled so loudly it was a wonder it didn't wake the household, so I crept into the kitchen. The plum duff was mostly uneaten, and I helped myself to a large slice.

Andrew surprised me and I jumped, almost choking on a mouthful. He banged me on the back until I stopped coughing.

'Mind, that's a very rich breakfast, even if you are carrying a lad.'

I nodded. 'My appetite is back at last.'

'No bad thing. You need to build yourself up for the coming bairn. It won't be long now.'

'Three moons or so. Two most likely.'

Andrew eyed my mother's satchel at my feet. 'Where are you going?'

'To see May and check on little Henry. He's never been a well bairn.' I busied myself with the plum duff so he wouldn't see the lie on my face.

'Well, he was certainly well enough last night when I chased the little menace out of the top field. You're fretting over nothing. If you're looking for something to do, you can come and give me a hand with the sow. Ma will see to Rose if she wakes up.'

My heart sank. But it wouldn't do to argue. 'Very well, but just let me stow Mam's satchel.'

'It's not the time for you to be lugging heavy things. Leave it for Ma to shift later.'

If Bett saw it, she was bound to look inside. 'Don't worry, Andrew, it's no weight at all.' I smiled to show how light it was. 'It'll only take a second to put it away. Besides, Rose might wake up and get into it.'

'Aye, it might be wise. Go on then, but be quick about it.'

* * *

Together, we walked along the river to the sty, with Andrew carrying the swill pail. An unseasonal sun had melted all but the snow on the hills. The melt water had transformed the earth to clarts and made it slippery underfoot, and my feet almost went from under me.

'Mind out! You nearly spilled the swill. Look down at your feet and watch your step. We cannot afford to have you lying around like a fine lady nursing a broken leg.'

'Sorry, Andrew.' It wouldn't do to irk him. But it wasn't just the clarts making me clumsy. My joints were already loosening, and I was more ungainly than I had been when carrying Rose. My belly was bigger and higher too. So, it was definitely a boy this time. Hopefully, he would take after the father who raised him and not the one who had made him.

The smell of the sty reached me long before the sight of it, and it forced me to breathe through my mouth. When she heard the pail rattle, the sow trotted out into the yard, but she seemed despondent, her head hanging low and her teats still swollen.

'She looks bereft, poor lass. She must be wondering where her piglets are.'

Andrew shrugged. 'Aye, she's a good right. Her piglets were all taken for suckling pigs.'

'Does she know, do you think?' The sow had sorrowful eyes. 'Hopefully not.'

He snorted. 'You're too soft. And you cared less yesterday when you were polishing off her husband. It's just how life is. Come, at least she has her swill to enjoy.'

There was nothing to say to this, and so I poured the swill into the sow's trough and watched her eating half-heartedly.

'Come, Jane, get back to fetch my breakfast. Mam can take Rose for a whilst afterwards since you were sound asleep last night when I came to bed.'

I clung to the wall and pretended not to hear him, but he gripped my shoulders and pulled me away.

'Stop your fretting over the sow. She'll have a new husband soon enough.'

In spite of what was coming after breakfast, this made me smile to myself. The sow was not the only one who would have a new husband soon enough.

21

John

Blood on Fire

Uncle James' cure was worse than being placed in an infirmary. Despite my protests that MacBain was nothing better than a witch, my uncle discharged me into that man's care. He bound my hands and hobbled my feet, and then forced me to follow him into his woodland shack as a prisoner. There was little point in trying to escape my confinement when my mind was so weak and feverish. Besides, MacBain, for all his ills, was a good physic and he would put me back in my right humours before too long. But he was also a dullard who lived amongst rabbits, and once I was well enough, it would be short work to get the better of him and make good my escape.

Once inside his dwelling, I was confronted again by his make-shift shelves crammed with pots and jars, a low fire and hundreds of rabbit skins lining the walls. The shack was warm and dry, and it smelt pleasantly of furs and medicinal herbs.

'Bend your legs, Sharpe, if you insist on breathing my air.'

I perched on the edge of a pallet, glad to take the weight off my feet for a whilst.

'You look bad, Sharpe. Your inner wickedness is starting to seep outwards and show on you. No bad thing. It'll make it easier for the innocents to see you for what you truly are.'

My mood darkened. This man showed no respect, which was foolish for one in his position.

'Watch your tongue, MacBain.' I rose to my feet.

He sighed and pushed me back down with one hand. 'Get back down before I succumb to temptation and do what I should have done years back.' He looked meaningfully at a large axe next to the fire. 'I should have cut you down a long time ago – many lives might have been the better and safer for it. Or, I could slip any one of a dozen poisons to you. A drop of hemlock would stiffen your limbs and freeze the air in your lungs. Your evil would be snuffed out and none would recognise the signs of poison.'

'Do you threaten me with murder now? My uncle will learn of this.'

'Ach, and he'll pay no heed, you being marked out as a romancer from an early age.'

'Guard your tongue, MacBain. If you murder me, you go against God and you risk your soul. If you own such a thing.'

'I'll take my chances. God would know it was an act to save the lives of many by taking the life of one. It's a chance I might yet take, so don't test me.' MacBain picked up a heavy poker and saw to the fire. 'For now, it's my misfortune that you must bide here whilst I mend what ails you. When you're restored to some semblance of a decent man, you may return to your uncle's care. But till then, you'll be lashed to a pallet. Do you understand?'

I nodded. He thought me deranged and it would do me no harm to play along. But all the time, I would be simply foxing him and watching and waiting. My mind would occupy itself gathering evidence against this man and looking for a chance to overcome him and get away.

'You needn't think of dosing me with any of your compounds whilst I'm here.' I jerked my chin at the array of pots jostling on the shelves. 'My soul has been imperilled enough as it is by being in proximity to you and your ilk.'

'Ach, you've no need of any remedies. Your blood is most likely on fire with whisky and it's addled your brain. You can be left to the wiles of nature. Sleep will be your best medicine. Sleep, plain food and no excitement.'

'And for this supposed cure, you will charge me good silver?'

'Aye, because I must put up with you whilst you heal, and there's not enough silver in Scotland to make that a bearable prospect. You might as well sleep a whilst, Sharpe, as I'm away to catch our dinner.' He pressed me backwards onto the pallet and bound me at my chest and legs. 'Once there's a stew bubbling, I'll take a proper look at you and see what needs to be done. Though truth be told, there's only one cure fit for you.' He grimaced at me and drew the back of his finger across his throat.

I closed my eyes against him. Contempt was the best way to treat this man. He'd learn the hard way. My temper would remain even, and I'd save my strength to plot his demise.

But even my busy mind needed rest. Despite my being tightly bound and unable to move, the strangely scented air soothed me into a healing sleep that was only somewhat fractured by the sights and sounds of demonic children and laughing witches chanting their poisonous prayers.

When next I opened my eyes, it was dark and the only light came from the fire and a pair of tallow candles lighting MacBain's table.

'So, you're awake finally, Sharpe. You've missed your dinner, but I've spared you some bread and cheese. I suppose you must eat if I'm to be paid.'

He placed a hard heel of bread and a hunk of yellow cheese near to me and then poured out a cup of ale. It was a simple repast, but my stomach was empty, and so I was glad of it. MacBain untied my right hand to let me eat. Now was not the time to argue about my preferred diet. It was important that he believe me a changed man, one cowed by the threat of the law. Although a greater authority governed me, MacBain didn't realise it, and so the wretched man didn't take his eyes off me whilst I ate.

'This ale is bitter although bearable, but the bread is so hard it has caused my gums to bleed.'

'Aye? Well that's a problem easily enough mended with acorn tea.'

'And my innards are cramping. Who knows with what cause?'

Would he heed my complaint? It was hard to tell. But as soon as I'd finished eating, he put a noose around my neck and untied my second hand.

'I'll permit you a single pass of the trees so you can purge yourself and loosen your limbs, and then it's back to the pallet for you. Don't get any ideas. I'm sure your uncle would understand should something happen to you. In fact, he might prefer it as his troubles would then be at an end.'

I didn't protest against this remark, as there was a chance MacBain might be right. Instead, I bowed my head humbly and allowed him to lead me outside.

When we returned, the old witch threw a rug made of earthy rabbit skins over me, and its warmth and weight lulled me and made me forget my failure to remove the polluted child from sacred ground.

For now, I must content myself with observing the barber. My uncle felt him beyond reproach because MacBain was a man, but I hadn't yet explained to him about Matthew Bulmer in Newcastle. And if men were witches in England, then they might also be witches in Scotland. Once all was well in my mind, there would be time enough to explain this to my uncle. He would learn how MacBain had introduced a succubus into my goodwife – and who knew what else he might be capable of. Once Uncle James understood, he would certainly remove the fetid corpse from the kirkyard himself. I sighed. All would be well. Uncle James loved me, and he would help me once he understood.

* * *

In the morning, MacBain appeared before me with a brace of rabbits slung over his shoulder and a selection of roots and firewood. He built up the fire and then started to skin and gut his prey.

'Come, Sharpe, stir your bones. I've been up for hours. I'll fashion a tasty meal from the forest floor, and then we can eat.'

I must disabuse the man, if only to avoid waste, or to prevent him forcing me to eat.

'MacBain, I eschew blooded meat and roots that grow beneath the earth. I eat only those leaves that grow above ground in God's good air.'

'Fussier than a maid.' MacBain shrugged. 'Well, I can make short work of two rabbits by myself, with nary a blink. In future,

I'll fetch just the one rabbit or fish for myself, and extra leaves with nuts and berries for you.'

'If I might just be loosened to gather a few bitter leaves.' I raised my bound hands.

'I'll set you to graze, if that's your will. But your hands and feet will remain bound. You can lower your mouth to the ground to eat.' He peered through the open door. 'Fear not, you won't be allowed to starve to death. Now, before I set you to grazing, give me your hands.'

I didn't like this but did as bade. The old man grasped my hands with his own, which were surprisingly hot. He pressed his fingers into my inner wrists and closed his eyes, nodding all the whilst. It gave me a strange feeling and one I didn't much like.

'What's that, what are you doing?'

'Just listening to the song of your blood. It's an old skill. Now, your blood sings to me that your life has been wicked, and that you have hurt women, many women.'

'Aye, there's no denying it.' I sniffed. 'But only those deserving of just punishment.'

MacBain dug his fingers harder into my flesh. 'Aye, the blood is singing a somewhat sorrowful song. Now, I'll need to put you right, and it will hurt – a great deal – but only for a short time.'

'Do whatever you consider necessary. But there will be no leeching this time.' I recalled my last sojourn here. 'And no mercury clyster either.'

When MacBain released my hands, I shook them hard as if trying to shake something free.

* * *

Despite MacBain's promise not to let me starve, the flesh fell from my body. Was the man testing me? But my will was strong, and he wouldn't have the satisfaction of seeing me give in. It was not easy. I ate no flesh, but this new diet contained no cheese, milk or eggs either. I began to slaver at the thought of eggs scrambled in cream, of thick slabs of bread slathered in salted butter, of ripe cheeses with a sharp tang. It was sinful to dream in this way, but there was nothing else left to me but food. There had been no whisky, and for the first few days, I'd quaked, my head filled with visions. Gluttony had never been a sin of mine, but food filled my every waking thought of late.

Whilst MacBain was boiling acorns one morning, I slumped back against the pallet and eyed him. 'She died a bad death, you know, Dora Shaw. I watched her burn, and the executioner didn't strangle her first.'

His big jaw clenched, and the muscle worked itself, but he didn't take the bait, instead stooping to test all the knots binding me.

'Silence, man. Else I forget myself and strangle you.'

'The old witch deserved what she got.'

The man's nostrils flared as he took in a great breath and his face flushed. So I'd finally rattled him, which was a good sign.

'Your game is obvious to me, Sharpe. You're taunting me to make me lose my temper in the hope I'll lose my wits at the same time. But it won't work. My heart is already filled with hate for you, and it's not possible for it to contain any more. You'll taste justice – proper justice – once your uncle sees sense and realises what you are. Meanwhile, feel free to waste your words on the air in my dwelling. But if I tire of you, then you'll be gagged and allowed to famish till he fetches you.'

This shut me up. It would do me no good to sap myself until I was a skeleton. If my strength was depleted, it would be hard to keep my mind keen. I would suffer in silence and plot my escape. There could be no going back to my uncle, so I would make for England and try to revive my living. But my clothes were tattered and still bore traces of grave dirt. Were I to attend a trial like this, the men of high standing would look upon me as naught better than a pauper. I needed new finery, which would restore my pride and give me a fighting chance. If MacBain didn't bleed me dry, there should be silver enough left to dress myself decently.

But there was little chance of getting away from MacBain. The wily barber loosened my hands and feet only long enough to eat and attend to my ablutions. He turned his back at these times, but he stayed close by, ready for any sound that might signal an escape. Even during my brief spells of exercise, I might only walk a few steps in a shuffling gait, and so there was no way of going anywhere.

After my ablutions, it was time to pray and then lie down to sleep under my rabbit-skin covering. It was not an unpleasant way to pass time. And once my eyes were closed, the world was my own, and no man might interfere with my thoughts. MacBain sat by the fire each night waiting for me to fall asleep and he was always awake at dawn, rebuilding the fire and gathering provisions. Despite his advanced years, he had an unnatural energy, which no doubt came from eating blooded flesh every day. Admittedly, my mouth watered at the smell of meat roasting slowly over the fire, but I didn't berate myself for this. Rather, I took pride in my ability to face temptation and overcome it. My Lenten fast lasted all year round, and I was the better man for it. Most importantly, it kept my head clear, which was necessary in order to plot my escape. And escape I must.

22

Jane

A Pale Green Powder

Revered Foster found me refreshing the Yuletide greenery in the church, and he frowned when he saw me.

'Good morning, Reverend.'

'Ah, there you are, Jane. You've a haunted look about the eyes. Are you sleeping at all?'

'No, not really. It's just hard to sleep lately.'

'But you've always slept better than most of the poor souls resting in the earth. What keeps you from your dreams?'

His eyes were so sorrowful that I didn't want to add my troubles to his burden. 'Just this little one.' I sighed and patted my belly. 'Except he's not so little. He makes it hard to get comfortable of a night.'

'Are you sure that's all it is? These are terrible times for you. They will pass, as times must, but the pain will stay fresh a whilst yet.'

He straightened the altar candle, but not before I saw the tears glazing his eyes. The Reverend knew all about pain.

'So, tell me, how go the plans for your departure? Tom tells me you're headed to a safe corner of the New World that his physician friend has told him about.'

'Then you know more than me, Reverend. It's been weeks since we last spoke. It feels as though Andrew has me in gaol of late. It's a wonder he hasn't followed me here to the church.'

'Aye, it is a wonder. Still, it's safer by far to keep apart from Tom than run the risk of Driver finding out and somehow preventing your leaving.'

'Andrew reads me too easily. Some days, it seems as if he knows something's afoot.'

'Surely only your mind playing tricks on you, Jane.'

'Maybe. Maybe. I jump at every shadow these days. Imbolc cannot come soon enough. But, oh, Reverend, how will we live without you? And you without us?'

He placed a hand on my shoulder, and its weight brought me peace. 'I will live happy in the knowledge that you are with Tom. You will live every day knowing that Rose is safe and with her rightful father. And Tom will be a good father to the little one when he comes. Knowing that you are all safe and happy will bring me peaceful dreams.'

I nodded and stepped back to look at the holly and the ivy. The pretty red berries against the glossy green. 'You should come with us, Reverend. You and Bill. We could all be together.'

He laughed then, and his chest gave a great wheeze. 'You don't want to be saddled with two old men. Besides, the sea would be the death of us both. We'll be well enough here. And we'll await your letters. Assuming Driver doesn't string us up . . .'

'Oh! He might at that.' This was a terrible thought. 'And what about the Bishop. Will you and Bill be punished? Or driven out?'

But the Reverend just smiled. 'Don't fret yourself. The Sunday after Candlemas, my plan is to denounce you both from the pulpit as adulterers. And Bill will disown Tom publicly. That should ward off the Bishop and the Drivers. When you write, use a false name, in case of gossiping messengers, and send your letters under clerical seal – I'll give one to Tom as my parting gift to you both.'

He enclosed me in his arms. Sadness washed over me and I closed my eyes. It would be pain beyond measure to leave this man, but there was no choice. In time, his health might improve and the sea voyage might become manageable.

'Besides, there's another good reason that you must go.' He sat down on a pew and drew me down next to him. 'It's not just Driver you need to fear.'

'What can you mean?'

From his breviary, Reverend Foster removed a letter with a broken seal and passed it to me.

'This is from a minister in the north of Northumberland. One of the many ministers I wrote to in the Borders. John Sharpe was operating there not so very long ago . . . and he may well still be in England.' He took my hands. 'You must go soon, Jane. My dreams are haunted, and I am so tired of late that it is hard to tell day from night and real life from dreams . . .'

Bile rose in my throat and I swallowed hard. 'You cannot think John Sharpe will come for me, surely?'

He paused. 'Well, the man is out there still. My greatest wish is not to alarm you, but it's right that you should know, so you can protect yourself . . . and Rose. It seems that, far from fleeing to Scotland, Sharpe has remained in England, peddling his evil views. The women in Berwick have fallen victim to him this time.'

'Oh, no! Not more women killed?'

The Reverend shook his head. 'No. Mercifully a military man recognised him for what he was, and he was given short shrift and chased from the town. We must pray he has returned to his homeland.'

My hands trembled. 'No woman is safe whilst that man breathes. None!'

The Reverend wheeled on me. 'Jane, guard your tongue, please! You mustn't be heard wishing death on anyone, let alone on that man.'

'Sorry, Reverend.' He deserved the apology, but my heart was not in the words. I took the letter and stared at it. 'This man is a slithering eel. He may not have killed any women this time, but the law has let him slip free once again.'

'Aye, that wicked man has thwarted the law at every turn – it must be his claim on godliness and virtue, however misplaced. But now he's slipped through the hands of the English lawmen twice. They must believe him higher than man's law. Either that or they've given in to the lure of silver.' He flicked the letter with the back of a fingernail. 'Sharpe was reputedly charging three pounds per witch, so he must own a heavy purse. That would be enough to buy off many sergeants.' He took my hand. 'Do you see what it means?'

'Of course. My life is in danger whilst John Sharpe roves the land, his heart filled with hate for cunning women. And Rose might also be in danger.' Even so, it seemed impossible that such a thing could happen here. Even though the Puritan fever had gripped Newcastle, it was hard to believe anything evil could come to Mutton Clog. 'But surely, he won't return to Newcastle. Not after what happened . . .'

'He might. My greatest fear is that the authorities have no interest in prosecuting the man since he's evaded justice twice already. The sergeants of Newcastle gave him passage and the townspeople might well welcome his return, even knowing him to be no better than a common murderer. They've fooled themselves for so long with tales of sorcery and Satan that it might be hard for them to see Sharpe through clear eyes.'

I took the letter and touched the seal. 'It amuses them, I expect, hearing these tales of witches, demons and satanic goings-on. It must bring some colour to the drab existence they've forced on themselves.'

'Take heart, Jane. If there was ever any doubt in my mind about you and Tom leaving, this letter has extinguished it. You must go. As soon as you can. As far as you can. In the meantime, I will write more letters.' He shook his head slowly. 'Even if you are out of harm's way, other women are not. He must be stopped. And others like him.'

Tears threatened to overwhelm me, as they so often did these days, and the Reverend placed his hand on my shoulder to calm me.

'Don't take on so, Jane. All will be well.'

'Does Tom know?'

'Not yet, lass, but I'll go to him next. You'll all be gone in a short time. And in the meantime, keep watch. Be on constant guard for strangers in your midst. But please don't distress yourself – this is mere precaution. You and Rose will be safe. I'm certain of it. We must have faith in God.'

'You mean it kindly, Reverend, but you have no way of truly knowing.' The pain in his eyes made me feel guilty, but I kept going. 'And putting my faith in God has not helped me in the past.'

146

He glanced at the altar and then back at me. 'You may be right, Jane. You may be right. Put your faith in me. Will you do that?'

I nodded, but my doubt was stronger than my faith these days.

He got up and moved towards the altar and then he was lost to the world.

'I'll leave you to your letters, Reverend, before Andrew comes looking for me.'

Letters wouldn't achieve much, but if they served to lessen the Reverend's sorrow and regret, then that might be purpose enough.

* * *

Rose tossed in her basket and her restlessness woke me. I slid from the bed so as not to wake Andrew, but he wasn't there. Her bedclothes were twisted around her damp form, and I lifted her into the kitchen only to find Andrew was already up and about.

'Jane? What are you doing up?'

'Rose is having a bad night of it. Can you clear the table so I can lay her down?'

'Oh, Rosie, you do look poorly.' He pushed everything from the table to the floor with one sweep of his arm. 'What ails the bairn?'

'Fever.' I laid her on the table and placed a hand on her brow. 'She's burning hot and we need to cool her down.'

'What do you need?'

'Whilst I strip her, can you get Mam's satchel please, and some honey?' I didn't need to tell Andrew how easy it was for small children to be carried away on the wings of fever after he'd lost his baby sister all those years ago.

He lit some candles and went in search of the satchel. Rose had such a high colour that she was almost puce, but there was no sign of any rash, which was a blessing. She was clammy to the touch and her temperature was so very high that she was sure to begin fitting at any moment. Hopefully, I'd woken just in time.

147

When Andrew returned, his eyes were hard and he held out Mam's satchel to me. It was open. Placed on top were the little vests and stockings for the new baby and Rose.

'Why are these hidden away?'

My heart lurched. How could I have forgotten to move them? Words failed me for a second, and then an idea formed. 'Oh, just my silly superstition. Not wanting to tempt providence . . . But the new baby has to have things ready for him. So, I thought it best to hide them away. Pretend they weren't there. You know, not wanting to tempt fate.'

He held up a pair of stockings. 'But these will fit Rose, so why are these are hidden away? What's afoot, Jane?'

'Nothing's afoot.' My voice came out higher than usual and would give me away, so I lowered it before speaking again. 'They're for Rose. For when the new baby comes. Or for her birth day. So she doesn't feel jealous of her new little brother when he comes.' My face was growing hotter, but the lies kept spilling from me. I dropped a kiss on Rose's forehead and stroked her cheek. 'Don't worry, little Rose. You'll soon be well. Andrew, please, can we talk about this later? Will you get the honey?'

'Aye, very well. You minister to Rose, then.' He looked at me. 'There'll be plenty of time for questions after. Will she be well?'

'If we can stop her from getting too hot. Whilst I wash her down, could you take the crock of willow from Mam's satchel. That should fetch down her fever and soothe any pain.'

He frowned at the crocks. 'Which is which?'

'Middle row, eight from the left. Open the crock and show me.'

He picked out the right one and removed the lid to reveal a pale green powder. I leant in and inhaled the soft, astringent smell that told me it was willow. 'Thank you, that's it. Mix a pinch with a spoonful of honey, forming it into balls the size of pearl barley.'

I watched him until he passed me a sticky mass, which I flattened and slipped under my little girl's tongue.

'It'll dissolve in the heat of her mouth and shouldn't choke her if I keep her upright. She can have another in a little whilst.' I continued swabbing her with cool water, but she seemed to be growing hotter. 'Andrew, Rose is still getting hotter, and I'm afraid for her.' There was a waver in my voice. 'Would you go and fetch Reverend Foster for me . . . and Tom?'

'I'll fetch the Reverend if you think he's needed.' His face stiffened. 'But Verger has no business in this household.'

'But, Andrew, Rose is . . . she might not . . .' I closed my eyes, praying to a God that I didn't, and couldn't, trust.

'He won't set foot in my house again. Do you hear me?'

I nodded. 'Then fetch the Reverend, please.'

'Aye. And I'll knock Ma out of bed in case you need help in the meantime.'

Once the Reverend knew of Rose's condition, he would rouse Tom. He'd have more power over the Drivers than me. And Tom should be here . . .

Whilst Andrew was gone, I wiped my eyes, dosed Rose again with willow and continued swabbing her with cold water, but she grew ever hotter. This sometimes happened. The temperature would reach a crisis and then begin to fall. It was the most dangerous time.

My daughter suddenly stiffened and began convulsing on the table, so I picked her up, cradling her gently so that she didn't knock her head on the hard table. Her little arms and legs thrashed, and tears ran freely from my eyes, landing on her forehead.

'Poor mite. Poor little mite. Fear not, I'll tend to you.'

Bett appeared and came and stood by me. 'Oh, Rosie! What'll become of her, Jane?'

I shook my head. I'd seen fits in small children before and they often passed, but it was a different matter when the child was my own. Rose's whole body was still burning as she shook in my arms. Oh, Rose, please don't leave me. I couldn't bear to lose you as well.

Eventually, Rose stilled and her little body fell limp. Her eyes fluttered, but she was still far too hot. The door opened and Andrew entered, his mouth set in a grim line, followed by Reverend Foster. But no Tom. I opened my mouth to speak, but Andrew gave me a warning look.

The Reverend came straight to Rose's side. 'How is she, Jane?'

'Not good, Reverend. But she's stopped fitting now, which may be a good sign. Andrew, we need a stream of cold air flowing in. Can you hang some wet sheets to cool the air?'

'Ma, fetch some sheets and water.' Andrew nodded at a ball of twine on a shelf. 'Reverend, make yourself useful and help me hang a string between the window and Rose.'

When Bett returned with dripping sheets, Andrew began hanging them.

* * *

Finally, in the early hours of the morning, the willow began to do its work and the heat started leaving my daughter.

'Will she live?' The Reverend hovered over me as I checked her. There was a catch in his throat. 'Will little Rose live?'

'The crisis is over, Reverend, but she's very weak.'

He frowned. 'What can else can you do?'

'When she awakes, I'll dose her with elderberry linctus. It'll act as a tonic and strengthen her until her natural fight returns. But she's out of danger.'

The Reverend wiped his eyes. He quickly took my hand and squeezed it before leaning to drop a few words in my ear.

'I'll go straight to Tom and let him know that Rose is well.'

Bett's gimlet eye saw this whispering and she bustled over, carrying a pile of little vests and stockings before her. 'Well, if the crisis is over, there's no need for the Reverend to be here anymore. It's best you get away and let Rose and Jane get some sleep. Now, Jane, I'll put these clothes in the drawer, it's no good them mouldering away in your mother's old satchel. Whatever were you thinking, lass?'

23

John

A Taint on Me

In the morning, I woke in a fever. Patsy Gillie and her ilk had left a taint on me, and my body was now covered in sores. Madness whirled around my head in the semi-darkness of the room. I was left in a queer state, lashed to my pallet, wall-eyed, looking at the rafters. Whatever surged in my veins withered my organ, and the prayers fled my mind. So, it was not even possible to avoid thinking about the contagion in my blood by forcing my mind towards God. Now, I was all alone in the world.

I put my hands to my face to examine myself. My wet lips were too loose and large for my face, and they blossomed from my beard like an indecent flower. Typically, I had dried white rinds for lips and these slabs of raw liver disturbed me, especially when I wetted them further by licking them with my thick tongue. I'd begun raving of late and dared not return to sleep in case I tried to engage myself or MacBain in lewd conversation. As it was, I needed to steel myself to keep myself clean for my return to work.

In normal times, whisky helped with purification, but MacBain had deprived me of my preferred medicine. I waved my hands before my face and the red sores on my palms horrified me.

'Witches, curse them, filthy, unclean women! Rotten to the core, the lot of them.'

MacBain came back then and looked me over. 'What are you shouting about now, Sharpe? Why so irate?'

'I'm sick. In the body this time, not in the mind. Don't stand there looking baffled, man. Can you fettle me, or not? Hand over one of your concoctions. Hand it over, MacBain, I've God's work to attend to.'

But MacBain only scowled at my outburst. 'You'll have to bide a whilst so I can look at your symptoms.'

He leant forward and examined the palms of my hands without touching them.

'Hmm. There's not much call to deal with the pox in this neck of the woods, but that's my best reckoning.'

'It is not the pox. As you must surely know, my vital organs have been infected by at least one known witch.'

MacBain had the temerity to raise his brows. 'Deny it all you like, Sharpe, but the sickness that ails you is one that's well known to me, even if not hereabouts.'

He returned, carrying a small book, which he opened and read.

'Now for . . . grandgore, there is no concoction that will truly help. There is only one true cure, but it's too late for the taking now. I don't envy you.'

'Stop speaking in riddles, man. I've warned you about this before.'

MacBain made a show of sighing. 'The only known cure is prevention – control of the appetites. Still, there are plenty in their graves through failing in that regard, and doubtless plenty more to come.'

'How dare you wish death upon me!' I shook my swollen fists.

MacBain put down his head, pretending to read his book, but really, it was to hide the grin that had taken over his smug face.

I lay, lintel-like whilst MacBain checked my symptoms. 'Aye, you've a fair collection of chancres about your person. Definitely the grandgore. A despicable disease. I've seen it in many of the soldiers I've treated over the years.'

The pox! How dare he? But what if he were right? How much credence should I give this man? As a barber-surgeon, he was just beneath a respectable physician in standing, but I knew him as a witch, a cunning man. Surely my blood was on fire again with a witch's contagion and the man was just trying to get a rise out of me.

'Let me see that book, MacBain. Hand it over!'

He propped the book on my chest. I tried to raise my head, but my neck ached and it was so dark that it was impossible to read. MacBain must have unnatural powers to see in such poor light. I shook my head and he took the book away.

'What can you possibly know, MacBain, about ailments and treatments? In the small villages in these parts, you must spend your waking hours stitching smashed heads and applying compresses to those suffering no more than the after effects of too much ale.'

'You give me short shrift. I've spent many years of my life following soldiers into battle and so I have more knowledge of life and death than might be expected from a country healer. Still, the pox is a troubling condition. And more troubling for me being a surgeon and knowing only too well what fate awaits you.'

I blinked. 'Aye, it would be better to leave me ignorant. Don't fill me with the horrors. There's enough in my mind to terrify me as it is.'

'You're not wrong, Sharpe. There could be nothing worse than knowing the pox is on the loose around your body.' MacBain took a draught of ale, wiped his mouth on the back of his hand and laughed. 'Best try not to think about it.'

But I did think about it. About how lust had brought me low. Was I somehow to blame in bringing this scourge upon myself? I flushed at my innocence. There was no blame attached to me. Hadn't that Gillie woman gone out of her way to tempt me? She'd hexed me so that I'd been unable to control my own lust. How had I been so gullible? I thrashed my head from side to side. But I was jolted from my remorse by MacBain grabbing my arm and almost dislodging it from its socket.

'Come, Sharpe, don't hurt yourself by falling.'

Then I lay still, panting and staring at MacBain, as if expecting an answer. He lashed me back in place and tried to prise free my fingers, which were now clutching his breeches.

'And now my once-smooth mouth has fallen to ruin – look, look.' I forced my jaws apart, revealing the bloody interior of my mouth. MacBain didn't even feign interest.

'Aye, Sharpe, it does look very sore and bloody, which is to be expected.'

'And that's not the worst of it. My nose is rotting so the smell never leaves me, forcing me to smell it and taste it every waking second.'

I peered up at MacBain, trying to grab his arm, wishing fervently that he might save me from this list of excruciating ailments. But the barber-surgeon now stood beyond arm's reach.

'Settle yourself down, Sharpe. One day, there'll be nothing. Your mouth will be clear, and your nose will cease its festering. The malicious aches plaguing your joints will slip away. Your hair will grow back and it will lose that rat-chewed look. You'll appear to be better, fully healed, and it'll be as though you're reborn. And after being ridden with chancres for so long, they'll soon enough go.'

This was welcome news. 'So these chancres, they will leave me?' A chance to be reborn. Yes! And then I'd be a better person, I would keep away from low places and common women who were too free in their ways. Reformed. That's it, a reformed character I would be. 'And so, I'll be cured then?'

MacBain laughed until he coughed. 'Cured? No, Sharpe, never. It's only a cruel jape. Any well-travelled barber-surgeon knows the chancres haven't really gone, but merely faded from the visible skin. Meanwhile, the nasty disease spirals its way down through skin, fat and muscle until fully unleashed into the blood so it may travel where it might.'

This news shrivelled my hope. I thought of the filthy disease touching my organs: my good heart, my passionate liver, my hardworking lungs and finally, my exhausted brain. It was a wonder to me that I'd thrown away my good health so willingly. Here I was, a man of God, but one brought low by the sin of lust – even if it was not my doing.

'You know the worst thing of this disease, MacBain?' I didn't wait for him to reply but barrelled on. 'My inner eye looks within now, and I see the chancres, unloading lesions everywhere, all over my lovely organs. One day soon, my clean white bones will be seized by the unholy taint.'

'Aye, the pox wastes men to death. Even in that fresh-scrubbed brain of yours, the disease will still be there – it'll just be sleeping.

The pox will burrow deep within you, just waiting to return and wreak havoc once more.'

I imagined it sleeping, worm-like, in the cushiony depths of my body, snugly hibernating.

'And how long will this hibernation last when it comes, do you know?'

'No way of knowing. It might be a few years. It might be thirty. It might never end. It could end the morrow.' MacBain grinned. 'There's no way of knowing.'

This was so unjust, this poisonous hex from the harlot at Berwick. She was another who had escaped justice and must be dealt with. 'So, even when I am grown clean, a giant clock will tick constantly over my head, reminding me that each second of clean living might be my last? For all I know, the dormant beast within might wake at any moment? And what might wake it?'

He counted on his fingers, looking far too cheerful for my liking.

'Strong drink and loose women, or a liking for little boys and fatty meat.'

'Well then, it won't awaken in me. I live the life of an ascetic and already eschew all pleasures of the flesh, living only on leaves and the weakest of ale. Oh, my clean days cannot come soon enough! Then my eyes might get better. When it's dark, I must peer at even the nearest things, which makes my life very hard to see. And yet, those same eyes of mine, which refuse to see in low light, perversely let in every drop of glaring bright light.'

'Well, that's a matter easily solved.' With that, MacBain threw a rug of rabbit skins over the window. 'There, darkness suits you better.'

So now I'm condemned to lie in darkness, else cover my face with veils like a widow. The thought of this sickness exhausted me, and I lay, eyes closed and slack-mouthed.

* * *

MacBain loosened my bindings, then reached out with both hands, grasped my wrists and pushed his fingers into the pulses, nodding as he listened.

155

'Am I improved?' My heart raced, waiting for the diagnosis.

'For now, your chancres have left you. But it is as I supposed, Sharpe. You have much to fear.' He let go of my hands and pulled the rabbit-skin cover back over me. 'The singing of your blood tells me that you won't make old bones. You've not much time left to you. So if you need to make your peace with God, don't leave it too long. You can return to your uncle the morrow.'

My mind reeled at this blasphemous prediction. But then a shadow slowly settled over my soul. Blasphemy it might be, but what if MacBain were right? It meant there was little time left to complete my work. How long was left to me? Surely God wouldn't take me before my errand was complete? Once returned to Uncle James, he would keep me under lock and key, and it would be impossible to return to Newcastle. There was no time to waste. This left me a mere night to escape. But how? MacBain was cunning, and big. It would take some effort to overcome him, especially in my weakened state. How would I overwhelm MacBain without risking my neck? It would be a perilous undertaking, but there was so little time left to me. There would be only one chance. I lay perfectly still. MacBain examined me for a long time. Was there pity there, or trust, because I hadn't tried to escape? Would he trust me to return to my uncle alone? I held my breath, waiting.

'Have you nothing to say, Sharpe? About my diagnosis?'

'Diagnosis? It is nothing short of a blasphemous prediction. That makes you guilty of witchcraft, MacBain! And I will see you swing for your crimes with my final breath! You will beg for your life just like Dora Shaw.' His cheeks purpled and his fists clenched at his sides, his breath coming in short pants. I sneered at him. 'And just like Kirstie Slater!'

The big man lunged for me then, but I rolled to the floor and he landed heavily on the pallet, which broke and sent him floundering. I snatched up the axe from the fire and knelt over him.

'In the name of God, Sharpe. Put down the axe.'

'How dare a tainted man such as you utter God's name?' My arms trembled as I held the axe over his head. My limbs were weak, but God lent me an avenging fury. 'You're nothing more than a common witch, with your herbs, and your fortune-telling ways. You cannot be allowed to live!'

I brought down the blunt head of the axe on the back of his head, and MacBain collapsed before me, blood trickling from his skull and pooling on the floor. His limbs were still, but there was a chance he still breathed. To be sure, I smashed the axe down on his head again and again until it was just a bloody mass.

* * *

It took me almost the whole of the night to bury the remains of the barber-surgeon. He wouldn't be missed until Uncle James came to seek me. And Uncle wouldn't think him dead. Only gone away on his travels. And he would think me escaped. Without a body, there could be no accusation of murder. No one would suspect he was buried beneath his own shack.

That was one more witch gone from the world, and without time to pray for his soul. But it was not enough. The devil still walked amongst us in the guise of cunning women. I couldn't, in all good conscience, let the Newcastle witch and her progeny live. My days were numbered now, and so I must pray to God to grant me time enough to complete His errand.

24

Jane

Forty More Days of Winter

My belly writhed. So, my overwrought mind had disturbed my infant's rest as well as my own. I placed my hands over my taut skin. Well, little one, if you want to share the same birth day as your sister and her father, you need to hurry into the world today. I smiled in spite of myself. My belly was high and this child wouldn't be born today. My judgement must have been off kilter last year and maybe there was another moon to go yet. The boy seemed in no hurry to join this world, for all his energy. My bodice was loosened to its furthest extent. If this child failed to come soon, the only garment to fit would be my cloak.

It would be best if he came after we boarded the ship that would take us to the New World. Still, the thought of crossing the great, dark sea in the belly of a ship to an unknown land filled me with unease. A perilous journey lay ahead of us the morrow, and we'd not be safe until we set sail some days hence. And who knew what would face us when we reached dry land? But we were strong, and we would be together, and we would be free.

My racing thoughts must have affected my child as he was so busy now that it would be impossible to return to sleep, and I lay awake, keeping vigil with the night. My back ached, and so I eventually slid out of bed, giving up all pretence of sleep. Rose and Andrew slumbered on and would no doubt sleep for some hours yet.

It was Imbolc and the day of Rose's birth, of Tom's birth and of his mother's death. This would be a hard day for him. I'd knitted Rose some red woollen mittens to match her Yuletide stockings, and I wished with all my heart that I might have knitted some mittens for Tom, but there was no way of concealing the crafting of a gift for him. It pained me to give him nothing on this day, but the morrow, I would give him his daughter.

The youngest maid would wear the candle-crown today – the wreath of lights. It had been Tilly Green last year, and now it would be Rose. It fell to the maid's mother to fashion a wreath from winter greens and the first flowers to poke through the earth. The first Candlemas bells usually drifted along the river banks in the heart of the valley where winter's breath was softer. It was still dark, but I would go there now because many tasks lay ahead of me today.

My last day in Mutton Clog. Every step I took today would be filled with portent. It would be the last day I walked the riverbank, the last day I would see the dear face of Reverend Foster. And it would be the last time I set eyes on Andrew Driver. It seemed hard to believe that I would be free of him at last, but I must mask my nervous state, else he get wind of something afoot and prevent us leaving. I would try to force all thoughts of leaving from my mind and just concentrate on my tasks.

Although it was morning when I crept from the house, the sky was still black and dusted with thousands of brilliant stars. I shivered but paused to look at them. They seemed so very near. But I couldn't tarry too long – if I hurried, then I'd reach the river before first light and pick the flowers whilst they slept under the gaze of the gentle gibbous moon.

The ground was hard and shone with frost, so I placed my feet carefully, especially where the roots of the trees showed through the earth like the ebony bones of long-gone giants. It felt like a long walk with such a heavy belly, and I walked slowly in case the movement should bring on the baby.

The river was frozen into a glistening white path, and clumps of sleeping snowdrops were massed along its banks. The cold from underfoot seeped through the soles of my clogs and journeyed up my legs. I stared down at a lone snowdrop and smiled.

Snowdrop, Candlemas bell, milk flower. Good for elderly people softening in the head, but with great caution for it is also poison. Too humble to turn its little face up to the mighty giver of light and life, the snowdrop stared down past its feet, as if yearning to return from whence it came.

I picked only as many flowers as necessary for the wreath of lights and for the church. Even though I took care to take only a few from each clump and to leave plenty behind, the drifts still looked ravaged. Before the cold overtook me, I plucked the lone snowdrop. It never troubled me to pluck a flower from the warm earth in July, but now, it filled me with guilt to pick this one after it had fought through soil so frozen it defied Bill and Tom's spades. But it was done now. A flower once plucked cannot be unplucked. A crow cawed from a low branch, perhaps echoing my thoughts, and then flapped away into the darkness. I peered at the sky and shivered. It couldn't be long until sun-up.

* * *

I walked towards the church and placed my hand on the door. I paused. This would be the first year that I'd arranged the Imbolc flowers myself. When I finally entered, the church was in darkness, so I lit a small beeswax candle to light my work. The sweet smell of the hive was heavenly, but it was wrong to waste good wax when the church was empty. Still, the Reverend was not here to chide me. It was only one small light, and the carnal stink of burning tallow seemed wrong in God's house and not fitting for the purification of the Virgin. I could almost hear my mother's voice in my ear and my face collapsed into a smile, remembering how much Mam hated the smell of tallow.

The church held centuries' worth of smells. At Yuletide, holly and ivy wreaths graced the pews, and all the greenery of winter was fetched inside for blessing and safekeeping. At Imbolc, the gentle smell of snowdrops permeated the cold year with the first lights of spring. At Ostara, primroses gladdened the eye with their bright colour and lifted the spirits with their bright aroma. At Beltane, bridal bouquets of hawthorn fell heavy on the senses. At Litha, corpses sweetened with decay, their corruption

160

not quite masked by roses or the scented smoke of forbidden incense. At Lammas, glossy, warm loaves bore the smell of home. But always, underneath these smells was beeswax, from the many candles burnt here. Of wood rubbed to a shine, warm wood that groaned and creaked and ticked depending on the season and the time of day. Of perfumed wine from the distant days of Holy Communion. Wax, wood and wine – all held still in the holy breath of this place.

As a pink tinge lit up the eastern window, I blew out the candle, sending up a spiral of white smoke, and I stooped once more to tie bunches of snowdrops to the altar. The low winter sun shone through the window then, making the dust motes come alive. The smell of beeswax and the gentle perfume of snowdrops hung in the air, and the old oak pews creaked as they absorbed warmth from the newly strengthening sun.

I stood back to look at my floral arrangements and pressed my hands into the small of my back to ease the ache there. The creak of the door opening behind me made me turn.

'Jane, is that you?'

'Tom! What are you doing here?' He shouldn't be here. I'd made a promise to Andrew. Yet, it wouldn't be the only promise to him I was set to break.

Tom ran to me and embraced me quickly before stepping back. 'A noise outside roused me, and then I saw the light in the church. Does this mean you're ready to leave now?'

'No, Tom, we cannot leave until the morrow, you know that. Although it might seem better to miss the Imbolc ceremony, if Rose doesn't take her part in the ritual, it'll raise the alarm—'

'Please, Jane. We should make away. The ship is almost ready, and we can hide on board until it's ready to sail. We'll be safer there than here. No one will suspect us of going to the New World. They'll never think to search a ship.'

'But, Tom, we cannot take away the Imbolc maid and leave the village without fortune for the next year.' I put my hand against his warm face and smiled up at him. 'One more day can do no harm. Please. It'll make me feel better about leaving the Reverend behind. And it'll give you one more day with your father. You cannot leave him today, of all days . . .'

He sighed and nodded, and then looked behind him. 'All the same, I'm going to stay here till you're finished.'

I smiled. 'There's no need. The sun's up. All that's left to do now is set out the candles. Then I'll go to the Drivers' and fashion a small wreath for Rose.'

'Aye, well. I'll wait here and see you safely on your way. Don't worry, no one will see me.'

He placed his hands on my shoulders and bent to kiss my forehead. 'Till the night, Jane. Come to the church once everyone is asleep. Be safe.'

I nodded. 'Till the night, Tom.'

* * *

Imbolc was halfway between mid-winter and spring. A time of purification and cleansing. And a window into the future. A future that could only contain goodness, joy and a life free from fear. The frost of the night had gone, the sky was blue and cloudless, and the sun shone brightly. But I frowned, knowing this meant that the white months were not yet over. Forty more days of winter were yet to come. What might this mean for our journey to the ship? And what would winter at sea be like? But I couldn't let these thoughts crowd my mind, or fear would freeze me here for life, so I would concentrate on preparing Rose for the ritual ahead.

* * *

Once dusk fell, we set off, watching our footing as the frost was back. In the darkened church, candles rested on every flat surface and the honeyed smell of beeswax hung in the air. It would be hard to sit in church today without my mother. If only she were with me now, to see Rose wear the wreath of lights. She'd have been so proud of her tiny granddaughter. I smiled to myself. And she would've made a better job of the decorations.

Finally, the procession began, and I led Rose through the door behind the Reverend. A green and white wreath holding small candles graced Rose's hair. She walked through the church, her

162

hair glittering with a constellation of tiny stars. Tom watched her, and I tried hard not to smile at him as the Drivers would be watching and they would see the secret that lived between us. Nothing must give away our plans.

Andrew ran a proprietorial eye over me and my daughter as we passed, and I forced myself to look on him kindly. All the children now stood behind Rose, clutching their family candles, walking forward slowly, waiting to have them blessed by the Reverend and to take the holy light back to their families. After a whilst, the church was lambent as every hand held a lit candle. Except for the Vergers. Tom must get his candles blessed! I willed him with my eyes. We'd endured enough darkness of late and could afford no more.

Tom stood and walked to the altar. Andrew's eyes were on him as he walked towards me and Rose, but Tom kept his head down. He held out his candles and Reverend Foster made the sign of the cross over them, then held out the large candle for Tom to take a light. Now, all the village candles were blessed. Together, we would celebrate the purification of the Virgin.

Rose lit up the church with her pretty smile. Tom watched her. How must he feel, being reduced to the status of a stranger, watching another family's joy? But at least this would be the last time. Soon, we would leave Mutton Clog as a family. But it wouldn't do to get excited now and raise suspicion, so I focused all my attention on my daughter, fixing the tiny candles in her hair so that no hot wax would drip down and scald her. I straightened my back and stole a glimpse of Tom.

Andrew met my eye, and a flush spread up my face at being caught. There would be trouble later. Often, I wondered whether Andrew had most wanted me, or whether he had most wanted to cause Tom pain. Perhaps both, though I couldn't see that Tom had given his former friend any cause for vengeance. Andrew had given Tom plenty of cause, but apart from that first fight, Tom had borne his burden with grace.

I felt both Tom and Andrew's eyes on us as I led Rose in a circle around the church, her flame-coloured curls catching the candlelight. As she passed by her father, Rose's large green eyes looked into his with the wide-eyed stare that only small children can manage. When the colour met its match, a smile broke out across his face. Our little girl smiled back, dimples winking. Tom clenched his jaw and dug his hands under his oxters.

His eyes were marred with worry. Had something happened with the voyage? There was no way of knowing or asking him. And I daren't speak to the Reverend or Bill in case we were overheard. For their own protection, the Reverend and Bill must not be involved in our escape. After the service would be the last time I ever saw them, and I wouldn't be able to say to Reverend Foster all the things I wanted him to hear. That although he was not my father, he was a father to me. That it broke my heart to leave him behind. And Tom would need to say goodbye to his own father. I ushered Rose on her way and Bill Verger stooped to speak to her.

Andrew glared across the church and crushed out the candlelight between his fingers as if grudging Bill this moment. Although Rose lived in the Drivers' home, she was born of Verger blood, and Andrew could never change that. But he would make me pay for this snatched moment. If I were fortunate, he'd only inflict one of his long and brooding silences that made me tiptoe around him. I resolved to make up with him. The worst possible outcome would be if Andrew stayed up all night shouting and we couldn't get away.

When we left the church, Reverend Foster was shaking hands with the men, Bill Verger at his side. Tom must have realised my dilemma, as he took his leave and crossed the graveyard to his shack.

Jim shook the Reverend's hand. 'A grand service, Reverend. Grand. And our little Rose the perfect Candlemas maid.'

Bill's eyes flickered at this, but he kept his face still. He looked from me to Rose, and in that look, were decades of loss. Tom's mother was buried in the graveyard. And now Bill would lose Tom and Rose. He held out his hand to Rose and then opened his fingers. In his palm was a carved black cat.

I caught my breath as Rose took it, smiling and holding it up to me. 'Gyb! Gyb!'

Oh, Bill, please don't give us away!

Andrew frowned and took the carving from Rose. 'What's all this, Bill Verger? Why are you giving my daughter a trinket? It's not for you to do.'

But the Reverend smiled at him. 'Settle yourself, young Driver. The verger always gives the Candlemas maid a small gift. It's a tradition. Now, you wouldn't want to break with tradition, would you, and bring down disaster on all our heads?'

I bit my lip. For the Reverend to use superstition to cover Bill's action was audacious after everything he'd ever said against it. But Andrew seemed reassured and handed the plaything back to Rose.

'Aye, well. That's alright then.'

Bill winked at Rose. He must long to reach out and ruffle her hair, but his hands stayed firmly at his sides. I drew in a deep breath and smiled at Bill. This was the very last time I would see him. Although I would see him every day in Tom and Rose.

The Reverend held out his hands. I took them, not speaking. All the words had left me. They were no good in front of the Drivers. I swallowed and willed this good man to know what was in my heart. He closed his eyes and placed one hand on my head and one on Rose's head.

'God bless you and go with you, Jane and Rose.' Then he quickly opened his eyes and addressed Andrew. 'More superstition, you see. Giving thanks for the Candlemas maid and her mother. Now on your way, the pair of you.'

He was struggling to contain his tears, and so I must not make it harder for him.

'Goodbye, Reverend. And thank you.'

25

John

The Makings of a New Witch

The journey back to England had been almost unendurable. My nights were spent abroad in dark forests, living in constant terror of wild dogs and cutpurses. In the daytime, I holed up inside hollow trees and burrows and all but froze to death. I stank of the earth and must have presented a pitiful sight, but now was the time for action and not for vanity. Back in my neighbour country, I was no longer a revered guest, but a fugitive, albeit one still on God's errand.

When the sharp peaks of Scotland had given way to the rounded hills of England, I'd thought about the degenerate harlot nestled in the heart of Berwick. She'd delivered a death sentence upon me, and for that, she must pay. But it was too soon since my troubles there and that town would still be alert to my arrival. Besides, my troubles had started with Jane Driver, and her curse must be removed first. Enough time had elapsed since August, and there would be less likelihood of my being recognised and arrested.

On the approach to Newcastle, the oppressive walls had reared before me, but there was no need to enter the town. Driver's mother had announced at her trial that she haled from Mutton Clog near Shotley Bridge, which sat on the River Derwent. So, I'd veered past Newcastle and followed the Tyne until it led me to the Derwent. From there, it was simply a matter of following the river south and west to Shotley Bridge. Whilst Mutton Clog appeared on no map, it would be a small matter to find the church of the false priest, and he would lead me to the great witch, Jane Driver. Thoughts of vengeance and glory lifted my spirits. Once I'd delivered this witch, the Lord would show His pleasure.

* * *

My way was lit only by the moon reflected on the white frost that feathered the ground and the trees. The river was frozen solid and the air was frigid. Nothing could do well in this weather. I struggled to keep my feet, and feared breaking a leg, but at last, I came to the hamlet of Shotley Bridge, which comprised but a few cheap huts. No lights shone from any windows and there were no signs of life.

There were no other buildings for a way until I passed a smallholding in the valley, but no lights shone there either. Further on, I came to a hill and saw the silhouettes of a church and house upon it. So this was where the witch's mother had lived with the false priest – a most curious state of affairs. Whilst the dwellings were in darkness, I made my rounds, distant enough from doors and windows so that no dogs wakened. By keeping to the shadows, it was possible for me to see without being seen. The church would be the best place to keep watch. The priest was close to the witch, and she'd no doubt appear beside him before too long.

The church at Mutton Clog was hunched on the hill. Close to, it was no thing of beauty, this toady lump, crouched darkly, as if awaiting its prey. On the approach to the church, I was struck by its foulness. This was a building fit only for the devil, and not for praising God. The path to the church led through a graveyard populous with ornate and menacing stones, with a verger's shack huddled to one side. At the boundary, a row of queer trees grew, festooned with spidery flowers, even though it was the depths of winter. No doubt this whole village was in the grip of witchcraft. I closed my eyes and prayed silently to God to protect me before creeping forward. The church windows flickered with strange lights that made the saints in the coloured windows come to life. So that's where the villagers were! Well, it would be a simple enough matter to hide myself away until the service was over to see who might come out.

The church was a building that appeared more ancient than it was. Of course, the stones were older than the church itself, and they must have been dragged up the hill on straining carts, and then exposed to the wind and rain until the elements weathered dimples in the stones. The church had coloured glass in its windows, which was an abhorrent vanity and a sure sign of the former idolatry that had taken place here. God didn't need to be praised with the fancy ornament and frivolity favoured by the papists.

Although it had taken the church centuries to see it, popery was a sin sent straight from Satan himself. These papists were nothing short of witches and magicians themselves. Every one of their words and deeds was tantamount to casting a spell. The high, ornate cathedrals defied manly logic – using their height and space to addle the brain. The coloured glass in the windows did no more than pollute the rays of God's golden sun. Music and singing heightened the spirit to a dangerous degree. Singing in strange tongues understood only by the priest must surely confound the innocent so they hardly knew of what they were at. And with mouths and hearts opened and made ready by singing, the devil was surely invited in to take up residence. During my vigil, I would pray for strength and fortitude.

* * *

When the church doors finally opened, a burst of sound and laughter preceded the congregation, who flooded out, clutching fistfuls of candles. The false priest and his verger stood outside shaking hands with men and blowing great clouds of vapour, so hot was the air that billowed from them. Of course, I held the priest somewhat to blame for my parlous state. But he was a man of God, of sorts, and one held in the thrall of a witch, and so I couldn't apportion too much blame to the man, weak though he may be.

A buxom young woman, fair of hair, left the church behind her parents, trailing two young siblings with her, and followed by what must be twin brothers. Then a stocky young man came out, clutching his hat in his hand, his shock of luxuriant black curls almost womanly. From behind him came childish laughter and a girl's voice. A tall, red-haired man came out next. The dark-haired man scowled at the sight of him, and his ill temper marred an otherwise pretty face. The red-haired man glanced behind him and set off across the graveyard to the verger's shack. The verger's son, evidently. I stared at the dark-haired man. Clearly of country stock. A strong working man. If he was typical of the local breed then they'd more than match me in physical battle. I'd need to rely on my wits and use stealth in my approach.

Next, came a goodwife, heavy with child. My heart began to race when I saw it was the bitch who'd escaped the hangman's noose. The last time I'd set eyes on the slattern, she was very different. Now, she was great with child and she struck me as an indecently ripe fruit, bursting with sweetness and temptation. Clearly, the brazen whore fed from Satan's teat. In August, she was a scrawny, shorn-headed witch with a slight curve to her belly. Now, a mere two quarters later, she had a cap of rich chestnut hair, she was full of face and had burgeoning breasts. Her great belly protruded with the makings of a new witch and her bodice was fully loose. How had she flourished in so few months, if not at the devil's behest?

The witch called out, 'Rose – Rose come here.' There came a flurry of noise and a small child ran to the witch's side, burying her hands in her mother's kirtle. Fittingly, she bore an old pagan name and one not suitable for a Christian child. The brat had a mass of red curls. Her legs were clad in scarlet stockings and her head was crowned in a wreath that flamed in the night air – the candles and plants no doubt held fast with filthy witch's knots. Her crown bore not the good leaves that God had sanctioned for the nourishment of man. No, these were Candlemas bells, and they were destined for no man's plate. What ungodly intent lay behind their presence, I knew not, but whatever it was, Jane Driver was teaching it to her child. The child's colouring made her an obvious witch. This colouring could be borne by man – I had hair of flame myself – but in the weaker vessel, the colouring indicated the devil's insidious approach.

The witch straightened the child's crown and addressed her. Her parentage puzzled me, for two dark-haired parents couldn't produce a child with colouring such as this. I wondered at the man's lack of suspicion. Yet another innocent cuckold who didn't know what imp he housed beneath his roof. But no matter, for his troubles would be over soon enough. This tiny witch would be slain along with her mother, else she inherit her powers.

Jane Driver spoke to the verger, and he passed something to her child. Her husband squared his shoulders and they didn't give until the priest addressed him. He gave off an animal strength that I knew enough to fear. But there was something between this woman and her husband – an anger that had gone cold and become hatred. Something was afoot here. The wench was certainly comely enough, and her flushed face and loosened bodice promised warm loins and soft, full breasts. My member rose in my breeks and I clenched my fists. The devil's bitch already had this man in thrall to her, and were I not careful, she'd have me as well.

The dark-haired man summoned his family to him and set off down the hill. The pregnant vixen led her spawn away from the church and they followed him until they were out of my sight. The woman was an abomination. What form of church would admit a witch? Perhaps the priest had been taken by the dark side, and his church made unclean. Or perhaps all those within were foul consorts of the witch.

For a moment, I thought of God's commandments. Murder was a sin. But God's instruction surely meant it was a sin to murder another man. A man was different. He was born to God, in God's own image and was therefore harder for the devil to infiltrate. Women were born to the devil, and this one and her children especially so. It would be a small matter to dispose of a child, especially a girl-child – for who would miss her truly? Only her witch mother, but she would soon die, along with the imp in her belly. Driver's husband might miss her, but he would soon find a replacement and wouldn't howl for too long.

But killing three witches would mean working quickly and most likely at night in the bitter cold. I need only bide my time and God would help me find a way. There could be no rest for me whilst there was still air in the witch's lungs. She would continue to breed and there would be no end to the scourge. The spilling of her blood would end the curse, cleanse my path and return me to my righteous position in the time left to me on this earth. I closed my eyes against the night and prayed to God for guidance. In my mind came the vision again of the owl rising in the night, wings outspread, taking the black lamb. It was good. He had decreed it.

26

Jane

No Longer Watching for the Moon

Halfway home, Andrew left with his father to go carousing in the valley with some of the farm lads. There'd be lots of ale and cider swallowed and the illicit cheer of seeking omens in the flames to make predictions for the coming year. I didn't want to take part, for I was afraid to see the future flickering in the firelight. A dangerous night lay ahead of me. And beyond that, a dangerous voyage into a new life. It wouldn't do to see what fate held in store for me, so I made the excuse of Rose being tired and needing to get home. This would allow me to prepare to leave without Andrew watching my every move. But my plan was thwarted when Bett insisted on coming home with us, and she was every bit as vigilant as her son when it came to watching me.

All the way home, Rose gave lie to my excuse by skipping to and fro, admiring her red stockings, refusing to remove the candle-crown and chattering to herself. When we arrived at the Drivers' home, I lit the candles on the wreath once more and stood her on a chair before the darkened window so she could see herself reflected in the glass, lights twinkling over her head.

'Who's that pretty girl, Rose?'

She pointed to her reflection and smiled, watching her twin's hand moving in harmony with her own. Once the tapers on the wreath had burnt down, I lifted it from her head, but Rose held out her hands, tears welling.

'No more for now, Rose. It's time for bed, little maid.'

She scrunched up her face and her complexion darkened, but even when she was being naughty, she made me smile. I lifted her down from the chair and placed her on the settle.

'Such a sulky girl, Rose! You're far too tired after so much excitement. Come, you can have a singing hinny with butter and some camomile tea with honey and then I'll lie with you until you sleep.'

Whilst batter sizzled on the griddle, I softened the dried flower heads with hot water to release their fragrant oils.

Bett yawned. 'You'll ruin that girl, pandering to her so. Wait till you have two under your feet, and then you'll rue it.'

I touched my belly and opened my mouth to speak but remembered that Andrew's little sister had died at birth. It wouldn't do to remind Bett of it, even if it was something she thought of every day.

'Well, it's her birth day, so it won't hurt this once.' I wanted Rose to be drowsy, so that when I took her out later, she'd be less likely to stir and wake the entire household.

Bett gave me a sharp look. 'And you should try to get something down yourself – you're almost skin and bone. Folk will think we're too poor to feed you.'

Bett was as proud as ever. But it wouldn't do to needle her in case anger kept her awake. So much depended on everyone sleeping soundly. At least Andrew and Jim would be half senseless with drink when they returned.

'The baby takes up so much room in my belly now that it's a struggle to eat.'

'Just like when I was carrying Andrew. You're having a lad.' She smiled at me then. 'Well, hopefully, the birth shouldn't be too far off. Have you agreed a name yet? How about Andrew? Or James?'

'Not yet, no.' A glance through the window revealed a cloudy sky, which was lit by the moon. Rose had been born in a winter storm, which were notorious for bringing on babies early. 'It's cloudy but calm, so we'll have snow, but no storm. This infant won't be born the night.' But even so, our journey would be hard-going.

'Well, he must come some day. Of that you can be certain. And he'll need a name. It's wise to have one ready . . .'

I saw the pain of Bett's lost daughter in her eyes. And now she'd lose me and Rose, too. I gave her a watery smile.

'James. He'll be named for Jim.'

Her eyes sparkled and she nodded. 'Good. I'll sleep the better for knowing the bairn has a name. Now, I know you had a difficult birth last time and it was only your mother's doing that saved you. But I'll be with you, and I've birthed plenty of cattle over the years. So you're not to worry.'

It was hard not to smile at this gruff assurance. 'Thank you, Bett . . . and sleep well.'

'You too, Jane.' She kissed Rose and rumpled her hair. 'Goodnight, Rosie. Now, I'll get to bed, for the morrow will be a hard day if there's to be snow, especially if the baby arrives.'

Whilst Rose had her supper, I drank some honey in warm water and pondered. The thought of giving birth preyed on me. Bett was right – I'd only survived Rose's birth because of my mother's skill. With this birth, I wouldn't have her comforting presence, or even my home. In all likelihood, this baby would be born aboard a ship, with only Tom to help me. How would he manage a birth?

It might be wiser to bide here until this baby was born – at least Bett would be with me. But that might mean waiting another year for a ship, and Andrew would be sure to get another bairn on me in that time. All my best efforts at prevention might fail me. We had to leave now.

At last, Rose's head began to droop, and she was barely able to chew. The camomile had done its gentle duty.

'Come, Rose, bedtime. Your eyes are closing.'

She nodded drowsily and slipped down from the settle, holding out her arms. I picked her up, kissed her and carried her to her basket. Once Rose was tucked up with her poppet, blankets snugly wrapped around her little form, her eyelids began closing again. Even though exhausted, she still fought sleep, and she kept squinting at me in the candlelight. Eventually, I blew out the light and leant forward to kiss her on the forehead.

'Goodnight, sweet Rose.'

* * *

When Andrew and Jim returned, it was late and their rowdiness almost woke Rose. Glassy-eyed and red-faced from too much cider and ale, Andrew staggered into the room, dropped a handful of half-burnt candles to the floor and collapsed next to me. He lay down face-first and started to snore. Nothing would shift him now until first light. No doubt the entire village had been roused if all the menfolk had returned home in this state. There would be angry faces and sore heads in the morning, but with fortune on our side, we'd not be here to see them. I yawned, struggling to stay awake. It wouldn't do to fall asleep and miss my chance, so I forced myself to stay awake, waiting for the snores around me to deepen.

In spite of my best efforts to stay awake, tiredness overtook me and dreams flitted through my mind. Fortunately, the screech of an owl awoke me in the early hours, but it was impossible to say whether the owl came from my dreams or from the real world. So tired was I of late that it was becoming harder and harder to tell one from the other. I sat up. Even though the room was bitterly cold, sweat ran from me. My belly was hard. There'd been no movement all day, and I wondered at the stillness. For a second, I felt a fleeting joy. No child would ease our passage to the New World and the life beyond. But this dark joy was quickly extinguished by guilt. It was wrong to wish a child dead, for I'd witnessed too many children born still. What had I become that I could wish away my own baby?

I crept to the window to find the source of the sound. I raised the curtain and rested my forehead on the cold glass, trying to peer into the dark whilst my heart-rate slowed. Snow had fallen heavily in the past few hours. On the sill was a dish of pinecones that Rose had gathered from the woods. I ran a finger over their sharp, dry scales. They were wide open, so the snow wouldn't lie long, however thickly it lay. I tied my belt, tucked my pruning knife into it, drew my cloak around me and slipped on my clogs.

The household still slept all around me. Snores came from Jim and Bett's room. Andrew lay flat on his back, chest rising and falling steadily, dark curls flopped over one eye. Rose lay curled in her basket, thumb tucked into her mouth. I kissed my fingertip and traced her brow with it. Her lips pursed as if to scold, but then fell back to repose. I tucked her poppet into my belt, drew a blanket over her and lifted her onto my hip. At the movement, Rose cried out in her sleep, and I stood still, staring at Andrew and holding my breath. His brow furrowed, he waved an arm and muttered. But then his face relaxed as if nothing had roused him. Heart thumping, I left him to his dreams, picked up Mam's satchel and stepped outside, closing the door gently behind me.

Outside, lying against thick waves of snow, were two-dozen hollowed rabbit heads, draped like silken glove puppets. Their eyes stared at the sky, but they were no longer watching for the moon. Empty skins – so someone wanted the meat but not the fur. I shuddered, wondering at the wastrel hunter who'd passed this way. Beyond the brainless heads, there were large footprints, set far apart. Someone had passed this way, but surely not Tom? He'd never be so wasteful. I listened for a sound signalling any-one nearby, but none came.

The air was so cold that I could taste it. The night was quiet. No birds. No wind. No dogs. All sound was muffled by the snow, so what of the owl that had startled me? I shivered, afraid that an unseen someone might be watching us, and I looked back to the house where the Drivers slept.

Perhaps Tom was putting away last-minute provisions for his father – that might explain such careless hunting. I stepped over the rabbit heads and pressed one foot into the first smooth footprint. Carefully, I tiptoed after the trail, putting my own feet into the footprints and following them past the barn. It was hung with ivy and thousands of icicles cascaded down the stone walls. Inside, the beasts slept on and no sounds came from within, beyond their soft breaths.

The footprints led up the hill to the church. It must be Tom – perhaps he'd made his way past the Drivers' home hoping to see if I was coming and he'd carried his prey with him to explain his presence at this hour.

The cold stole my breath and walking up the steep hill bearing the combined weight of Rose, my belly and Mam's satchel made my thighs and lungs burn, but I dared not pause and so I contin-ued, panting, with fog streaming from my mouth.

When I entered the graveyard, I paused at Mam's cross. 'Goodbye, Mam, you gave yourself to save me, and I'll honour your sacrifice by making a good life for Rose, me and the baby. I'll always carry you in my heart.' I shifted Rose's weight, kissed my fingertips and touched them to her cross. 'Wish us well, Mam.'

There were no candles burning in either the manse or the Vergers' shack, which must mean Reverend Foster and Bill were abed. Over at the church, a faint light flickered through the stained glass. My heart lifted. Tom was inside waiting for us. This very night, we'd be on our way to a new life together.

With a final look at my mother's cross, I walked to the church. Once inside the vestibule, I saw that the nave was suffused with a low light. But the light was on the floor, which was not a proper place for a candle. That was not like Tom. Something wasn't right. Was he sending me a secret message to set me on my guard? A smell pervaded my senses. It was one I knew all too well, but it was something never before smelt in this sacred place. It smelt of old corruption and my belly roiled. This was a tallow candle, and we kept no tallow candles here.

The moon silvered the stained glass, casting an eerie light across the pews. When I peered beyond those pews that were doused in moonlight, and beyond the feeble pool of light cast by the candle, there was a change in the shadows of the dark side of the church. Why didn't Tom show himself to me? I dared not call out in case it was someone else. What if Andrew had followed me? My progress up the hill had been so slow that he could easily have cut behind me and entered through the vestry.

My back ached, so I put down Mam's satchel and laid Rose on the bench in the vestibule, tucking a hassock beneath her head, and covering her with my cloak so she was hidden in the darkness. She'd be warm enough and safe there whilst I found Tom. I considered the Vergers' shack. Should I just go there? But that risked rousing Bill and would make him a conspirator in our plans.

Should I turn back? But if it was Andrew, he must already know something was afoot and going home wouldn't help now. Whether it was Tom or Andrew in the shadows, once he realised I was here, he would show himself. I closed one eye, then opened it and closed the other, trying to adjust my eyes quickly to the darkness. I stilled myself, hearing only the creaks made from the wooden pews and the altar as they lost the warmth of the day and took on the chill of the night. I breathed as softly as I could, hearing the pounding of my own heartbeat in my ears. But when I held my breath, I became convinced there was another breathing alongside me. Although I could hear no more, I sensed a second heartbeat in the church. But was it Tom or Andrew? Still, I didn't move, and listened carefully for Rose lest she awake alone and be afraid.

There! A tiny creak that was not from the wooden pews or the altar, and a movement in the shadows. Slowly, I turned my head towards where the sound had come from. Behind the altar, there was a patch of darkness that was denser than the surrounding air. I fixed my gaze on it, trying to gauge its height and shape. It wasn't tall enough to be Tom, or his father. But was it broad enough to be Andrew? Might it be the Reverend? It was so dark that it was impossible to know. But whoever he was, he moved ever so slightly. It became clear to me now that the shadow was certainly not tall enough to be Tom. If it were Andrew, how would I explain why I was here with Rose?

My mind began racing. It would be simple. We had only my mother's satchel with us, and so it would be easy to say I'd brought Rose here for a blessing. That I feared for her fever once more. He wouldn't believe me, but he couldn't prove anything. At worst, it would mean a day of sulking and raised voices and hands. But he would also watch me more closely, and that would make it harder to get away again. If Andrew were here, it would be better to go home after all. Better than being caught. Had he seen or heard me? Might it be possible to flee? I was ungainly, and would be slowed down by carrying Rose, but if I took care not to reveal myself, I could leave before Andrew caught me.

But then the shadow moved side on and the candle revealed his profile. It was not Tom. It was not the Reverend. It was not Andrew. What business had this strange man in the house of God? Fear squeezed my heart and my feet were as lead. Then I thought of Rose, alone in the vestibule. Where was Tom? If I screamed, might it bring him running? Had the stranger done something to Tom? But my voice was frozen in my throat. Whoever this man was, somehow, I must draw him away from Rose. I would run out of the vestry and then when he was lost, double back to fetch her. In any case, Tom must come before long, and he would find Rose there.

My fingers furled around the pruning knife at my belt. I flung my knife to the left of the main door and the shadow darted after it. This gave me a slight chance, and I raced away from Rose towards the vestry, clutching my belly, with my heart pounding. As I hoped, the sounds of the footsteps paused and then they came nearer to me. I tried to run faster, but then came a blow to my head and my feet went from under me.

27

John

In the House of God

The bulbous moon shone through the blasphemous stained-glass windows, its silver light tainted by the hues of idolatrous saints. The candle at the foot of the altar flickered and its weak light illuminated the altar. There was little shadow left in the church, apart from the corners either side of the main door. The witch must not see me else she scream or flee, so I stayed in a shadowy corner, trying to quieten my breathing. She was brazen, out in the night and walking into a darkened church. Her powers were so great that even standing in this sacred place had no effect on her. But even though this church was popish, it was still God's house, and He would lend me strength to overcome His foe.

The witch walked towards the candle. She was cautious, perhaps sensing all was not well as she glanced over her shoulder every few steps. I would wait until she was at the altar, the point furthest away from the door, and furthest from the manse and the verger's shack where the old man and his son lived. Here, there was less chance of escape for her, and there was less chance for anyone to hear her screams. It wouldn't do for the false priest and the big verger to come to her aid. Because she was in the house of God, her satanic master's powers would be weakened. This was my best chance. It would have been better were the small flame-haired witch with her. But the child's powers would still be in their infancy, and I could easily deal with her later.

As the moon rose higher in the sky, more light flooded through the windows and it made me visible. I slid along the wall, to press myself into the furthest corner. Although my breathing was soft, and I'd made no sound at all, the witch followed my move into the shadows. Her supernatural senses were working in her favour, and I would need to take more care. She stared into the corner of the church for a long whilst, and I was careful to lower my gaze else the moonlight reveal my eyes. But she must not have seen me after all, and so I breathed more easily.

Then came a clattering of metal next to the church door, mere feet from where I stood, which made my heart lurch. Someone must be coming into the church. I darted towards the sound, too late to realise that the bitch had foxed me into revealing myself and she began running towards the altar. Damn her! She must know of another exit. The witch would get away and raise the hue and cry. And once she was off sacred ground, her dark powers would rise and put me in greater danger.

But the girth of her belly made her slow and I caught up with her easily. A blow to the head felled her and she collapsed to the floor without a sound. The blow had rendered her unconscious, but I needed to work quickly. The false priest would be asleep or in his cups, but the big verger might be near. I pulled my knife from my belt and held it up to God. As it turned, the moon's light glinted off it. The blade hadn't been cleansed by prayer, but there was no time. I raised the witch's kirtle and put my left hand under the curve of her belly. I had watched this cut performed on my own goodwife. Even so, the task sickened me. Driver's indecent belly was hard, the skin felt thinly stretched and her flesh was hot. The devil's spawn writhed beneath my hand, surely aware of what it faced. I pricked the thin skin underneath her belly with the tip of my knife, quickly sawing back and forth to get the full blade in.

As I pierced the witch's belly, there was a great giving way – a feeling of pressure escaping, as if the devil himself had been trapped in her belly – and her hot blood coursed over my hands, the noxious stench sickening me. The knife must have also pierced the veil of sleep and she awoke and began to thrash, her eyes and mouth wide, her claws scratching at my eyes and throat.

Before she could scream, I cuffed her hard at the temple and she was still again. I should have cut her throat, but she had to be alive until I delivered her spawn.

Quickly, I continued sawing at her belly until there was room enough to plunge my hands into her. Blood boiled up to my elbows, but finally, the slithery infant was within my grasp. I wrenched it from its mother's belly and hacked through the pulsing serpent that joined him to his mother. The witch was fortunate – due to my merciful nature, she would die of a swift and peaceful exsanguination.

A moan came from the witch and her eyelids began fluttering. The newborn gasped and then mewled. I kicked the witch in the head to silence her and carried the infant to the altar. The infant's skin was blue – further proof of his satanic nature. I placed him on the altar cloth, pinned him down with my left hand and raised the knife high in my right.

'God, I will spare this child from damnation, but forgive me for what I must now do in your name. So be it.'

I pierced the infant's belly with the tip of the knife. He drew in a gasping breath and screamed, and the unholy noise almost caused me to drop the knife. Before my nerve dissipated, I quickly slit his belly, all the whilst struggling to hold on to the howling, writhing child, whose screams bounced off the church walls. Such a terrible sound must bring people running. The princeling's strength must come from his true father, and I shivered in the presence of this evil. The force of the life leaving his body was strong. It was taking too much time. And someone might arrive and save him. In my panic, I was forced to cut his throat to snuff out his life. This was a merciful end. It was fortunate that he had scarcely drawn breath, and his few minutes of life would mean he was not able to stain the earth with his dark soul. My act would spare mankind from an eternity of evil.

The candle flickered as the blasphemous child's lifeblood flooded from him. It was good work and he was quickly rendered still.

My reverie was interrupted when the door opened and the church was flooded with moonlight. There stood two tall men in shadow, one broad at the shoulder. The vergers. There came a small squawk and both men turned. The big verger shoved his father out and pulled the door shut behind him. The red-haired spawn must have been out there sleeping. I bit my knuckle to stop myself crying out. The chance to kill all three and I'd missed it! I crept beneath the altar cloth. The verger might not find me if I remained still. But once the brat was safe, his father would raise the hue and cry. My heart pounded – there was no time to lose.

The verger moved towards the altar and the flickering candle revealed the infant. When he saw my handiwork, he put his hand to his mouth and retched. Then, he cast his eyes around until they fastened on the dying witch and a great howl broke from him. Might I overpower him in his grief? He was a big man, and rough with it. I'd slaughtered the witch and her imp, but my errand was not yet complete. So, I must stay still and quiet and watch for my chance to escape and then finish the girl-child.

28

Jane

The Moon Was Falling

There was a great pressure, as if the moon was falling to earth and pressing on me. I put my hands to my belly. Why was it flat and cold? Why was it wet? What were these soft shapes that sent screaming pains through me when I touched them? My breasts were full, but where was my baby? Why was I on the floor? Had someone torn my infant from my belly? And where was Rose? Had that same someone taken Rose? Was this a dream? A nightmare? Would it end soon?

I saw Rose taking the kern baby from the corn dolly's womb. Corn cut from the Drivers' fields. The dolly wore a garland akin to that worn by me on the Beltane night Rose was made. It was fashioned in my image. Had Rose stirred something in hell and led someone to tear the child from my womb? I must try to wake up. But the screams of my baby cut through the silence and told me this was no dream. I had to save him. But when I clutched my belly and tried to stand, the darkness took me.

The door opened and moonlight filled the church. My head swam and I fought to keep my eyes open. There was no strength left in me and my limbs felt all bone and sinew. My eyes couldn't focus and I gazed blankly. But I could hear running footsteps, long strides. A gagging sound and then a terrible howl.

'Jane? Dear God!' Words struggling through sobs. 'Jane, it's me.'

Someone took a step towards me. I tried to call out, my parched lips struggling to make a word.

He leant over me. 'Jane? It's me, Tom.'

It didn't sound like Tom. Great gulping breaths and words juddering as he spoke. I blinked at him. His face was wet with tears. He scrubbed his arm across his eyes and held out a trembling hand.

'Oh, Jane, Jane. Come here.'

He knelt beside me and pulled me into his arms, baulking as he did so. My body shook and his tears flowed, hot on my skin.

'Jane! Dear God, what's happened to you?' His voice felt very far away, but he was close as he put his hand to my belly, pushing and shoving and then gripping my flesh.

As a fresh wave of agony coursed through me, I grasped Tom's arm and clawed him.

'Jane, oh, God. Sorry to cause you pain, but I need to staunch this bleeding.'

'Rose?' It took all my strength to say her name.

'Da's got her . . . we heard screams . . .' He buried his face in my neck, weeping. 'Jane, who did this to you?'

A memory came back to me, but I was too tired to make sense of it.

'Man.'

'What man? Driver?'

A thought swam back to me. A voice I knew. 'Sharpe.'

'Sharpe? The witch-finder? Your son was ripped from you by John Sharpe? What brings him here? What could make a man so evil?'

Evil. Or mad. The moon was almost full. The countryside was lit almost as if it were daylight. Its waxing power must have addled Sharpe's mind. A scream was building inside my chest, but no sound would come. There was no strength left in me.

'I must find him before he finds Rose and Da. We'll send up the hue and cry and get all the men out as soon as I stop this bleeding.'

I looked up at Tom, pleading with my eyes.

'Never fear, Jane. Rose will be safe whilst me da has her.'

Tom kept pressing on me, but I was shivering.

'Baby . . .' No sound came out, but Tom must see my lips move.

He didn't respond. Then, my son was dead. So many people had been snatched from me. And now my son. The earth began falling away from me. Tom rested his lips on my brow and kissed me, hot tears falling from his eyes into mine. There were no words to tell him what had happened. It was so hellish, it couldn't be real. My lips moved, soundless.

This act had happened to another Jane in another life. I closed my eyes. My poor mite had passed without a blessing. I would pray for him now and hope the prayer found its way to him. That my mother would be waiting for him. And for me.

My lips moved again. 'Baby?'

'Save your strength, Jane. Please don't try to speak. Just stay with me. Oh, please, Jane, please. I cannot bear to lose you again.'

Great sobs racked his body. I shook my head, but the movement asked too much of me and so the movements slowed and then I was still. Was it possible to bear so much suffering and live?

'Jane, something's wrong – you shouldn't bleed like this.'

The moon was nearly full; it would bleed me dry.

'Help me save you, Jane. Tell me what to do.'

I forced out a whisper. 'Rev . . .'

'The Reverend? Da was going to rouse him – wait, you cannot mean . . . No, Jane. No!' He swallowed, but his voice came out full of tears anyway. 'You're strong. You'll live. I'll make you live. I can sew you up. Da will send help. Only, you have to stay with me, Jane. Please, please, God, spare Jane.'

He pulled me closer, but still the coldness seeped into me.

'Please stay awake, Jane.' He patted my face, his body shuddering as he wept. 'Stay with me, for Rose and for me. We need you. God, dear God, please help us.'

Oh, Mam, if only you were here. You could save me. There was not enough air and my breath became hoarse. No more words would come now.

'Jane! Look! The bleeding's slowed. Have you strength enough to hold your belly together? Let me find your mam's satchel and I can sew you up. You'll live. I promise you'll live. Oh, God, please help Jane. Please save her.'

Tom's words tired me. Pains swept through my body, and the air was very thin. I was cold as stone and longed to pull the night over myself and take a long sleep.

'No, Jane, you mustn't sleep. Please, God, divvent let her sleep! I love you, Jane. Stay with me. Please stay with me, Jane.'

Tom took my hands and gently touched the inside of my wrists. My heartbeat was very slow now.

'Please, God, look after Jane and let her live. I cannot bear to lose her and for Rose to have no mother. Oh, please . . .'

He wept again, and I was grateful for his silence so I could concentrate on breathing. He held me carefully, and I was shocked at how close my bones were to the air, as if I were dead already. My breath began to rattle in my throat and Tom took in a long, juddering breath then. So now he knew.

'Jane. I'm sorrier than you can ever know. I'll pray for your soul and for your salvation, and I'll be there for Rose, for all the days of her life. I promise you!'

His tears soaked my face. But there was no pain. No tears came from me.

Tom kissed me, and I felt his whole body shaking.

It was a lifetime ago when we jumped the rush . . . with me wearing the May crown. We made Rose that night, in the warmth of the dying Beltane fires and the frail light of the rising sun. Rose was a child of the elements, and she was strong. She would survive me. But no woman could ever be strong enough when men like John Sharpe walked the earth.

'Please speak to me, Jane, don't leave me. I cannot bear to live without you. . . . Rose will be safe with me, Jane. Sharpe won't draw breath long enough to hurt her. This is my vow to you. Only don't leave me. Please . . . stay with us.'

His sobbing echoed around the church. My mother was dead. My son was dead. Now, I would go to them. Tom loved me, and he loved Rose. He would care for Rose always. He would end Sharpe. It was enough. My grip on this life started to loosen, and as life slipped away from me, my eyes closed against the moonlight, and the darkness entered me.

29

John

To the Flame

The witch must be no more because the big verger hunkered over her, weeping without shame. When he finally stood, he rubbed his hands over his face and walked towards the door. Now was my chance. Whilst he left by the main door, I'd escape through the vestry before he returned with a mob and barred the doors. But in my rush to escape, I slithered on a slick of blood and floundered on the floor. I crept into the corner and tried to calm my breathing.

But the sound of my fall fetched him racing back. The candle on the floor guttered and died as he snatched it up and placed it on the altar. But not before it revealed the pool of blood shimmering black in the candlelight. Such an unnatural quantity of blood. Proof of the witch. No natural woman's body contained this much blood. I held my breath, keeping my eyes cast down so the whites of my eyes might not catch the moon and give me away. That dull metallic smell filling my senses dizzied me. My heart whirred, no longer beating but fluttering. My senses were alive, my ears pricked, nostrils flared, arms and legs primed for whatever work came their way.

'Don't move, Sharpe. I have a hunter's eye, and my bow is trained on you.'

The man had no bow trained on me – the tremor in his voice gave lie to his claim. I stood still, but trembled. The shock of the killings had rendered me weak. I should have left long since. Now, I'd lost the element of surprise that had helped me overpower the witch. She was small and ungainly, but this man was young and vigorous looking, and he was strangely in possession of his nerves for a man grieving. My only weapon was my eating knife, which would be of little use against him. The verger would no doubt keep his distance whilst he had the advantage. My best ruse would be to fox him into moving in one direction whilst I fled in the other.

'Why have you done this to my lovely Jane? And to her little bairn?' He paused to weep. 'She did no wrong and was good all the days of her life.'

My heart lifted at the sound of his sorrow. There was a distinct waver in his words, so he was weak after all, and may be easy to overcome.

But he spoke through his tears. 'Don't move, Sharpe. Or I swear afore God that I will slaughter you where you stand.'

His breathing was shallow and rapid, and wracked with sobs. Then I heard his breath no more. He must be holding it so that he might better hear me and work out my position. This confirmed there was no bow trained on me because he couldn't see me. Right now, he couldn't be sure whether I was quarry or hunter. Something skittered – a stone? It startled me. A knife flashed towards me. I raised my arm to deflect the blade, which slashed my arm but missed my throat. I slashed with my own knife, but the assailant grabbed my wrist and squeezed until my blade clattered onto the stone floor. Then he wrenched my arm up my back, forcing a sharp cry from me.

'Stop, man, or I will surely bleed to death.' The coppery smell of my own blood galled me.

'Not if I can help it. You won't die so easily by my hand.' He grabbed my arm so hard it almost left its socket. He grunted. 'You'll live. More's the pity.'

He removed my belt and bound my arm so tightly the pain dizzied me, and it was a struggle to remain conscious.

'There. It won't matter if you lose an arm. You won't need it where you're going.'

This soothed my terror. He hadn't killed me. No doubt the verger was a good Christian who knew it was wrong to kill a man. My path to freedom was clear.

'Please, let me go. Like you, I am God's servant. I have silver aplenty. Let me go and I will reward you amply.'

A blinding crack sent me reeling backwards into a heap.

'Keep your silence. And don't say anything that might tempt me to strangle you. Not because I fear any stain on me conscience, but because it would be too easy a death for you.'

He bore down on me and grasped me by the jerkin, yanking me upright. I should keep my own counsel lest he break my back. So, the verger wouldn't take a bribe easily. He must be more in thrall to the witch than to God. He would delight in hurting me.

I began to sweat profusely and knew this was not good. But now the furious verger had me in his power, it might be better to bleed to death. I began to pray.

'Dear God, please have mercy on your servant–'

He shook me like a runt. 'Save your prayers for Rose, since she must grow up without her mother and brother.'

'So the devil-sent girl is yours! Be warned, for she will soon join her mother and brother.'

He snorted. 'You'll not get near me daughter. And divvent think you can goad me into ending your life early.' He yanked hard on the belt until it felt as though he might sever my arm. 'You'll feel true justice afore this night is out. Besides, there's nothing of the devil in my daughter. The only devil-sent thing hereabouts is you.'

My mouth opened, but the verger showed me his back. He couldn't stand to look at me. He was an unnatural man and had a deranged look about the eyes.

'Aye, devil, turn your back on me. Another one that cannot bear the gaze of God's true servant.'

When he spoke again, his voice was cold. 'I've spent my whole life in the service of God. I've helped people all me days, but all you've done is hate people and make up stories of devils and demons. You sent my lovely Jane and her mother and son to dreadful deaths . . .' He paused to find his words, and when he spoke, he was crying again. 'Dreadful deaths without so much as a prayer for their departing souls. I cannot bring them back, but I can end you.'

My blood boiled and my eyes bulged. But I wouldn't speak. Instead, I began praying again. 'Dear God, please bless and keep–'

'Aye, Sharpe, you do well to pray for whatever mercy God might show you.'

He heaved me up and put me across his shoulders. The giant had an unnatural strength as he carried me to a pillar and lashed me to it. The sky glowed roseate through the coloured windows, and I feared what the day might bring. I began to buck and writhe against my bindings. As the verger bent to his knots, I snapped at his face, my teeth gnashing like a rabid dog. But he cuffed me at the temple, and the dawn was swallowed by night.

* * *

The weeping verger returned, accompanied by the false priest, who stared at first one corpse and then the other. His lips moved, but no sound came out. A prayer of some sort, a silent one. He leant against the altar, with his head in his hands, trembling and weeping. In his anguish, he sounded like a woman. When he finally looked up at me, his eyes blazed with an unholy fury.

'John Sharpe. What hatred resides in your heart that you can tear a child from his mother's belly and then slaughter them both? And in my church.'

I looked from the priest to the wet-eyed verger, and an idea formed in my mind. God had given me good wits and they might save me now to continue His work.

'Untie me, dear priest, I bear terrible tidings. The witch and her lover conspired to deconsecrate your church by means of a diabolical sacrifice. See what they have wrought? An altar fit for the devil.'

The verger gave a terrible moan and backhanded me across the face, his unchristian hatred pulsing through his hand.

My nose gushed blood and almost choked me. I appealed to the priest. 'You are a man of God, you must protect me from this common brute.'

But the priest would not hear my plea. 'Quiet, Sharpe, whilst I consider what justice to mete out.'

'But you are mistaken! This is not my doing.' My eyes were wild in my head. 'This is the doing of crazed witches – I am innocent.'

The priest stood over me. 'You are soaked in the blood of a girl who was once my ward. You have dealt Jane, her mother and her infant the most terrible ends imaginable. And now you hope to dupe me with lies that wouldn't fool a child.'

He took some holy water from the font and sprinkled it around the destroyed child. He kissed its forehead and made the sign of the cross in holy oil.

'Blasphemer! You cannot baptise a child once it's dead. This one has already gone back to the devil. You're too late.'

The priest ignored me, continuing to bless the child. The verger stepped towards me. Up close, his eyes were wet and red, and his face was white. He pointed a trembling finger at me.

'There is only one here who has gone to the devil and that is you, John Sharpe. You've sent Jane's bairn to limbo. And you'll go to hell for it.' He looked upon his slaughtered lover and then put his head in his hands. 'You're an evil man. Or a sick one.'

I clutched at this. 'Yes – sick, that's what I am. Someone must help me. God, help me in my hour of sickness! The sergeants will never execute a sick man. I must be helped, not hanged.'

The priest had moved to the body of his ward and he began blessing her. The verger knelt and put his face so close to mine, I could see the red veins in his eyes.

'For a sick man, your wits appear sharp enough. But you may be right. The sergeants and crowner will never hang a sick man. Besides, hanging's too good for you.'

I smiled to myself. A certain stay of execution. And then I would manage to elude my persecutors and slip back to Scotland. I was good at sliding into the shadows and moving back and forth across the border. And this time, none would find me.

The priest came and put an arm around the verger. 'For now, Tom, we must bury our dead. Can you and Bill move the earth? I cannot bear to put Jane and her son in the crypt. The thought of infants lying in the cold there used to terrify her as a child.'

'Aye, Reverend.' He swayed a little. 'Me and Da will break the frozen earth somehow ... suppose we get every man in the village to help and it takes all night.' He crossed the nave and knelt beside the witch's body. 'The sooner Jane and her bairn are laid to rest the better.' He leant down and kissed the corpse tenderly. 'I'll place you and your bairn with me mother, Jane, and it may bring you both a measure of peace.'

They would be buried in sanctified ground. I railed against my bindings. Did they not realise what they did? God help me escape and prevent this new blasphemy!

* * *

They tied me to a chair and locked me in the crypt along with a dozen corpses, which were covered only in sacking. If I was not mad when they put me in here, I would certainly be mad when I came out. If I came out. It was freezing – no doubt they hoped I'd simply perish so none had to answer for my death. But God wouldn't let them treat His servant in this way, He would see fit to punish them. And my rage would keep me warm in the meantime.

I drew my cloak to my spare frame and tried to ignore the dead villagers behind me. Their unseeing eyes were already turned towards eternity. Yet, I felt watched by them, judged even. But there was only one fit to stand in judgement of me, and I was prepared to face His terrible majesty.

For hours or days – I knew not which – I shivered in the crypt, imagining witches' sabats being danced in the church above my head. In my insomnia, my eyes beheld visions that my mind knew couldn't be real. Terrible sweats seized me and tremors wracked my body.

Pale light seeped through the keyhole and into the dark crypt, but it was impossible to know whether it was the light after sunrise or before the gloaming. Finally, there came the sound of bolts being drawn. I would watch for any chance to flee. When the door was heaved open, light illuminated the crypt and the sight of the lifeless forms surrounding me caused me to shudder. These corpses who had sat vigil with me through the night.

At the door stood five men: the false priest, the big verger, his father, the witch's cuckold, and a man who must be his father. The witch's cuckold was pale and his black eyes were vacant, and he seemed unable to speak or move. He had a sick look to him and his father kept a restraining hand on his shoulder. But the verger's green eyes burnt with hatred. He was strongly built and appeared capable of tearing me limb from limb. But he wouldn't kill me, or he'd have done so in the church. So my hide was safe for now.

The priest placed before me a platter of bread and cheese, and a pitcher of ale. He then untied one hand and removed my gag.

'Eat.'

I longed to cram the food into my mouth, but it wouldn't do whilst these men stood over me. And it was not seemly for a man about to be judged. But I needed my strength and wits, and food would sustain me through what lay ahead. Finally, with five men standing over me, I fell upon the food, ravenous. It had been so many days since I'd eaten properly, it was little wonder I'd begun to have visions. I should have eschewed these rich foods, but my animal appetites had the better of me. I drained the bitter ale without guilt at how fleshly weakness swept through me. Had I been presented with a woman, I'd have taken her gladly. The ripe flesh of Jane Driver had inflamed me. Clearly, she was able to use her demonic power to infect my mind still. She'd shown no shame, flaunting her brazen, swollen body and breasts. It was no wonder that she had five men in thrall even after her death. I had to think hard and drive a wedge of some sort between these men.

'So, men of Mutton Clog, now you will try me and execute me most unfairly, without a proper hearing.' When I spoke, my voice held a treacherous waver.

The priest stared evenly at me. 'You will be tried by fair men, true men of God.'

I thrashed helplessly against my constraints. 'You? You? You are no man of God. Your heart is so blackened with the desire for revenge that you cannot possibly be fair. And yet, you will decide my fate.' To my shame, I wept. 'It's not fair. It's not right. At the very least, there should be a magistrate appointed to oversee my trial.'

The verger spat at my feet. 'You'll have a fairer trial than you gave Jane and her bairn.'

I quailed before him. 'The sergeants will learn of this. News will leach out. You'll all swing. Your souls will be in peril.'

The big verger laughed without mirth and fastened my gag again. 'Not one man here will say a word of what goes on. Whilst you breathe, Rose is in danger, and I'll cheerfully trade me soul to keep her safe.'

At a nod from the priest, three of the men each took a leg of the chair I was tied to. The witch's cuckold seemed dead to the world and so the priest took the fourth leg. I'd been so cold for so long that their nearness warmed me. They carried me out, and their uneven heights and gaits made me pitch and toss sickeningly. The gag on my mouth prevented me from shouting for help, but it didn't prevent me from trying. My mouth was dry and my head pulsed. The fear made my scalp contract and I sweated, despite the frigid air. They carried me into the manse to a suffocating room where a great fire roared and placed me right next to it. So, they'd basked in luxury whilst making me suffer in the cold crypt. Well God would see me right.

The cuckold's father settled his son next to the fire and dropped soft words into his ear. The verger removed my gag none too gently and stepped back. The priest took out his Bible. He had piercing eyes in his gaunt face and they were filled with rage.

'You cannot give me a fair trial. You're filled with hate and a lust for revenge, driven by the loss of your common hearth woman.' I spat on the floor. 'It's obscene in a supposed man of God.'

The false priest stared at me and didn't blink. I could see the hatred burning in his eyes. He cared not that I'd desecrated his debased church, only that I'd taken his woman from him. I wouldn't humble myself before such a man and I turned my head away from him.

Finally, the priest spoke. 'We've decided what to do with you, Sharpe. You, who have eluded man's law so many times . . . If we give you to the sergeants, you may escape, and whilst you have breath, you'll use it to slaughter Rose. You're adept at turning the tables to your own favour – with such words that can turn allegedly learned men.'

Despite the warmth from the fire, a shiver ran down my back. My teeth chattered and my shoulders shook, yet not one man spared me so much as a piteous look. They hadn't an ounce of compassion between them.

'So, then. You will murder me in cold blood?'

'No. Not murder.' The priest held up his Bible. 'Execute.'

He inverted a large hourglass and watched the pale sand pouring through the narrow waist. The angel of death was etched top and bottom. This man fancied himself God's servant.

'There is no other way, Sharpe. We don't fear for our eternal souls. God will understand our purpose. Man's law permits the hanging of an urchin who steals a loaf to line his hungry belly. Is that justice, truly? We must look back to an older time, when the law was not there just to protect the rich from the poor. To a time of true justice.'

The heat of the fire had become unpleasant, my face began to prickle with sweat, and I tried to turn away from the flame.

'John Sharpe, you cut an infant from his mother's body and left her to bleed to death. You desecrated the altar by slaughtering an innocent babe on it. You have sullied the church.'

I shook my head violently.

'In August last, you put sixteen women and one man to death as witches – on the scantest of evidence. Had you not been stopped, there would have been another dozen. There are no doubt scores more we do not know about. We will not pause to hear your plea. You are drenched in the innocent blood of Jane Driver and her unborn infant. That blood speaks of your guilt. The five men here present will bear this dark secret to protect Rose. It is a secret that might one day poison our souls, but we are all five strong, and we can bear the stain to preserve a child. We answer only to God. You are a dangerous conniver and a cruel murderer, and you must face justice. As punishment, in the name of God Almighty, you will be taken from this place and put to death in a manner concordant with your sins.'

The fiendish man made the sign of the cross over the four men as he dared pronounce on my life. A sickening cramp wracked me and my bowels went to water.

'You will die, Sharpe, as many have died at your hand – without benefit of clergy. No man will pray for your soul. Nor will you be allowed to pray for your own soul. You will die unshriven. You have silenced so many. In return, you will be silenced. Now, we will take you.'

At that, the priest and three of the men seized a leg each of the chair and carried me on a jolting walk to the graveyard. I flailed in my chair, hoping to loosen my bonds, but these were solid knots.

In plain sight of the bright moon was a mound of wood. A pyre! I began thrashing against my bonds. They couldn't burn me! I gnashed my teeth. They had no right to put me to the flame like a common heretic! I railed against my gag and writhed in my seat, but nothing moved, and the harsh ropes of my bindings gouged the skin of my wrists and ankles. Tears of rage burst from my eyes. Without any ceremony or word, they lifted the chair onto the unholy pyre. The cuckold stood before it, looking up at me with eyes devoid of life.

The verger steadied the chair. 'Divvent trouble yourself, Sharpe, it's not as cruel as it looks. The smoke will finish you long afore the flames get to work. You'll be unconscious afore you feel too much pain.'

He tucked dry moss into the centre of the pyre and took a fire steel from his pouch, along with some flint and tinder. I bucked and reared and managed to tip the chair backwards, but succeeded only in cracking my head as I landed. Blood dripped from the wound. But I was still on the pyre, now staring up at the moon, which continued to rise. The verger climbed up and righted the chair. This time, the two older men held me steady, so I couldn't tip myself again. The verger struck the flint and immediately caught an orange spark of burning steel on the tinder. This, he bundled into a nest of dried moss. Blowing into it to kindle a fire, he placed the burning nest into the waiting hands of the priest.

The priest raised the bundle above his head to the moon. Finally, he had realised his duty to God and would put me to death with a prayer at the very least.

'May God have mercy on my soul.'

But the false priest prayed only for himself, and then placed the burning nest into the kindling beneath my chair.

The kindling crackled as the flames caught it, suffusing me with warmth and smoke. I longed to protest against this injustice. Had I not shown mercy, by letting the women of England go to their deaths by hanging? Yet, I was not to be afforded this same mercy. If they wouldn't grant me benefit of clergy, then I must pray for my own soul. But the sensations of my body soon began to outweigh the desire to pray and my thoughts began to circle in on themselves.

With a candle to the flesh, a quick pass and there is no pain – only a thin dusting of soot.

But hold the candle still and there is pain. And the acrid tang of searing flesh.

The flesh cannot bear the flame. If it can move, it will. But now, my flesh could not move and so must bear the flame.

Unable to grease the executioner's palm, I screamed my prayer to an oblivious God as the kindling caught. The complicit breeze took the flames up the faggots, taking my scream up to the skies. My eyes filled with tears that would soon dry to black salt on my warming skin. Smoke from green wood flooded my lungs. Choked me. Stole my breath. But it was not enough. The flame hadn't yet touched me.

Then, the thin skin around my ankles prickled. It scorched. It blistered. The flame devoured the hairs. The thick skin on my feet began to blister. Then the night was filled with one sound only.

Screaming.

Screaming.

Screaming.

It must bring the villagers. There was hope yet. But there was no one there. Only the five men who had condemned me. Now even they seemed absent. They had fallen silent. They mattered not. They would go home. To sleep. To wake. To live.

I would breathe no more.

The flame caught my wool cloak. Here lay mercy. My cloak began to burn. Thick black smoke rose around me. The wool almost froze on my skin as it burnt.

The smoke was drawing in. I was screaming inwardly. Sucking back all that rage. Taking all that anger, along with the smoke, and drawing it down deep inside my lungs. Holding it there.

Choking.

Coughing.

Praying.

The burning in my chest moved outwards to meet with the burning wool. As the inner flames rushed to meet the outer, my lungs imploded.

At last, the condemned one was free.

Afterword

After writing *Widdershins*, I really thought I was done with the story of Jane Chandler and John Sharpe. But then the characters kept reappearing in my mind. I tried to ignore them, but they continued to haunt me with their unfinished business. I realised that they wouldn't go away until I wrote them out of my head.

In particular, I felt honour-bound to give Tom Verger some more space on the page. In early drafts of *Widdershins*, Tom had his own point of view, and he occupied a third of the book, which at the time ran to just shy of 130,000 words. I was due to submit *Widdershins* for my MA in Creative Writing at Manchester Metropolitan University. Although there was no formal upper word limit, there were rumblings about changes to the MA, including the introduction of a cap of 80,000 words. Whilst the official advice was that a book should be as long as it needed to be, I thought it might be prudent to cut the word count and avoid any risk (whether real or imagined) of being marked down for an over-long novel.

In the earlier version with three points of view, the reader was perfectly aware at all times that Tom was alive and still at sea, but Jane and the other Mutton Clog residents had no knowledge of this (with the exception of Andrew Driver). So, with a few clicks of the keyboard, Tom's point of view vanished forever, along with all of my research into seafaring and naval medicine. Sorry, Tom – you were my favourite character as well. This meant that Tom's survival was then a surprise to most readers, although many of you have told me that you realised what Andrew was up to and that you guessed Tom was alive and well.

And Tom wasn't the only one with a story that needed telling, because in real life, the Scottish witch-finder got away from Newcastle and lived to tell the tale. According to John Wheeler's deposition in Ralph Gardiner's book, *England's Grievance Discovered in Relation to the Coal-Trade* (1655), the witch-finder proceeded to Northumberland and began to try women for three pounds per head. He was prevented by Henry Ogle, but yet again, the witch-finder escaped to Scotland. Gardiner states that the witch-finder was eventually jailed there and then executed after confessing to causing the death of more than 220 women in England and Scotland.

I decided that John Sharpe should be put to death by Jane's loved ones, just in case he slipped away again. I certainly didn't want to risk this horrible man haunting my dreams anymore in case he compelled me to write a third book about him. So, now he's finally gone from my imagination, I can sleep at night again.

I found these two books gruelling to write because of the grim nature of what went on in the seventeenth century. And I know that many of you have found *Widdershins* gruelling to read. Perhaps it's just as well that I took my critique group's sound advice and lightened up *Widdershins* – it really was a very grim read in its earliest iterations!

My next book is also set in the seventeenth century, but I've promised myself it's going to be much more cheerful. Let's see how that works out . . .

About the Author

Helen Steadman is the author of *Widdershins* and its sequel, *Sunwise*. She lives in the foothills of the North Pennines, and she particularly enjoys researching and writing about the history of the north east of England. Following her MA in creative writing at Manchester Met, Helen is now completing a PhD in English at the University of Aberdeen. You can find out more about her writing at helensteadman.com and you can follow her on Twitter at @hsteadman1650, on Instagram at @helensteadman1650 and on Facebook at www.facebook.com/helensteadmanauthor.